For Johnny, because he hasn't had a book dedicated to him yet.

AUTHOR'S NOTE

Welcome to book five in the Isle of Man Ghostly Cozy Series. I hope everyone is enjoying spending time with Fenella, Mona, and their friends.

Because Fenella grew up in the US, this book is mostly written in American English. The setting is, however, the stunningly beautiful Isle of Man, a UK crown dependency in the Irish Sea.

This is a work of fiction. All of the characters are products of the author's imagination. Any resemblance to actual persons, living or dead, is entirely coincidental. The shops, restaurants, and businesses in this story are also fictional. The historical sites and other landmarks on the island are all real; however, the events that take place within them in this story are fictional.

My contact details are available in the back of the book. I love hearing from readers, so please don't hesitate to get in touch.

I

"You look wonderful, " Shelly said with a sigh as Fenella turned around slowly in front of her. "That's the most gorgeous dress I think I've ever seen."

"It is nice," Fenella agreed, checking her appearance in the full-length mirror on the bedroom wall. "And it fits perfectly."

"Everything in Mona's wardrobe seems to fit you perfectly," Shelly said. "I wish I had a wardrobe full of incredible dresses and gowns that all fit me as if they were made for me."

"You should go through Mona's things," Fenella suggested. "I'm sure some of them would work for you."

Shelly shook her head. "You've already given me one dress from Mona's wardrobe. I can't possibly take anything else."

Fenella didn't bother to argue. She'd have plenty of opportunities in the future to offer her deceased aunt's clothes to her closest friend. She didn't need to push the issue today. Not while she was trying to work out what to wear for an important evening out.

"That's the one," Shelly said firmly. "Don't even bother trying on anything else."

"You don't think it's too revealing?" Fenella asked, blushing slightly at the low-cut neckline.

"Not at all," Shelly replied.

"Donald will love it," Mona said from her seat on Fenella's bed.

Fenella looked over at her aunt and frowned. "I don't want to give Donald the wrong idea," she said hesitantly.

"Oh, he already has the wrong idea," Mona laughed.

"I'm sure it's too late for that." Shelly's reply repeated Mona's sentiment. "But, honestly, can you imagine finding anything else that looks that good?"

Fenella looked in the mirror again. She did look much more fabulous than normal in the stunning black gown. "I suppose not," she admitted.

"So that's the matter settled," Shelly said. "And I know you have plenty of shoes that will match. Do you want me to stay and help with your hair and makeup?"

"I'll be fine," Fenella replied. She'd been doing her own hair and makeup for all of her adult life. Now in her late forties, she couldn't imagine how her friend could do anything more than get in the way.

"Maybe I'll pop home, then," Shelly said. "Gordon is coming over later and I really should run the vacuum. Smokey's fur seems to get everywhere."

"Meeroww," the large grey cat complained. She was stretched out on the floor near the door while Katie, Fenella's kitten, bounced around the room.

"Never mind, you know I love you anyway," Shelly told the cat as she got up from the desk chair in the corner of the room. "Let's go home and get ready for our visitor, shall we?"

"Things seem to be going well between you and Gordon," Fenella remarked as she followed Shelly and Smokey to the door.

"They are," Shelly agreed. "Which is worrying in its own way."

Fenella chuckled, but she knew exactly what the woman meant. Shelly had been widowed less than a year earlier and Fenella knew that getting involved with another man hadn't been in Shelly's plans. Gordon Davison was an old friend, though, and the couple were slowly working their way toward something that might have been a romance but was maybe just friendship. At least that was how Shelly always described it.

At the door, Shelly stopped and turned to give Fenella a hug. "I'll only squeeze gently so I don't wrinkle your dress," she said. "Have a wonderful time tonight."

"You, too," Fenella told her. She smiled as she watched the woman walk back to her own apartment, right next door.

Although they'd only known each other for a matter of months, Fenella felt closer to Shelly than she had to any friend in a very long time. Shelly was over ten years older, but the age gap was insignificant to both women. When her husband had passed away unexpectedly, Shelly had taken early retirement from her years as a teacher. She'd sold the home she and her husband had shared and bought the apartment next door to Fenella's aunt.

Shelly insisted that Mona had been instrumental in helping her deal with her loss, dragging her out and insisting that she start embracing life. As far as Fenella could work out, Shelly's idea of embracing life seemed mostly to consist of dying her hair red, talking to absolutely everyone, and wearing incredibly bright colors at all times. Whatever Shelly had been like before her husband died, Fenella thought she was wonderful the way she was now.

"It is the perfect dress," Mona told Fenella as she walked back into the bedroom. "It's very flattering on you."

Fenella looked in the mirror again. Mona was right, of course. She usually was, which was slightly annoying. It was possible that Mona was the ghost of Fenella's recently departed aunt, which was the explanation for her presence that Fenella preferred. Seemingly equally possible was that the woman was a figment of Fenella's imagination. If that was the case, Mona's tendency to always be right felt wrong somehow.

"I'm nervous about tonight," Fenella said.

"Why? You're going to a party with a wonderful man who will treat you like a princess," Mona replied. "There's nothing to be nervous about."

"Donald makes me nervous," Fenella admitted.

"The right dress, shoes, hair, and makeup will help build your self-confidence," Mona told her. "Besides, you've nothing to worry about with Donald. He's nothing special, you know."

"He's very rich," Fenella countered. "And far more sophisticated than I am."

"You could learn to be sophisticated if you wanted to bother. I don't recommend it. It's much more fun to be naughty and a little scandalous."

"You should know," Fenella said dryly. When she'd found out that she'd inherited her aunt's entire estate, Fenella had nothing but vague memories of the woman who had lived on the Isle of Man for her entire life. Mona had visited her sister, Fenella's mother, in the US on occasion, but it had been over thirty years since Fenella had seen the woman.

When she'd arrived on the island, Fenella had been surprised to learn that Mona had amassed a small fortune, but no one was exactly certain where her money had come from. Rumors about the woman and various wealthy men were often whispered to her, but Fenella had been unable to substantiate any of them, and she didn't really want to try.

Mona laughed. "I've told you many times that you shouldn't believe most of the stories about me," she said. "Nearly all of the people who had firsthand knowledge of my affairs have long since passed. What's left are a number of people who like to tell stories, often with embroidery to make the stories more interesting."

"Do you have a boyfriend in the afterlife?" Fenella changed the subject.

"Let's not worry about me, not tonight," Mona said. "We have to get you ready for your evening with Donald. Now, you're going to the Seaview in Ramsey, aren't you?"

"Yes, that's what Donald said," Fenella agreed.

"It's lovely there, although it is getting a bit tired. I wonder if Jasper and Stuart have any plans for remodeling. They'd probably struggle to find the time, I suspect. I imagine they're booked nearly every weekend all year. It is the best place on the island for a special event."

"As I understand it, tonight is pretty special."

Mona shrugged. "Everyone always thinks their parties are special. I'm sure this one will be much like every other charity event that gets held at the Seaview, except that tonight Patricia Anderson will be the one acting as if she's the most important person in the world."

"Who's Patricia Anderson?"

"The woman who has been head of the Manx Fund for Children since it was founded thirty or more years ago," Mona told her. "She's a horrid and nasty woman who thinks far too much of herself."

"What did she do to you?"

"Refused my help," Mona snapped. "I offered to help with the charity when she first started it, but she assured me that she didn't need any assistance. Over the years, I offered to assist with various events, but she never allowed me to get involved in any way. Oh, I was welcome to contribute generously to them, but only if I did so anonymously."

"Why?" Fenella had to ask.

Mona smirked. "She thought I was sleeping with her husband," she replied with a shrug.

"Were you?"

"Was I what?" Mona asked after a long pause. "Sorry, I lost track of the conversation."

"Were you sleeping with Patricia Anderson's husband?" Fenella asked flatly.

"No," Mona replied. "But it suited him to have her and others think so, and I didn't object."

"Why?"

"Why didn't I object? Because I simply didn't care. Oh, I would have liked a chance to do some sort of charitable volunteer work, and Patricia made sure I was shunned by nearly everyone, but beyond that it simply didn't matter."

"Why did he want people to think he was sleeping with you?"

Mona smiled smugly. "Let's just say it would have given him a certain cachet in some circles."

Fenella stared at her aunt. "I'm not sure I understand what you mean," she said after a moment.

"I'm sure you don't," Mona laughed. "But let's not worry about that. What shoes are you going to wear?"

Fenella pulled open the wardrobe and dug out a pair of black shoes with low heels. “These are comfortable,” she said.

“And geriatric,” Mona replied. “Those must be yours. I certainly didn’t own anything that unattractive.”

“They are mine, and if I wear them my feet won’t hurt by the end of the evening.”

“If you wear the black shoes that are third from the left in the first row of shoes, your feet won’t hurt either. I had them made for me, and I believe you’ll find that they’re unbelievably comfortable.”

Fenella eyed the strappy stilettoes warily. It took her a minute to work out exactly how the straps were meant to crisscross, but once she’d fastened the necessary buckles, she stood up hesitantly. After a few cautious steps, she turned to look at Mona. “I hardly feel like I’m wearing heels,” she said. “They’re practically magic, these shoes.”

“I told you you’d like them,” Mona replied.

A loud ringing noise cut through the conversation.

“Hello?”

“Maggie? Is that you?”

Fenella swallowed a sigh. “What do you want, Jack?” she demanded. When she’d inherited Mona’s fortune, Fenella had sold her house, quit her job as a university professor, cut her ties, and moved to the Isle of Man. Leaving Jack Dawson, her boyfriend of over ten years, behind had been one of her easier decisions. In the US, she’d gone by Margaret, her middle name, as that was easier for people to spell and pronounce. Jack was the only person who called her Maggie, and she’d never liked it.

“It’s July,” Jack said.

“Yes, it is. Is that supposed to mean something to me?”

“You moved over there in March,” Jack replied.

“Very good. You were paying attention,” Fenella snapped.

Jack sighed. “Don’t you think you’ve had quite enough time to come to your senses?” he demanded. “I think it’s high time you moved back to Buffalo. You can move in with me. You don’t even have to find your own house this time.”

Having her own house was probably one of the factors that had allowed her to stay with Jack for so many years. That she’d never once considered moving in with the man, not even in their earlier and happier years, should have told her everything she needed to know about the future of the relationship. It had been easier to ignore all of the problems in favor of having someone in her life, but now that she'd broken free, she knew there was no going back. Convincing Jack of that was proving more difficult.

"I'm not coming back," she said.

"I thought you'd say that. And I know why you're saying it. You're lonely and unhappy, but you don't want to admit that you made a terrible mistake. I understand, and I'm here to help."

"I'm not lonely or unhappy."

"Here's my plan," Jack said, ignoring her reply. "I'll tell everyone that I'm dying, and then you can come back to nurse me through my final days. Once you're back, I'll stage a miraculous recovery and we can live happily ever after."

"I'm not coming back."

"Not even if I'm really dying?"

"Are you really dying?"

"Well, no, well, yes, I mean, of course, we're all dying, aren't we? That's why it wouldn't be a total lie, just an exaggeration. It's the perfect plan, isn't it?"

"It would be a good plan," Fenella admitted grudgingly, "if I wanted to move back to Buffalo. But I don't want to move back. I'm happy here. I've already built a new life for myself here. There's nothing in Buffalo for me anymore."

"What about your brothers?" Jack demanded.

"None of them live in Buffalo," Fenella replied.

"No, but they're all in the US and they're all getting older. You shouldn't be so far away from them."

Fenella swallowed hard. Jack wasn't to know that he'd hit on a rather sore subject. She missed her four brothers dearly. "They are all happy and healthy," she said. "And not any of your concern."

"We were together for ten years. They're like family to me now," Jack protested.

"Really? What are their names?"

"John, Jacob, um, James, and, um, Joshua," the man said.

"You're close, but you're only guessing," Fenella said dismissively. While she'd seen her brothers frequently when she'd lived in Buffalo, Jack had never accompanied her when she'd visited them and rarely spent time with them when they'd visited her. Jack hadn't liked any of the men and Fenella knew the feeling had been mutual.

"I'm not," Jack said stubbornly.

"What are their wives' names?"

"Darling Maggie, let's not fight. I miss you," Jack changed the subject.

Fenella took a deep breath and just barely stopped herself from being too cruel. "I'm sorry," she said. "But I'm happy here, and I really need to go. I have plans for later."

"A date?"

"Yes, a date."

"With a man?"

Fenella chuckled. "Yes, with a man."

"Am I that easy to replace?"

She needed another deep breath to stop herself from saying yes. "This isn't about you. I've moved halfway around the world and I have a new life. Donald is part of my new life."

"Donald? What's he like? What does he do?" Jack was a professor at the same university where Fenella had formerly taught.

"I'm not having this conversation. Look, Jack, you really should stop calling me. You need to find someone new."

"But you understand me. Dating new people is exhausting. You have to tell them your life story and listen to theirs. It's always so boring."

"So learn to enjoy being single," Fenella suggested.

"Life was so much easier when you were here," Jack said, his tone dangerously close to whining. "You did my laundry and ironed my shirts and you took me grocery shopping and told me what to buy. You handled all of my little problems for me."

"But you're an adult who can handle his own problems."

"That reminds me, where is my brown suit?"

"Your brown suit?"

"You know the one. You never liked it. You didn't get rid of it, did you?"

Fenella sighed. "It's an ugly suit, but I didn't get rid of it. I told you when I left that I was going to drop it off at the dry cleaners for you. You spilled soup on it at the February faculty lunch, remember?"

"Soup? What kind of soup?"

"I don't remember, and I can't see what difference it makes," Fenella said. No amount of deep breathing was going to help now. She could feel herself getting fed up with the man on the other end of the phone line.

"So my suit is at the dry cleaners?"

"Maybe. You were meant to pick it up months ago. They might have given it away by now."

"They can't do that!"

"I think they can. I stuck the ticket from them on the board in your kitchen. I'll bet there's some fine print that says how long they have to keep abandoned items."

"I didn't abandon that suit, you did."

"Yes, well, all the more reason to be glad you've seen the last of me, right? Look, I really have to go. I hope you find your suit. And I hope you find someone lovely who doesn't mind looking after you. Bye."

Fenella put the phone down and looked over at Mona, who rolled her eyes.

"Ten years?" Mona asked.

"It seemed like a good idea at the time," Fenella muttered. She sat down in front of the makeup mirror in the corner of the room and began to dig through her makeup.

"You should take a quick shower first," Mona told her. "Then you can put your hair up when it's wet."

"I wasn't going to put it up."

"You should. It's that kind of evening."

Fenella glanced at the clock. She would have to rush if she was going to fit a shower in before Donald arrived. Looking back in the mirror, she tried pulling her shoulder-length bob into a twist. Half of it fell down immediately and the rest stuck out at awkward angles.

"Once it's wet, it will go up easily. Use the silver clip in the bottom drawer," Mona said.

As she headed for the shower, Fenella wondered how she'd reached the point where she took nearly all of her advice from the ghost of a ninety-one year-old-woman. Half an hour later, after Mona had talked her through applying her makeup and pinning up her hair, Fenella couldn't help but smile at herself in the mirror. Mona might be old and dead, but she knew a lot about hair and makeup. And she had fabulous clothes.

"I look wonderful," she said softly as she smoothed away a fold in the dress.

"You do. Donald should be impressed," Mona said.

"I doubt it. I'm sure he's used to dating gorgeous supermodel types in their twenties."

"He has done, in the past," Mona agreed. "Maybe he's grown up a little bit lately. You aren't at all his type, but he seems determined to win your heart. Or maybe it's just your body he's after."

"I'm not sure what he's after," Fenella said, feeling a rush of apprehension. "I'm nearly fifty and at least ten pounds overweight. He could do so much better."

"Nonsense," Mona snapped. "You're pretty enough, but more importantly, you're smart. Donald likes beautiful young women because they make him feel younger, but he's interested in you because you challenge him. He knows he can't just buy you a few trinkets and get you into bed. He's going to have to work hard to gain your affection and the man loves a challenge."

"I don't like feeling like a prize to be won," Fenella complained.

"It's better than being an item that can be bought," Mona said. "You're just playing with Donald, anyway. We both know that, even if you won't admit it to yourself yet. You're not really interested in him, you're just enjoying the attention after all those years with that horrid professor."

"I'm not playing with him," Fenella protested.

Mona shrugged. "It wasn't a criticism," she said. "Men love these sort of games."

"I hate games."

"Yes, and I can't imagine why. Life is too short to take it seriously."

"Says the woman who died at ninety-one."

"Yes," Mona said wistfully. "I was hoping for considerably longer. I was meant to be having dinner with a new man the day after I passed. I hope he was devastated."

"Shall I look him up and ask him?"

"There's a thought. But no, what if he's found someone else and forgotten all about me? I'm probably better off not knowing. This way I can imagine that he's sitting at home every night pining for me."

"Yeah, sure," Fenella muttered.

Mona laughed. "I left more than one man pining for me over the years," she said. "I should look a few of them up now and see what they're doing with their afterlives."

"I'm not even going to ask you if you can really do that or not," Fenella said. "You won't give me a straight answer, anyway."

"My dear girl, has it occurred to you that you really don't want to know?"

"What do you mean?"

"I mean, if I were totally honest with you about what happens after death, dying would lose all of its mystery. It is your last great adventure and you should go into it without any knowledge of how it will turn out."

"I hate surprises," Fenella replied.

Mona laughed again. "You don't, really. I remember when you were maybe ten and I came to visit. I brought you..." A knock on the door interrupted the story.

Fenella crossed to the door and opened it.

"You look wonderful," Donald said, his eyes moving from her pinned-up hair down to her strappy shoes. As they made their way back up again, very slowly, Fenella felt herself blushing.

"Come in," she invited. "I just have to give Katie her dinner and I'll be ready to go."

Donald followed her into the kitchen. As she filled Katie's food and water bowls, the tiny, mostly black kitten darted into the room.

"Merow," she said in a conversational tone.

"I told you I'm going out tonight," Fenella replied. "I won't be terribly late and I'll try not to disturb you when I come in."

"Mereww" Katie answered, nodding her head.

"You two understand each other," Donald said with a laugh.

The kitten had dashed into Fenella's apartment only a few days after Fenella had arrived on the island. She'd made herself at home, and now Fenella couldn't imagine living without her. "She's very good at communicating with me," she told Donald. "And at getting her way."

Donald laughed. "But these are for you," he said, handing her a bouquet of beautiful red roses.

"You shouldn't have," Fenella said. She put the flowers on the counter and began to look around the kitchen for a vase.

"Try the cupboard next to the refrigerator," Mona said. "On the top shelf."

Fenella pulled down an expensive-looking crystal vase. "Isn't this lovely," she exclaimed. The apartment had been fully furnished when she'd inherited it, right down to plates and pots and pans in the kitchen. She knew she ought to go through everything, just to see what all she had, but she also enjoyed discovering things she didn't know were there, like the stunning vase.

"Mona had exquisite taste," Donald said.

Fenella filled the vase with water and then carefully unwrapped the flowers and added them. "They're beautiful, thank you," she said, glancing at the man. He looked even more handsome than usual in a tuxedo that had clearly been custom-tailored for him. His grey eyes twinkled behind his glasses as he watched her looking at him.

"I hope I'll do," he said after a moment. "The tuxedo is a new one, just arrived from my tailor yesterday. If you don't like it, I can rush home and change into a different one."

"You look very distinguished and sophisticated," Fenella said. "I'm terrified of you."

From behind Donald, Mona shook her head. "Never let the man know he has the upper hand," she said.

Donald chuckled. "Fear is the last thing I want you to feel when we're together," he said. He crossed to her side and pulled her into his arms. "Maybe I can set your mind at rest." He ran a finger down her cheek and then slowly lowered his lips to hers. When he lifted his head, he gave her a satisfied smile. “Better now?” he asked softly.

“So much worse,” Fenella replied, feeling as if she were drowning in a sea of emotions.

“Stop acting like a schoolgirl with a crush,” Mona hissed in her ear. “Take a deep breath and pull yourself together.”

Fenella followed her aunt’s orders, as that was far easier than trying to work out what to do by herself. She took a small step backwards, away from Donald, and smiled. “I think we should be going,” she said.

“If we must,” Donald replied. “We could skip the party and just stay here, getting better acquainted,” he suggested.

“Laugh and then say something about maybe already knowing him too well,” Mona spoke in her ear again.

Fenella chuckled. “I think we might already know each other too well,” she said, hoping Mona knew what she was doing.

Donald laughed. “Not even close,” he told her. “But let’s get to the party. It should be an interesting one.”

Picking up her handbag, Fenella followed the man out of the apartment. She wasn’t surprised to see the limousine waiting at the door for them.

“Everyone will be using them tonight,” Donald said as the driver shut the door behind them. “Like all of these charity events, tonight is about making the right impression.”

“On whom?”

“No one in particular,” Donald said. “The island’s elite social circle, I suppose. We all know how we’re meant to behave at such events, and arriving by limousine is the first step. Of course, having a beautiful woman on my arm is important as well.”

“Oh, dear, and you’re stuck with me,” Fenella blurted out.

Donald laughed. “If you’re fishing for compliments, I’m happy to supply them. You look stunning in that gown and I love what you’ve done with your hair. I’m sure I won’t be the only man at the party tonight who won’t be able to take his eyes off of you.”

Fenella blushed again and shook her head. “I wasn’t fishing,” she said. “I have a mirror.”

“Then you know I’m right,” Donald said. “In some ways you

remind me of your aunt. Even in her eighties, when she was at a party she was the center of attention. She had a way of walking into a room and making everyone take notice. In that dress, you could do the exact same thing."

"It's Mona's dress," Fenella said dryly.

"Why am I not surprised?" Donald grinned at her. "Just promise me you won't flirt too outrageously with all the other men tonight."

"I won't flirt with anyone," Fenella promised. "Not even you."

"And sometimes you're nothing like your aunt at all," Donald told her. "She flirted with everyone all the time."

The car pulled up in front of the Seaview a moment later. The hotel's doorman pulled open the car door and helped Fenella out of the car. A few flashbulbs popped as Donald took her arm.

"Press?" she questioned.

"For the back pages of the glossy magazines about the island," he told her. "They always feature photos from charity events."

Inside the sumptuous lobby of the hotel, they were greeted effusively.

"Donald, darling, thank you so much for coming," a tall blonde woman who looked around thirty said, offering her hand and then pulling Donald into a hug. "It's going to be quite an evening. We have some wonderful auction items. I'm counting on you to bid early and often."

"Melanie, meet Fenella Woods," Donald said, taking a step away from the woman. "Fenella, this is Melanie Anderson-Stuart. Her mother founded the Manx Fund for Children, and Melanie has been working with the charity since she could walk."

"It's very nice to meet you," Fenella said politely. She offered her hand and the other woman touched it lightly.

"Mother would like me to take over in the next year or two," Melanie said. "But I'm not sure I can live up to her legacy."

"I'm sure you'll do a wonderful job," Donald replied.

"Do you really think so?" Melanie asked, gazing into Donald's eyes. Fenella felt an irrational urge to slap the other woman.

"Of course I do," Donald told her. "And I'm sure your husband thinks so as well. Where is Matthew?"

"I thought everyone knew that Matthew and I aren't together any longer," Melanie said lightly. "He decided he wanted children and I simply couldn't go along. I've spent my entire life working with underprivileged and abused children. I simply couldn't imagine having one of my own."

"I am sorry to hear that," Donald replied.

"Oh, it's fine," Melanie said. "It just means I'm single again, which is exhausting. I think I'm too old to go through all of this again."

Donald laughed. "My dear, you're a mere child. I'm sure you have men beating down your door at all times."

Melanie shrugged. "Not the right ones," she said. She leaned toward Donald and smiled up at him. "Maybe I need an older man," she said softly.

"I'll see if I can think of any that might suit you," Donald said heartily. "Or maybe Fenella knows someone? What do you think, darling?" he asked, slipping an arm around Fenella's shoulders.

Fenella hid a smile as Melanie's face fell. "I can't think of anyone immediately, but I'll certainly give it some thought," she replied.

"Gee, thanks," Melanie replied sarcastically.

"Look, there's Carl," Donald said. "I'm sure you need to speak to him. We mustn't keep you from doing your job."

Melanie frowned and glanced at the door. A short, bald, and portly man had just entered. He stood in the doorway, scratching his head. "Carl," Melanie said with clearly fake enthusiasm. "How are you?" She took a step toward the man. Donald quickly began to lead Fenella down the corridor away from her.

"Sorry about that," he told her as they walked. "Melanie is a bit of a handful. She always has been."

"She's beautiful," Fenella replied.

"I've known her since she was two," Donald said. "She's only a few years older than my son. I have no interest in getting romantically involved with her, although I get the impression she doesn't share my sentiment."

"She was definitely flirting."

"And I only have eyes for you," Donald said. They'd reached the ballroom now and Fenella's breath caught when she saw the beautifully decorated room. She'd been there before, but she'd forgotten how gorgeous it was.

"Let's get some champagne before we mingle," Donald suggested.

An hour later, Fenella was quite tired of mingling. Donald had introduced her to dozens of people, and she'd already forgotten all of their names. A few men had tried flirting with her, but Donald had interrupted every attempt. Equally, a few women had made suggestive remarks to him, but he always made sure that they understood that he was not interested.

"Are you bored yet?" he whispered to Fenella as they exchanged empty glasses for full ones.

"A little bit," she replied.

"I'm sorry. Things will pick up once the auction starts," he assured her.

"Donald? How are you, darling?" a voice said from behind them.

The pair turned around. Fenella smiled at the elderly woman in the long black dress. She had to be over eighty. Her hair was white and gathered on the top of her head into what looked like a cloud. She was wearing thick glasses and too much lipstick.

"Phillipa, how lovely to see you," Donald said. "And Paulette, don't you look lovely tonight," he added. "Fenella, this is Phillipa Clucas and her daughter, Paulette."

Fenella shook hands with the older woman and then her daughter. Paulette was also wearing a long black dress. She was probably around sixty, with dark hair liberally streaked with grey, pulled back in an unflattering ponytail. She smiled at Fenella as they shook hands, but the smile didn't reach her eyes.

"Who did you say this was?" Phillipa asked Donald.

"Fenella Woods," he replied. "She's Mona Kelly's niece."

Phillipa took a step backwards and stared at Fenella. "And you have the nerve to stand there, acting like it doesn't matter," she shouted. "Acting like you've no idea who I am, or what harm has been done to me."

2

Fenella felt her jaw drop. She looked over at Donald, but he looked as confused as she felt. "I'm sorry, but I don't believe we've met before," she said hesitantly.

"I'm sure your aunt has told you all about me, though, hasn't she? No doubt she's bragged to you about how much time my husband spent in her bed, and how they probably laughed about me, sitting at home, totally unaware of what was happening," the woman said, nearly yelling the accusations.

Conscious that nearly everyone in the room was watching, Fenella struggled to work out how to reply.

"Mona passed away in January," Donald said, taking Fenella's hand and squeezing it tightly. "Fenella moved to the island in March."

"And you don't mind living in the flat where she seduced other women's husbands," the woman retorted, her eyes flashing. She took a step closer to Fenella. "You should be ashamed."

"Now, Phillipa, that's hardly fair," Donald said. "You've never even met Fenella. Take it from me, she's nothing like Mona."

"No? She's here with you, isn't she?" Phillipa snarled.

"Mum, you have to stop," Paulette said, pulling on her mother's arm. “Remember what the doctor said about your heart. It isn’t good for you to get upset, remember?”

“How can I not get upset?” the older woman shot back. “I shouldn’t have come tonight.” She shook her head. “I should have stayed home and mourned your father, but that doesn’t feel right. He wasn’t the man I thought he was. He wasn’t the man you thought he was, either.”

Paulette nodded. “I know, Mum, but it’s no good shouting at Fenella. She never even met my father. What her aunt did isn’t her fault.”

Phillipa looked at Fenella and narrowed her eyes. “She doesn’t even look sorry,” she snapped.

Paulette sighed and slid an arm around her mother. “Let’s go home,” she suggested. “We can open a bottle of wine and watch some television and forget all about everything.”

“I wish I could forget that easily,” Phillipa said. “But I can’t.”

“I’ll ring Dr. Quayle,” Paulette told her. “He can come and give you something to help you sleep.”

“I don’t want to sleep,” Phillipa argued.

“Where’s Paul?” Donald asked.

“He’s running late,” Paulette told him. “Otherwise I’d let him deal with my darling mother.”

“Do you want me to ring for a taxi for you?” Donald asked.

Paulette shook her head. “I drove, just in case we needed to make a quick exit.”

“We aren’t leaving,” Phillipa announced. “She should leave,” she added, sneering at Fenella.

“What on earth is going on over here?” an imperious voice cut through the air.

“Patricia, how lovely to see you,” Donald said as the woman who’d spoken joined their group.

This has to be Patricia Anderson, Fenella thought. She looked so much like her daughter that Fenella might have taken them for sisters if she didn’t know better. Patricia’s dress was fire-engine red. It was low-cut and far more daring than Fenella’s, even though the woman had to be over sixty.

"Why did I hear shouting?" Patricia asked, looking at each person in turn.

"She's Mona Kelly's niece," Phillipa said in an accusatory tone.

Patricia raised an eyebrow. "That explains a lot," she said almost to herself. She turned and smiled at Fenella. "I'm Patricia Anderson. It's a pleasure to meet you."

"Fenella Woods," she replied. "Donald tells me you're behind the wonderful charity hosting tonight's event."

"Yes, indeed, it's been my life's work," Patricia told her. "Mona was a very generous supporter of what we did. She always insisted on giving anonymously, of course. She never wanted to draw attention to her kindness."

"She had an affair with my Paul," Phillipa shrieked.

"Fenella did?" Patricia said incredulously.

"No, Mona did," Phillipa replied.

Patricia raised an eyebrow. "I find that difficult to believe," she said after a moment. "But I can't see what difference it makes. Both Paul and Mona have passed now, after all."

"It matters to me," Phillipa said with tears in her eyes. "It matters to me a great deal."

Paulette put her arm around her mother. "Come on, Mum, let's go home," she said. Before the other woman managed to object, Paulette began to lead her away.

"That was unpleasant," Patricia said as the others watched the pair leave the room. "Deeply unpleasant."

"Paul only passed a few months ago," Donald said. "It seems that Phillipa is taking it quite badly."

"Clearly," Patricia's tone was icy. "There's no excuse for such behavior, though. Tonight is about the Manx Fund for Children, not Phillipa's personal vendettas. Ms. Woods, I am sorry that you were subjected to that. I hope it won't put you off supporting our good cause."

Fenella swallowed hard. "No, of course not," she muttered. She hadn't planned on bidding on anything in the auction or making a donation, but perhaps she was going to have to do one or the other. Having quit her job to move to the island, she'd been pleased to find that she'd inherited enough to allow her to stay at home and work on the book she'd always wanted to write. Her budget didn't allow for many extra expenses, though. Sipping her champagne, she tried to work out exactly how much she could afford to spend to try to stay on Patricia Anderson's good side.

Patricia chatted with Donald for a moment before deciding that she needed to speak to someone on the other side of the room. Fenella blew out a sigh of relief as the woman walked away.

"Are you okay?" Donald asked, pulling her close as soon as Patricia was gone.

"Not really," Fenella admitted. "Phillipa scared me, and Patricia worries me."

"You mustn't worry about Phillipa. She's obviously not herself since her husband died, but she's eighty-five and mostly harmless. I'm sure shouting at you has completely worn her out," he replied.

"I just hope I never see her again," Fenella said fervently.

"And you mustn't let Patricia bother you either," Donald continued. "She's only interested in one thing, and that's raising money for her charity. She bullies everyone mercilessly until they donate, but as it's a good cause, we don't complain."

"I just don't know that I can afford to donate much," Fenella murmured.

"You're my guest tonight," Donald said. "I'll donate enough for both of us."

"I can't let you do that," Fenella objected.

"Of course you can," Donald said with a wave of his hand. "In fact, I insist on it. When you start getting invited to these things yourself, then you'll have to start making your own donations, but tonight you are my guest."

Fenella opened her mouth to object again, but decided against it. As she didn't feel she could afford to make a donation, perhaps Donald was right.

He gave her a tight hug and then kissed the top of her head. "Now stop worrying," he whispered in her ear. "Have some more champagne and relax."

Half an hour later Patricia was nearly ready to start the auction.

Donald pulled Fenella into the front row of seats near the stage. "You'll have to let me know what you want," he told her. "I'm sure you deserve a present for getting through tonight."

Fenella sank into her seat next to Donald and closed her eyes. All she really wanted right then was to go home and talk to Mona. Asking her aunt whether she'd had an affair with Paul Clucas or not was going to be awkward, but it needed to be done. Fenella wasn't sure why, but she felt she needed to know whether Phillipa's anger had been misplaced or not.

"I'm sorry, but may I just have a minute of your time?" a timid voice asked in Fenella's ear.

She opened her eyes and jumped as she realized that Paulette Clucas had slid into the seat on the other side of her.

"Oh, I didn't mean to startle you," the woman said quickly. "I took Mum home and got her to bed, but I had to come back to apologize. She really isn't herself at the moment, and I'm terribly sorry that she shouted at you."

"I hope you can get her some help," Fenella said after an uncomfortable pause.

"I'm doing everything I can to help her," Paulette assured her. "And I have Dr. Quayle on speed dial."

"How difficult for you," Fenella murmured.

"You've no idea," Paulette retorted. "But I'd really like to explain. After everything that was said, you deserve a proper explanation. I don't suppose you'd be willing to have tea with me tomorrow?"

"Tea?" Fenella repeated, her mind racing.

"They do a proper tea on Sunday afternoons here," the woman replied. "It starts at two and it's just about my favorite thing in the world. My mum started taking me out for Sunday tea when I was a little girl. It was something we did without my father or my brother. It was just for the girls." She stopped and shook her head. "I'm sorry. Whenever I have to talk to someone about something upsetting, I try to make it over tea here. It feels like home to me."

"It sounds lovely, but there's no need," Fenella told her.

"But I really want you to understand," the woman said fervently. "And I want to talk to you about Mona, as well."

"I believe we're ready to begin," Patricia said from the stage. "If everyone could find seats, please?"

"I have to go," Paulette said. "I can't afford to bid on anything and I should get home to Mum anyway. Sunday tea? Please?"

"Sure, why not?" Fenella replied, feeling flustered.

"Thank you so much," the woman replied, beaming with delight. "I'll see you then."

She was gone, swallowed up by the crowd looking for seats before Fenella could change her mind.

To Fenella the next hour seemed to drag on forever. She was eager to get home to talk to her aunt and bored with the seemingly endless auction. Expensive jewelry, high-priced electronics, and exotic vacations came under the hammer, and the well-heeled crowd bid each item up to ridiculous prices. Donald bought a few paintings, none of which Fenella could imagine hanging on her walls.

"Let me buy you this necklace," Donald urged as a diamond and ruby pendant came up for auction.

"I really wouldn't wear it," Fenella told him.

"What about this bracelet?" he asked a few minutes later as an emerald bracelet was showcased.

Fenella shook her head. "I rarely wear bracelets. They just get in the way." And that one is gaudy and horrible, she added in her head.

The last few items were all vacations and Fenella was relieved when Donald didn't offer to buy her any of those.

"I'd love to take you on holiday with me somewhere wonderful," he said quietly during the bidding. "But I don't intend to announce my intentions by buying the holiday in front of a huge audience."

When the auction was over, Donald grinned at her. "Yet again you've managed to avoid letting me spoil you," he said. "This can't continue, though. Sooner or later you're going to have to let me buy you something wonderful."

"I don't feel comfortable with you buying me things," Fenella countered. "I can't imagine that changing."

Donald chuckled. "I must have a better imagination than you do," he said. "I can imagine all manner of things." He winked as she blushed. "I have to go and pay for all of my art," he said, getting to his feet. "Then we can get out of here."

Fenella stood up and wandered toward the buffet tablets. Donald had joined a long line of people clutching checkbooks, so she picked up a plate and selected a few things to nibble on while she waited.

"So you're Mona's niece," a voice said from behind her.

Fenella turned around and forced herself to smile at the stranger. "I am, yes," she said.

"I'm Anne Marie Smuthers," the woman said. "Mona and I were friends, after a fashion." Anne Marie was grey-haired and looked at least eighty. She was wearing a very old fashioned looking blue dress that just about matched her eyes and clutching a small handbag with one hand and the handle of a cane with the other.

"It's nice to meet you. I'm Fenella Woods," Fenella introduced herself.

"Yes, I've heard about you. You and Donald are together, I understand," the woman replied.

"We came to the auction together," Fenella replied.

"Don't get too attached to him. He's like his father. He won't be interested once he's taken you to bed."

Fenella nearly choked on her onion tart. "Thanks for the warning," she muttered after grabbing a glass of champagne and taking a sip.

The woman shrugged. "Mona would tell you the same thing if she were still around. She understood men far too well. She warned me about marrying Herbert, but I didn't listen."

"Did she?" Fenella asked, wondering who Herbert was.

"Oh, yes. As I said, she understood men. She knew what he was like and why he wanted to marry me, but I thought we were madly in love." The woman sighed and then laughed. "Only the mad part was right, though. I was mad to ever marry the man."

"I am sorry," Fenella said, glancing over to see where Donald was in the line. There were still several men in front of him and no one seemed to be in any hurry.

"It was fun for about ten minutes," the woman replied, waving a hand. "And then Herbert was kind enough to crash his car and eliminate himself from my life."

Fenella felt her jaw drop for the second time that evening. “My goodness,” she gasped.

Anne Marie caught her eye and then began to laugh again. “I’ve shocked you,” she said happily. “No one expects little old ladies to say such things, but it’s true. He was a horrid man who married me for my money and then cheated on me with my closest friends. And Mona was one of my closest friends. I wasn’t at all sorry when he met his explosive end.”

And now I have yet another thing to talk to Mona about, Fenella thought. “How interesting,” she murmured, checking again on Donald’s place in the line.

“Interesting? That’s one word for it,” Anne Marie said. “That was sixty years ago, you know, and I’ve been happily on my own ever since.”

“That’s great,” Fenella said.

“I would have taken back my maiden name if I could have, but women didn’t do such things in those days,” the woman said. “Of course, I did a lot of other things that women weren’t meant to do. I really should have gone back to my maiden name.”

“You could change it now,” Fenella suggested.

“That would be too much bother at my age. I don’t really mind, not after all these years. I’ve had a great many other men in and out of my life and my bed since Herbert died and not one of them ever persuaded me to change my name again.”

Fenella was relieved to see that Donald was now writing his check. Anne Marie Smathers seemed to be taking great delight in shocking her and she was eager to get away. “I never married,” Fenella said. “That was one decision I never had to make.”

“Marriage is highly overrated. Of course, most of the men I took as lovers over the years were already married to other women, so that did limit my remarriage possibilities, but that was absolutely fine with me. I enjoyed my freedom far too much.”

Fenella nodded. “I’m enjoying my freedom as well.”

“Watch out for Donald, then,” the woman said. “He’s not the faithful type, but he does like being married. He’s had three wives already, you know. Men like that romanticize being married and are always surprised when their marriages fail.”

"Sorry that took so long," Donald said as he joined them. "Anne Marie, you look wonderful tonight."

"I was just warning your friend about you," the woman replied.

"Oh, dear, I should have interrupted sooner," Donald said with a smile.

"She's new to the island. She doesn't know what you're like," Anne Marie countered. "Just like your father, really. He always appeared to be devoted to whichever wife he was currently with, but behind her back he always had at least two or three lovers."

Donald flushed. "I'm nothing like my father," he said sharply. "I think it's time to go," he told Fenella.

"I didn't mean to upset you," Anne Marie said. "I loved your father dearly, you know, and he was always totally honest with me. Not all of my former lovers afforded me the same courtesy."

"It was lovely to see you again," Donald said.

"And you," the woman replied. "If I were a few years younger, I'd be trying to win you away from Ms. Woods."

"No doubt," Donald said. "Shall we?" he asked Fenella.

"It was nice to meet you," Fenella lied to the other woman.

"It was lovely to talk to you," Anne Marie replied. "Mona was lucky to have family. I've no one at all. My estate will all go to charity."

"But that won't be happening for many years yet," Donald said. "Good night."

"Good night," the woman replied. She turned and took a few steps toward the center of the room. One of the waiters stopped and spoke to her, eventually offering his arm and then leading her toward the door.

"Let's get out of here," Donald whispered to Fenella. "I'm tired of all of these people."

Fenella didn't speak until they were in the car, heading for Douglas. "I thought you enjoyed these sorts of evenings," she said.

"I usually do," Donald replied. "But tonight wasn't especially enjoyable."

"Why not?"

"You were shouted at by one elderly woman and then told goodness knows what by another," Donald replied. "I wasn't expecting either of those things to happen, not at a charity auction."

"It was a rather strange evening," Fenella admitted.

"Phillipa and Anne Marie have both been friends with Patricia forever," Donald told her. "Your Aunt Mona was part of their social circle, along with many of the other women who were married to the island's wealthiest men. I think Patricia keeps inviting them out of a sense of obligation. It isn't like any of them can afford to make the sort of large donation that Patricia expects from the rest of us."

"Phillipa seemed to be, well, mentally unstable."

"She may be. Her husband, Paul, passed away fairly recently. I don't think she's taken it well. I feel sorry for Paulette."

"I'm meeting her for tea tomorrow," Fenella said. "She wants to apologize for her mother's behavior."

"She would. She's that sort of person. Her brother, Paul, Junior, ought to be doing more, really. I'll tell him that the next time I see him."

"I'm not sure I want to know about Anne Marie Smathers," Fenella said.

Donald laughed. "She's unconventional, but then so was Mona. The two were very close friends in their youth; at least, that's what I've been told. At some point they stopped speaking to one another, although I've never heard the same story twice as to why."

"Anne Marie suggested that Mona slept with her husband," Fenella said.

"With Herbert? I would have credited Mona with better taste," Donald replied. "But it's possible, I suppose. I know for a fact that after Herbert's death Anne Marie began chasing after every man that Mona looked at twice. Their rivalry was the talk of the island when I was a young man."

"Really? I can't imagine."

"It was a different time. Women were meant to be wives and mothers, and both Anne Marie and Mona took a different path. Anne Marie was widowed very young, and of course Mona never married. I will say that Anne Marie's reputation was far wilder than Mona's. She had a number of affairs and never did anything to hide that fact. Mona was considerably more discreet, even mysterious, which only added to her appeal."

"I'm not sure I want to know, but did you get involved with either of them?" Fenella asked. As soon as the question was out of her mouth she regretted asking it.

"I'm only fifty-seven," the man replied with a chuckle. "Anne Marie has to be in her eighties and Mona was older than that. They were both friendly with my father, but I was too young to attract their notice when they were in their prime."

"Friendly with your father? Do I want to know?"

"I'm sure he had an affair with Anne Marie. She said as much tonight, and I know my father wasn't one to turn down a willing woman. I can't comment on his relationship with Mona, though. I know they were friends, but how far that friendship went, I don't know."

"The food was lovely," Fenella decided she'd had enough of the uncomfortable subject. "And you bought some interesting art."

"I did, although I can't imagine what I'm going to do with most of it. I keep buying more at every charity event I attend. I'm rapidly running out of wall space in my offices around the world."

"What about at home?"

"You've never seen my home," Donald replied thoughtfully. "I must have you around for dinner one night. You can see for yourself how little room I have left for more art."

"Maybe you should stop buying it," Fenella suggested.

"I should, but I'm lazy," he told her. "It's the easiest thing to buy at these auctions. Many of the pieces go for less than what I'd pay for something similar in a gallery, and I can buy four or five pieces and look extremely generous. If I had someone to give it to, I would have bought jewelry tonight," he added.

"It looks like rain," Fenella remarked, changing the subject again.

Donald laughed. "You're avoiding the issue," he chided her. "But yes, it does look like rain. I hope it's fine on Tuesday."

"I do, too," Fenella said. "It's my first Tynwald Day and I can't wait to see it."

"Are you sure you can't attend with me?" Donald asked.

"I'm quite sure," Fenella replied. Shelly had invited Fenella to attend the island's national day ceremony with her many weeks earlier. Peter Cannell, another neighbor, was also joining them, and they were planning to spend the day at St. John's enjoying the spectacle.

Donald would be sitting with various important people, watching the ceremony from the grandstand. Fenella was quite happy to sit on a blanket on the grass with her friends for the event.

"It still amazes me that the island's government meets outdoors once a year," Fenella said. "And that anyone who wants to can petition the government about whatever concerns they have."

"I believe it is fairly unique," Donald said. "But the island is a small country, so it can do things that larger countries couldn't possibly manage."

"I'm fascinated by the whole event."

"It's a fun day out. You'll have a chance to try different Manx products, hear Manx music, and see Manx dancing. There will be Vikings, street theater, and bands, and at the end of the evening, fireworks."

"Shelly said it's one of her favorite days of the year," Fenella replied. "As long as it doesn't rain."

Donald nodded. "That's always a problem, of course, but there are marquees for some things."

"Marquees?"

"I believe you'd call them tents," Donald said with a grin.

"Well, rain or shine, I'm going."

"I'd love to join you after the ceremony. If Shelly won't mind."

"You're more than welcome, of course. Shelly's inviting everyone she knows to join us."

The limousine pulled up in front of Fenella's apartment building and stopped.

"You don't have to come in," Fenella said quickly.

"But I will, anyway," Donald countered. The driver opened Fenella's door and helped her out of the car while Donald climbed out the other side. Before she'd taken more than a single step, he was offering her his arm. At her door, Fenella dug around for her keycard.

"I can never find the stupid key," she muttered, digging through her small handbag.

"You could just come home with me," Donald suggested.

Fenella blushed and focused her efforts. "Got it," she exclaimed, pulling the card from the bag. She unlocked her door and pushed it open.

"Thank you for a lovely evening," she said to Donald.

"It wasn't lovely, but it was better with you there," Donald told her. "Thank you for giving up your evening to make mine better."

He leaned forward and kissed her very gently. Fenella returned the kiss, once again nearly overwhelmed by the physical chemistry between them.

"I could stay," he whispered as he lifted his head.

"I'm not, that is, I can't, I mean," Fenella stuttered.

Donald smiled. "I promised I won't rush you, but I'm also not going to stop offering," he said. "One of these days you'll change your mind."

"Or you'll give up," Fenella suggested.

"Maybe. But not any time soon," Donald replied. He pulled her close and kissed her again, this time anything but gently. When he lifted his head, he grinned at her. "Would you like to change your answer?" he asked.

Fenella reluctantly shook her head. She really wasn't ready to take things to the next level with the man.

"I'll see you on Tuesday, then," he told her. "Take good care of yourself until then."

Fenella nodded and then shut the door behind the man. Katie bounced into the room as the lock clicked.

"Merrroowww," she said.

"You had your dinner," Fenella told her. "All you get now is more water."

Katie stared at her for a minute and then padded off to the kitchen. Fenella followed and refilled the animal's water bowl. After a moment's hesitation, she took a treat out of the box in the cupboard and gave it to the animal. Katie gobbled it up and gave Fenella a satisfied smile.

As she washed her face and combed out her hair, Fenella tried to decide how she was going to ask Mona about the things she'd heard.

There didn't seem to be any easy way to bring up the subject, but she didn't feel as if she could simply ignore the stories. Feeling fortunate that Mona wasn't around at the moment, Fenella got ready for bed and climbed in. Katie was already curled up in her usual spot in the exact center of the bed.

Tomorrow she would have to talk to Mona before she headed back to Ramsey for tea with Paulette, she decided. Too bad she wasn't looking forward to doing either of those things.

3

Katie woke Fenella at seven the next morning. "I gave you a treat before bed," Fenella complained as the kitten jumped up and down on her chest. "You could have let me sleep for an extra hour."

The animal just looked at her and then jumped off the bed and ran out the door. A moment later Fenella could hear her complaining loudly in the kitchen.

"I'm coming," she said, sighing deeply as she pulled her bathrobe on over her pajamas. She filled up Katie's food and water bowls and then started a pot of coffee. There was too much on her mind for her to go back to sleep. While the coffee was brewing, she showered and pulled on jeans and a T-shirt.

"How was the party?" Mona asked when Fenella walked back into the kitchen a short while later.

Fenella turned and looked at Mona. The woman didn't look a day over thirty, and Fenella had to admit that she was beautiful. This morning her hair was pulled up in an elaborate chignon and she was wearing a pretty summery dress. Mona was tall and slender and she looked far more well-rested than Fenella felt.

"It was interesting," Fenella replied. "I got shouted at by Phillipa Clucas, which wasn't very pleasant."

"Phillipa Clucas shouted at you? That doesn't even make sense. I don't think Phillipa has ever shouted at anyone in her life."

"Well, she shouted at me, although it was really you that she was angry with."

"Me?" Mona shook her head. "What could I have possibly done to upset Phillipa? We always got along well when I was alive."

"She wasn't very happy that you'd slept with her husband," Fenella said dryly.

Mona looked at her for a moment and then began to laugh.

"I'm not sure I think it's funny," Fenella said eventually.

"I'm sorry, but the very idea that I would sleep with Paul Clucas is quite hilarious," Mona told her. "Did you meet the man?"

"He's dead."

Mona stopped laughing. "Oh, I am sorry to hear that," she said. "I didn't realize. Poor Phillipa, she relied on Paul for so much. I imagine she's quite lost without him."

"She was with her daughter last night."

"Oh, yes, Paulette. Such a dreary and dull woman, but devoted to her mother, of course."

"I'm having tea with her this afternoon at the Seaview," Fenella said.

"Yes, well, do see if you can find out why Phillipa thinks I slept with Paul. I'd love to know, even if it is a rather horrible idea."

"Why?"

"He was ghastly," Mona replied. After a moment, while Fenella sipped her coffee, she shook her head. "I'm not being fair," she admitted. "I might have been tempted by him when we were young if he hadn't been married to Phillipa. But Phillipa was so madly in love with the man that I knew she would be hurt if he cheated. I did try to avoid married men who had wives who loved them, you know."

"Did you?"

"I did," Mona said firmly. "Anyway, Paul was a terrible flirt, but I don't think very many women in our social circle succumbed to his rather dubious charms. I'm sure he probably found one or two that were willing."

"Phillipa must have known," Fenella suggested.

"I always thought she chose not to know. She was busy with the children. Paul was out nearly every night, enjoying the social scene. I assumed at the time that Phillipa was simply turning a blind eye to whatever he was getting up to."

"Maybe I'll find out more at tea," Fenella said.

"You'll struggle to stay awake once Paulette starts talking," Mona replied. "She's never done a single interesting thing in her life, that woman."

"She seemed very nice."

"Yes, well, you have fun. Sometimes I'm glad I'm dead and I don't have to observe social niceties anymore."

"No social niceties in the spirit world?" Fenella asked.

"None at all," Mona said happily.

"Anyway, after that awkward encounter, I had another uncomfortable chat with Anne Marie Smathers," Fenella said.

"No doubt she told you I slept with her husband," Mona said. "I was being unfair to Paul, really. Herbert was a dreadful man. Paul wasn't nearly as bad by comparison."

"So you didn't sleep with Herbert Smathers?"

Mona sighed. "I wish I'd had as exciting a life as everyone seems to think I had," she said. "But really, my reputation was built almost entirely on gossip and innuendo. I didn't have anywhere near the number of lovers people thought I'd had. As we're making comparisons, I was an angel compared to Anne Marie."

"She did tell me that she'd had several lovers after her husband died."

"After and before," Mona corrected her. "Those two were ill-suited from the start, but Anne Marie wouldn't listen to anyone in those days. She probably still won't."

"She said he married her for her money," Fenella recalled.

"Perhaps. Although he wasn't exactly poor himself. And my goodness, but he was gorgeous," Mona said with a sigh.

"But not nice."

"Oh, no, not nice at all," Mona agreed. "Although he could be overwhelmingly wonderful when he wanted something from you. And once he'd latched on to Anne Marie, well, she didn't have a chance. He flattered her and spoiled her and convinced her to marry him in less than a month."

"Wow, that's fast."

"Anne Marie always said that was the happiest month of her life. Once they were married, the real Herbert came out, though."

"I'm not sure I want to know more."

"He simply lost interest in Anne Marie," Mona said. "He made no effort to hide the fact that he was chasing other women. Anne Marie was meant to be grateful that he'd married her and simply look the other way."

"How dreadful."

"It was terribly unpleasant. I refused to get mixed up in it. In fact, I even went to the US to visit your mother for a few months to get away from the man. He could be incredibly persistent and I didn't want to be persuaded."

"Anne Marie said he died in a car accident."

"I was still in the US when he died, so I can only tell you what I heard," Mona replied. "He definitely died in a car crash, but I've always wondered whether it was an accident or not."

"What do you mean?"

Mona shrugged. "As I understand it, the car blew up and was completely destroyed. If anyone had tampered with anything, the evidence was gone."

"You think Anne Marie killed her husband?"

"Anne Marie or maybe someone else's jealous husband," Mona suggested. "The police investigated and the whole thing was officially ruled an accident. I'm just telling you how I felt at the time."

"Why does Anne Marie think you slept with Herbert?"

"I'm sure he told her that I had," Mona replied. "That was one of his arguments when he was trying to get you into bed. He was going to tell everyone he'd taken you to bed, so why not go ahead and do it?"

"What a horrible man," Fenella exclaimed.

"Yes, I can't say I was sorry to hear about his death."

"Didn't you ever talk to Anne Marie about it?"

"Never. In our social circle there were a handful of affairs over the years. No one ever talked about them directly with the people involved, although we all talked about everyone behind their backs. Mostly, the people involved preferred to pretend it wasn't happening. That way families could stay together."

"Well, Anne Marie is talking now," Fenella said.

"Now that I'm dead, no doubt she'll be happy to throw around all sorts of accusations. I wouldn't be surprised if she tried rewriting history. In time, I'll come to be the woman that drove her and Herbert apart. That is, unless someone else dies as well. There are so many women that she could attach blame to, really."

"What about Phillipa Clucas?"

"What about her?"

"Did she have an affair with Herbert?

"Oh, goodness, no," Mona chuckled. "Phillipa was faithful, the poor dear. She was mostly oblivious to what was going on around her. I can't imagine that Herbert even noticed her, really. Anyway, as I said, she was busy with her children for many years."

"You said Paulette has a brother?"

"Yes, Paul, Junior," Mona replied. "Both children were named after their father, which tells you something about how devoted Phillipa was, doesn't it?"

"I suppose so."

"But there was a third child," Mona said. "I nearly forgot about Paula."

"Another one named after her father."

"Yes, she was, but she wasn't well," Mona told her. "I never knew exactly what was wrong with the child, but she needed care around the clock, which was one of the reasons why Phillipa was so busy all the time. She didn't like having anyone else look after Paula."

"What happened to her?"

"She passed away quite young. I can't remember the whole story, but I do know that Phillipa was devastated. She had to be hospitalized for several weeks. Paul, of course, used that as the perfect opportunity to take up with someone else."

"Poor Phillipa," Fenella remarked.

"Yes, she's had a difficult life, really. She chose the wrong man to marry. So many women make that mistake."

"Maybe that's why I've never married," Fenella said.

Mona laughed. "But it's so much easier now," she said. "You can simply get a divorce if things don't work out. In my day you were expected to stay married for life, no matter how bad things got."

"So people cheated."

"That was certainly easier than trying to get a divorce in those days."

"I suppose I should be grateful that I live now, then."

"For so many reasons that have nothing to do with what we're talking about," Mona replied.

Fenella poured herself another cup of coffee. "How much of all of this do you think Paulette knows?"

"I wouldn't have thought that Paulette knew anything about her father's indiscretions, or attempted indiscretions, I should say," Mona replied. "Did she seem surprised at what her mother was saying?"

"No, not really," Fenella said after some thought. "She just seemed embarrassed."

"Someone must have said something to Phillipa. Maybe Anne Marie said something. Although she's a fine one to be pointing fingers at me when it comes to Paul Clucas."

"Anne Marie had an affair with the man?"

"She did. It actually got quite serious. It wasn't long after Herbert died. Phillipa was pregnant with one of the children, I can't remember which. Anyway, Anne Marie and Paul were suddenly everywhere together and there were rumors that he was going to ask Phillipa for a divorce so that he could marry Anne Marie."

"And then what happened?" Fenella demanded when Mona stopped talking.

"I'm not sure," Mona said with a frown. "One day they were inseparable and the next day they weren't speaking. A few weeks later he began flirting with Margaret Dolek and that was that."

"Margaret Dolek?"

"Another woman from our crowd," Mona told her. "Her husband traveled a lot for work, but I don't know that she ever actually cheated on him. She just enjoyed flirting."

"I don't understand why married people behave like that," Fenella said.

"As I said, it was a different time," Mona told her. "Imagine that your father insisted that you marry some man that he chose for you not long after your eighteenth birthday. You do as you're told and have a couple of babies, but you're miserable. Then you meet a wonderful man who woos you and tells you all the right things to make you feel loved for the first time in your life. You'd be tempted to listen, and maybe to cheat as well, especially if you knew that your husband wasn't faithful."

"Maybe," Fenella said.

"It was all a long time ago," Mona told her. "All of the people involved are either dead or old. It can't possibly matter anymore."

"It seems as if it still matters to Phillipa."

"Perhaps tea with Paulette won't be as boring as I'd initially assumed," Mona said.

Fenella changed into a light and summery dress for the afternoon tea.

"Everyone will be dressed up," Mona told her. "Afternoon tea is an occasion."

Since she hadn't yet taken her driving test, she rang for a taxi. "Wish me luck," she said to Mona as she headed out.

"Don't dawdle," Mona instructed her. "I want to hear what Paulette says about me."

The taxi driver chatted about the weather and local news while he drove, but Fenella was only half listening. When they arrived at the Seaview, she gave him a generous tip as an apology and then walked into the elegant lobby for the second time in as many days.

"How may I help you?" the man behind the reception desk asked.

"I'm meeting someone for afternoon tea," Fenella replied.

"Afternoon tea is served in the south dining room," he informed her. "If you follow the light blue carpet down the corridor, you'll see the dining room on your left."

Fenella followed the instructions and soon found herself standing in the doorway of yet another beautifully decorated room. There were a dozen or so tables spread out around the large space but only a handful of them were occupied. It took her a moment to spot Paulette Clucas at a table in one corner.

"Ah, Fenella, thank you so much for coming," the woman said, rising to her feet as Fenella approached the table. Paulette was wearing black again, this time an unflattering skirt and top that were at least one size too small for the plump woman. Her hair was in a ponytail again and her face was free of makeup.

"I hope your mother is okay," Fenella said as she slid into the chair opposite Paulette.

"She's, well, she has good days and bad ones," Paulette told her. "She was doing so well yesterday that I agreed that she could attend the party last night. That didn't go very well, though, did it?"

"Obviously, I didn't mean to upset her."

"It wasn't you," Paulette said. "It was hearing Mona's name that upset her. She'd always thought of Mona as a friend."

"Good afternoon," the waiter interrupted. "Is it afternoon tea for two?"

"Yes, please," Paulette said. "Unless you'd rather have something else?" she asked Fenella.

"No, afternoon tea sounds wonderful," Fenella replied. "It will be my first ever."

"Oh, my, I can't imagine," Paulette said. "Afternoon tea is one of the greatest joys in my life."

"I'll be back momentarily," the waiter told them with a bow.

"When I was a little girl my mother would take me for a proper grown-up tea once or twice a year. It was our special time together and it always felt, I don't know, magical or something. Paul wasn't invited because he was a boy and Paula was just a baby, but mother and I would come here and sip tea and eat cakes and talk about everything and nothing."

"It sounds wonderful."

"It was that and more," Paulette said, her eyes shining with remembered happiness. "My mother had a difficult life. Our afternoon teas were an escape for her."

"And for you."

"Oh, my life wasn't that bad. I had my mother, you see, and she was devoted to all three of us children. I didn't understand why my mother was sad all the time, or why we never saw very much of our father, but I didn't know to care until I was much older."

"I wonder how many people actually had happy childhoods," Fenella said, trying to lighten the mood.

"Very few, I would imagine," Paulette replied. "There were happy moments in my childhood, but overall it wasn't good. As I said, my father wasn't around very much. Times were different then, of course. Men weren't expected to play an active role in raising children in those days."

"No, that is true."

"Tea for two," the waiter said as he pushed a large tea trolley up to the table. He unloaded two pots of tea with matching cups before settling a large tiered stand in the center of the table. "Finger sandwiches, pastries, and cream cakes," he said, gesturing toward the stand. "If you'd like more of anything, or everything, please let me know." He gave each woman a small plate that matched the tea service before he turned and walked away.

Fenella's mouth was watering as she helped herself to several different items. When her plate was full, she smiled at Paulette. "It all looks delicious," she said.

For a few minutes neither woman spoke as they began to eat. Eventually, Fenella washed down a bite with a sip of tea. "This is fabulous. I can see why you have happy memories of doing this."

"When I got older, we used to go for tea more often," Paulette said. "Sometimes as often as once a month. But that was after, well, after something awful happened."

"I'm sorry," was all that Fenella could think to say.

Paulette sighed. "It's been so many years, you'd think I could talk about it easily, but I can't. Perhaps because my mother can't stand to be reminded."

"Can I get you another plate of cream cakes?" the waiter asked.

Fenella jumped slightly. She hadn't heard him coming up behind her.

"Oh, I am sorry," he said quickly.

"I think we could use more cakes," Paulette said with a nervous giggle.

"Right away, madam," the man replied.

He was back only a moment later and Fenella was delighted to see several small chocolate cakes on the plate he delivered. She helped herself while Paulette poured herself some more tea.

"If you talk to anyone on the island, you'll soon hear the whole story," Paulette said. "I may as well tell you everything."

"Please don't, if it makes you uncomfortable," Fenella said quickly.

The other woman shook her head. "I want you to understand why my mother behaved so badly last night. You should hear the whole story."

Fenella took a big bite of cake. Chocolate made everything better, even sad stories from many years ago.

"I'm the oldest," Paulette said. "My mother always told me that she'd hoped and prayed for a little girl when she found out she was pregnant with me. She and my father hadn't been married for very long, but she was already very lonely. She wanted someone to be her friend, I suppose."

"Hence the afternoon teas," Fenella suggested.

"Yes, I suppose so. I was far too young to properly enjoy them when we first started going, but I don't suppose my mother had anyone else with whom to go anywhere. Anyway, about two years later my little brother came along. I believe my father was happier with a son than he had been with a daughter, but that didn't mean he spent any more time at home, just that he sometimes took Paul, Junior, with him when he went out."

"Their own version of your afternoon tea."

"Something like that," Paulette agreed. "But only very occasionally. Anyway, a few years after Paul came along, my mother had another baby. This time it was another girl, Paula, but something went wrong. My mother was never certain whether Paula's problems were caused by an error in the delivery room or something that had happened during the pregnancy, but something went wrong."

"Could it have been something genetic?" Fenella asked.

"Perhaps. As I said, my mother never knew exactly what went wrong, but Paula had lots of problems. She never progressed past infancy, really. She could hold up her head, but she never managed to sit up on her own or walk or talk. My mother, of course, dedicated herself to Paula's care, but it was exhausting and endless. She didn't trust anyone else to look after her, except for her own mother."

"How difficult for all of you," Fenella murmured.

"Yes, it wasn't easy. My grandmother used to come and stay for several days at a time, two or three times a year. That was the only time my mother would ever leave Paula's side. As long as Paula was doing okay, we'd go for our afternoon tea, though. My mother always insisted on making sure we got to do that." The woman's eyes filled with tears.

"I'm very sorry," was all that Fenella could think to say.

"As I got older, I tried to help more, but Paula was, well, difficult to deal with, really. She would slap at me when I tried to feed her or shout when I tried to dress her. My mother was the only one who could manage her, although my grandmother could handle her for short periods of time. I was fifteen when my grandmother passed away."

"More tea?" the waiter asked. This time Fenella had seen him coming. She found she was glancing around the room a great deal, trying not to stare at the woman across from her who was pouring out her heart.

"Yes, please," she said quickly. The man replaced both teapots before bowing again and walking away.

"I'm sorry," Paulette said. "I'm dragging this out because I hate talking about it. I'll skip over some of the more maudlin bits and simply tell you that my baby sister died that summer, no more than three months after my grandmother had gone. My mother was, obviously, devastated."

Fenella nodded. "Losing a child is the most difficult thing in the world," she said. While she'd lost her only child in the very early stages of pregnancy, Fenella felt a tremendous rush of sympathy for Phillipa Clucas.

"Her heart simply gave out, apparently," the woman said. "The doctors said they weren't surprised. Apparently, they'd warned my mother that she might lose Paula at any time. My mother only told me that after her mother died. I was trying to persuade my mother to hire someone to come in to look after Paula for a few hours now and again. My mother wouldn't even consider it." She shook her head. "My mother had been warned. She knew Paula's heart was weak, but she still fell to pieces when Paula died. She had to be hospitalized for several weeks and it was nearly a year before she began to pull herself together."

"How awful for you and your brother," Fenella said.

"It wasn't easy. I was fifteen. I dropped out of school to look after Mum. My father didn't know what to do about the situation, so he just avoided it for the most part. My brother started spending most of his afternoons at my father's office, which was good for him, I suppose, but left all of the care for my mother on my shoulders."

"I can't imagine."

"Mum improved slowly," Paulette said, giving Fenella what looked like a forced smile. "And it was a long time ago. I'm well over the trauma of it all. When I look back now, it's all a dark blur, the year or so from when my grandmother died until the time when my mother began to improve. By then I'd decided that I didn't want to go back to school. Instead, I stayed at home as a sort of companion to my mother. Here we are, thirty-odd years later, and I'm still doing the same thing."

The waiter dropped off another plate of pastries and cream cakes as Fenella tried to work out how to bring the conversation around to Mona again. She still didn't know why Phillipa thought that Paul had had an affair with Mona.

"My father retired about ten years ago," Paulette told her as the waiter walked away. "As soon as he stopped working, he started playing golf five or six times a week. Mum used to joke that she saw more of him when he was working than after he retired. My brother used to play with him, at least on the weekends. He's taken over the family business, which pleased my father, I'm sure."

"Is he married? Does your mother have grandchildren?" Fenella asked as the questions popped into her head.

"No. I suppose seeing how miserable marriage made our parents for all those years, neither Paul nor I were ever tempted to try it ourselves. I had a few suitors when I was much younger, but nothing ever came of any of it." She glanced down at her outfit and waved a hand. "I know it's hard to believe now, looking at me, but I wasn't unattractive when I was younger. My father had a great deal of money, as well, which made me even more appealing. That may be why I stayed away from romantic entanglements, really. I could never be certain if men were interested in me or in my family's money. I'm not sure why Paul never married."

"Perhaps he's simply never found the right woman," Fenella suggested. "I've never married, either."

Paulette nodded. "But I invited you here today to apologize for last night," she said. "All of this has been a very long-drawn-out explanation for what happened last night."

"I'm not sure that I follow."

"It seems that my father decided, once he'd retired, to write his memoirs," she explained. "He passed away before he did much more than make a few notes," Paulette said. "My mother accessed them on his computer after his funeral."

Fenella nodded, anticipating what was coming next.

"She was devastated with what she found," Paulette said sadly.

"Let me guess, he claims in his notes that he had an affair with Mona," Fenella concluded.

"I've no reason to doubt what he wrote," Paulette said.

Fenella bit her tongue. She had every reason to doubt Paul Clucas's words, but she couldn't very well explain that to Paulette.

"My mother says she's only glanced at what's there. I'm trying to persuade her to delete the file without looking at the rest of it," Paulette told her. "From what I've seen so far, I'm certain that Mona wasn't the only woman he slept with behind my mother's back. Having seen how she reacted to meeting you last night, I really don't want her to find out about anyone else."

"I can understand that, but how can you be certain that your father was telling the truth?"

"He had no reason to lie, not when all of the cheating puts him in a bad light," Paulette argued. "Anyway, it all makes sense. It explains the long hours he was meant to be at work, and the weekends away. Now I know why he was never around and why he was so distant when he was at home."

"I'm sorry," Fenella said. She was tempted to argue further, but she didn't want to add to the other woman's obvious upset. At the end of the day, it probably didn't matter that Paulette and Phillipa thought that Mona had had an affair with the man. They were both dead, after all.

"Thank you," Paulette said. "I know you didn't know Mona, but I remember her from my childhood. She was incredibly beautiful and glamorous and sophisticated. I remember her visiting my mother when I was very young. She always looked like a princess to me in her fabulous clothes. Her makeup was always perfect and she never had a hair out of place. I don't know how she did it, but I know my mother was intimidated by her, even though they were meant to be friends."

"I'm sure she didn't mean to be intimidating."

"I don't know what to think now that I know that she had an affair with my father. I don't really understand how she could pretend to be friends with my mother after that."

Again Fenella bit her tongue. There had to be a way to convince the other woman that her father had lied in his book, but she needed to think it through before she started arguing.

"Anyway, my mother hasn't been herself since my father died, and this latest news has just about sent her over the edge. I'm doing my best to keep her happy, but it isn't easy. She insisted on going to the party last night. Once my sister passed away, she got herself involved in various charities, and she's still keen to support them. I never imagined that she'd behave as she did, though."

"It wasn't a problem," Fenella said. "I can't imagine how she must have felt, reading your father's notes. I hope you can keep her from reading any more."

"Luckily, she was so upset by what she read in the beginning that she had to stop. I've told her the computer isn't working properly now, but she's already said that she's going to talk to my brother about it. He's good with computers. It won't take him long to realize everything's fine. I really don't want him reading the notes, though. He doesn't need to know the truth about our father."

"Paulette, there you are," a voice called from the doorway.

The woman looked up and frowned. "Speak of the devil," she muttered.

[illegible]

Fenella looked curiously at the man who was rapidly walking across the dining room toward them. He was better looking than Fenella had imagined he would be, with dark hair liberally sprinkled with grey. He was wearing dark trousers and a light sweater and he looked fit and trim. As he sat down next to Paulette, Fenella couldn't help but think that he looked far more than two years younger than the woman.

"I rang the house and Mother said you'd gone out," he said. "This is the only place I could imagine you going."

Paulette smiled tightly. "You know I love my Sunday tea."

"Yes, but you usually bring Mother with you," he replied.

"I decided to meet a friend today instead," Paulette told him.

The man looked over at Fenella and smiled warmly. "I'm Paul Clucas," he said. "I'm sure we haven't met."

Fenella took the offered hand. She was surprised to find that the man had stunning blue eyes that didn't seem to go with his dark hair. "Fenella Woods," she said.

"Ah, but I've heard about you," the man said, holding her hand for a moment longer than necessary. "You're Mona Kelly's niece, aren't you? The entire island is talking about you."

"Oh, dear. What a dreadful thought," Fenella blurted out.

Paul chuckled. "Oh, we aren't saying anything awful, I assure you," he said. "But it isn't every day that a beautiful and single American woman arrives on the island. Donald Donaldson was lucky he met you early on or he'd have a great deal more competition for your company."

Fenella felt her cheeks go pink. The man was entirely too charming.

"Stop flirting," Paulette snapped. "Fenella is my friend."

"But what's this I hear about Mother causing a scene last night?" Paul asked his sister. "Patricia Anderson rang me this morning to ask me why I wasn't there to help keep her under control."

"Patricia Anderson is a meddling old..." Paulette was interrupted by the waiter.

"Can I get you some tea, sir," he asked Paul.

"Oh, I wasn't planning on staying," he replied. He looked over at Fenella and grinned. "But as the company is better than I'd expected, perhaps I will have a cuppa and a few cakes."

"Please don't," Paulette said. "This is my afternoon out. I don't want to spend it with you."

"Sisterly love," Paul said mockingly to Fenella. "I spent my entire childhood being incredibly jealous of my sister and her amazing tea parties with Mother. She would come home and tell me all about the endless supply of fairy cakes and tiny finger sandwiches until I would run and beg my mother to let me come along the next time. Mother always said maybe, but never ever followed through. I should think, now that I'm nearly sixty, that I should be allowed a fairy cake, shouldn't I?"

Fenella looked from one sibling to the other and then shook her head. "You can't possibly put me in the middle of this fight," she said. "I have four brothers. I know how impossible brothers and sisters can be."

Paul laughed. "You're right, of course. This is between my darling sister and me. Please, please, please, big sister. Can I stay if I promise to behave?"

Paulette frowned at him and then sighed deeply. She took a sip of her tea and then looked over at Fenella. After a moment she blinked and then gave her brother what looked like a fake smile. "Of course you can, baby brother," she said. "If I'd known how much it meant to you, I'd have insisted that Mum invite you along years ago."

A moment later the waiter arrived with Paul's tea and another tray full of delicious goodies. The women sat silently while Paul filled a plate with treats and took his first bites.

"I can't believe I've missed out on this for all these years," he said after a short while. "You and Mother were mean to me."

"It was our one chance to have some time, just the two of us," Paulette defended herself. "You were always off with our father anyway. This was our break from Paula."

Paul glanced at Fenella before looking back at his sister. "I'll assume you've bored Fenella with our entire family history, then," he said. "But that can't be why Mother was shouting at her. What happened last night?"

"It was nothing," Fenella said.

"It wasn't. I can ring Patricia back and get all of the gory details if you two won't tell me what happened," Paul replied.

"Mum has it in her head that our father cheated on her with Mona Kelly," Paulette said. "When she met Fenella, she started shouting at her about it, that's all."

"That's all? That's horrible," Paul said. He covered Fenella's hand with his. "I am so terribly sorry. I can't imagine what came over my mother."

"It's fine," Fenella said. She pulled her hand away and helped herself to another of what she would call a cupcake but that Paulette had called a fairy cake. She wouldn't want any dinner at this rate, but stress always made her crave sugar and chocolate.

"Father was writing his memoirs," Paulette said. "Mum found some of his notes on his computer."

"And he claimed he had an affair with Mona Kelly in those notes? Listen, I remember Mona. If I were ever going to write my memoirs, I'd claim I'd slept with her too. She was gorgeous, even if she was thirty years older than me."

Fenella hid a smile behind a biscuit. Mona will love hearing this part of the conversation, anyway, she thought.

"You don't think our father was telling the truth?" Paulette demanded.

"He always had a flexible approach to the truth," Paul replied. "I don't think I'd be surprised to learn that he had affairs, but I think Mona Kelly was out of his league, that's all."

"It doesn't really matter," Fenella interrupted the debate. "What matters is that your mother believes that he did and she's angry at me as a result. All I can do is try to avoid events where she's likely to be present."

"You shouldn't have to work your life around my mother's schedule," Paul said firmly. "I'll talk to her. I'm sure I can persuade her that she's wrong about Mona. I want to see these notes," he added, looking at his sister. "I've told you before that I want to go through the computer our father used at home. It's still company property, you know, and the company is mine now."

"Mother owns half of the company," Paulette countered. "And she uses the computer now herself, as do I. If you want to come and have a look at what's on it, we can arrange that, but we'll have to work around Mum. I don't want her upset any further."

"I don't want Mother upset, either," the man said. "But I won't have her shouting at random people at parties. We need to see what else is on there and get rid of it before Mother has a chance to discover it."

"Mum should know what our father did," Paulette argued.

"Why? Why not just leave her in peace with her memories?"

"She deserves to know the truth after all these years."

"Do you think she really wants to know?" Paul countered. "Our father was never around when we were growing up. Don't you think she at least suspected that he was being unfaithful? She never confronted him about it, at least not as far as we know. If she was prepared to ignore it for nearly sixty years of marriage, why should she have to have it thrust in front of her now?"

"She sits in her dressing gown and talks and talks about what a wonderful man he was," Paulette said bitterly. "She's mourning for a man that I've discovered never actually existed. He lied to her and he cheated on her, and by extension on us. I don't know what she knew or suspected while our father was alive, but I can promise you she was blind-sided by what she read on that computer."

"And now she's all worked up about it and we don't even know if any of it is true. It sounds to me as if he was writing a heavily fictionalized version of his life, incorporating his fantasies into what really happened. Surely it would be kinder to Mother if we could persuade her to believe that."

Paulette shook her head. "I won't be a party to hiding our father's lies," she said. "Mum might be having difficulty dealing with the issues, but in the end she'll be better off for knowing the truth."

"I hope you're right," Paul said softly. He turned to Fenella. "I do apologize for dragging you into the middle of our little family feud," he said. "Perhaps I could buy you dinner tonight by way of an apology?"

Fenella shook her head. "That's a very kind offer, but I already have plans for tonight," she said, making a mental note to call Shelly as soon as she could. Surely Shelly would be free to join her for a drink in their favorite pub so that Fenella wouldn't feel that she'd lied to the man.

"It's getting late," Paulette said, getting to her feet. "I shouldn't have left Mum alone for this long. I'd better go. Thank you for joining me for tea and for listening to me babble endlessly," she said to Fenella, giving her a tentative smile.

"It was my pleasure," Fenella said. "I hope your mother is okay."

"Oh, I'll take good care of her," Paulette said. "I always do."

"I'll stop over on Tuesday to look at the computer," Paul said. "It's Tynwald Day, so I won't be working."

"Mum and I are going to St. John's for the ceremony," Paulette told him. "Mum will probably want to stay out there for most of the day. Maybe you can come around next weekend."

Paul hesitated and then nodded. "Next weekend, then, but no later. That computer needs to be gone through and I need to talk to Mother."

"Yes, I'll tell her. She'll be pleased to hear that you're going to visit," Paulette said.

Paul nodded and he and Fenella watched as the woman picked up her handbag and headed out of the room.

"Now, Fenella, just how serious are you and Donald?" Paul asked, sliding his chair closer to hers.

Fenella popped a bite of cake into her mouth and chewed slowly while she tried to decide how she wanted to answer the question. There was something about Paul that she didn't like, so she didn't want to encourage his attentions, but she also didn't want him telling everyone on the island that she and Donald were seriously involved. "We're taking things very slowly," she said, opting for the truth. "I ended a ten-year relationship when I moved here and I'm not really ready for a new man in my life just yet."

Paul smiled and took her hand. "When you are ready, I do hope you'll consider me as a possible contender," he said, giving her hand a squeeze.

"I'm flattered," Fenella replied, "but I don't think your mother would be happy if she heard that we were dating."

"I can handle my mother," he told her. "Paulette has the best of intentions, but she doesn't always do what's best for Mother. I'm sure I can persuade her that this whole thing about Mona and my father is a falsehood."

"Do you really think it is?" Fenella had to ask.

"I don't know," Paul shrugged. "I know that my father had affairs. He didn't bother trying to keep them a secret from me, even if my mother and sister didn't know. But I meant what I said earlier. I think Mona was out of his league. There were always rumors about Mona and men who were much wealthier and more important than my father. And then there was Maxwell Martin, of course."

"Maxwell Martin?"

"No one has mentioned him in relation to your aunt?" Paul asked. "He owned the hotel where Mona lived from the age of eighteen until her death. Of course, it became flats in her later years, but as I understand it, Maxwell had the largest and most lavish flat built for her. I assume that's where you're living now."

"Yes, of course," Fenella replied. "I'd heard that she was involved with the man who had owned the building, but no one ever told me his name."

"He was fabulously wealthy," Paul said. "It wasn't just that hotel that he owned. He had property all over the island. As I understand it, he used to give Mona a piece of property every year for her birthday."

"Really?" Fenella said. She really needed to go through the piles of papers that her advocate, Doncan Quayle, had given her. He'd told her that she'd inherited Mona's entire estate, and he was regularly depositing checks into her bank account, but Fenella hadn't really asked any questions. Was it possible that she owned other property around the island?

"They were the island's most glamorous couple in the forties and fifties," Paul told her. "Made all the more exciting by the fact that they seemed to break up every other weekend. I wasn't lying when I said that I remember Mona from my youth. I was fascinated by her. In fact, I was crazy about her. I used to follow her around at parties, just staring at her. She was always sweetly amused by me, and always kind."

"I'm sorry I missed all of this," Fenella said.

Paul laughed. "I was at the party the night she and Maxwell announced their engagement," he said. "I was about eighteen and I had my first girlfriend with me. We had a huge fight because I was so upset that Mona was engaged. I was also at the party a month later when they had a huge fight and she threw her engagement ring into the sea. It was rumored to have been worth thirty thousand pounds, which was a huge fortune in those days."

"It's a lot of money now," Fenella murmured.

"Yes, well, as I understand it, no one ever found the ring. Maxwell was furious, of course, but they were back together a few weeks later. Neither ever mentioned marriage again, though, at least not publicly."

"So if Mona was involved with Maxwell for all those years, she couldn't have had an affair with your father," Fenella said.

"Unless that was one of the things that Mona and Maxwell fought about," Paul suggested. He shrugged. "In that social circle, it always seemed as if everyone was sleeping with everyone else. When I finally reached maturity, I was disappointed to find that most of it was just flirting and teasing."

"As fascinating as this conversation is, I really should be going," Fenella said, eager to get home to talk to Mona and feeling very much like she deserved that drink with Shelly.

"I have my car outside. Can I give you a ride home?" he asked.

Fenella hesitated. She wanted to get away from the man, but a ride home would be convenient. "That would be great," she said after a moment. As they got to their feet, the waiter came over.

"Are you ready for the bill?" he asked.

"I thought my sister took care of that," Paul said.

"Unfortunately, she did not," the man told him.

"I'm happy to pay my share," Fenella offered.

"Oh, no. I'm sure Paulette invited you as her guest. She was just happy to stick me with the bill for all three of us. I do love my sister, you know, some of the time, anyway." He handed the waiter his credit card, and when the man returned with the slip for him to sign, he added a large tip.

"Thank you so much," the waiter said as he took back the paper and his pen.

"Thank you. Everything was very good," Paul told him. He offered Fenella his arm. "Shall we?" he asked.

Fenella felt she had no choice but to take the offered arm. They made their way out of the restaurant and out of the building. The sleek bright red sports car that was parked in the no-parking zone in front of the building beeped as they approached. Paul opened the passenger door for Fenella and then climbed into the driver's seat.

"You're lucky you didn't get a ticket," Fenella said as they pulled away from the Seaview a bit too quickly for Fenella's comfort.

"I gave the doorman twenty pounds to let me leave the car there," Paul said airily. He drove them back across the mountain at high speed, whizzing around corners and passing slower cars almost recklessly.

Fenella found herself closing her eyes every time he went around another car. To her mind, there was often barely enough room for him to do so safely.

"Sorry," he said after she'd opened her eyes and let out an involuntary shriek when she saw the huge truck that they were speeding toward. Paul slid his car back into the correct lane, just inches in front of the car he'd been going around. He reached over and took Fenella's hand. "I love to drive fast," he said. "And there are no speed limits on the mountain road."

"I hate it," Fenella said, pulling her hand away. "If I'd known you were in such a hurry, I'd have called for a taxi to take me home."

Paul slowed the car down abruptly. "I'm not in a hurry," he said. "I was just having fun. But I wasn't thinking. The faster I go, the sooner you're home. I should be enjoying your company while I have the chance."

Fenella bit her tongue and looked out the window at the glorious scenery. The island really was the most beautiful place she'd ever seen. Paul drove the rest of the journey at a more sensible speed. When he pulled up in front of her building, he frowned. "You don't have a doorman, do you?"

"No, we don't," Fenella said. "But it's not a problem. I can just jump out here."

"Don't be silly. I'll walk you to your door. It's the gentlemanly thing to do," he replied. He checked the traffic and then did a U-turn and parked in a spot just across from the building.

Try as she might, Fenella couldn't work out how to open the car's door. Paul opened it for her and then helped her out. "There's a trick to it," he said, standing far too close to her for comfort as she emerged.

Fenella took a step backwards, nearly tripping over the curb. Paul slid his arms around her. "Steady now," he said in her ear.

She only just resisted the urge to bring her knee up sharply into his groin. "I'm fine," she said, quickly stepping sideways away from him.

"Let's go, then," he replied, offering her his arm. She took it out of a sense of obligation and let him lead her across the road and into her building.

"I have to admit that I'm curious," he said as the elevator rose. "I've heard stories about Mona's incredible flat. I've always wanted to see it for myself."

"It's nice, but I don't think it's anything too spectacular," Fenella told him.

She opened her door and walked inside, with Paul on her heels. The floor-to-ceiling windows that faced the promenade flooded the room with light. Fenella felt as if she were seeing the place for the first time when she saw the look on Paul's face.

"It's definitely spectacular," he said as he turned slowly. "And the furniture is special as well. I'm sure nearly all of it is antique."

"Maybe," Fenella shrugged. "I just like it because it's comfortable."

"Whom have you brought home now?" Mona asked from the kitchen doorway.

Without thinking, Fenella opened her mouth to reply, but she was interrupted by Katie's sudden appearance.

"Merow," Katie said loudly.

"You have a cat," Paul said, sounding surprised.

"I do. Katie adopted me just a few days after I arrived," Fenella explained. "I opened the door and she ran inside. I thought someone would come to claim her, but no one has."

"She's lovely," Paul said. He bent down and ran a finger down Katie's back. "We weren't allowed to have pets when I was a child. Mother had enough to worry about with Paula, I suppose."

"Do you have any pets now?" Fenella asked.

Paul stood up and stared at her for a minute. "I don't," he said eventually. "The idea simply never crossed my mind. I suppose I think of pets as something you have as children, not something a grown man would have when he lives on his own." He bent back down and rubbed Katie's tummy for a moment.

"That must be Paul Clucas, Junior," Mona said. "He does resemble his father, although not much, I have to say. He looks much more like his mother, unfortunately. He used to follow me around at parties when he was younger. I always thought he was sweet, but not too bright."

Fenella quickly swallowed a laugh.

"I'm rather too busy with work, of course," Paul said when he stood back up again. "It wouldn't be fair to an animal, the hours that I work. He or she would never get fed on any sort of schedule."

"That probably rules out a dog, but cats are more flexible," Fenella said. "Or there are always fish," she added.

Paul laughed. "While your little kitten is adorable and I can see the appeal of having one, I don't think a fish would be anywhere near as satisfying a companion."

"Thank you for the ride home," Fenella said, hoping the man would hear the goodbye in her tone.

"You're very welcome," he replied. "I was coming this way anyway. I have a flat here in Douglas, although it isn't as nice as this one."

"I do love Mona's apartment," Fenella agreed.

"Surely it's yours now."

"Oh, yes, of course, but it still feels like Mona's to me."

"If you ever think you want to sell it, please give me first refusal," the man told her. "I'd love to have those views every morning and evening."

"I can't imagine selling it," Fenella replied. "I love it here."

"You don't intend to go back to the US, then?"

"No, not at all. I sold my house and all of its contents when I moved. If I did go back, I'd have to start all over again."

"You could take all of this with you," he suggested, waving an arm.

"Or I could just stay here and enjoy it," Fenella replied.

"I hope you do," Paul told her seriously. "And I really would like to take you to dinner one night soon, if you don't think Donald would mind too much."

"Donald isn't in a position to mind," Fenella said.

"In that case, how about dinner tomorrow night?" the man countered.

Fenella flushed. "I don't think I can do tomorrow," she muttered.

"Make sure he takes you somewhere extravagant," Mona said. "Paris is lovely this time of year."

"What about this weekend?" Paul suggested.

Fenella crossed the room and looked at her calendar on the wall. It was depressingly empty. "Friday?" she asked.

The man pulled out his phone and tapped on it for a moment. "Friday works for me," he said. "I'll collect you at seven. Do you have a favorite restaurant on the island yet?"

"Not really," Fenella said. "I'm happy just about anywhere."

Paul nodded. "There's a lovely little place in Port Erin with amazing sea views. I know your views are stunning, but I think you'll like it anyway."

Fenella glanced over at Mona, who shrugged. "The food is excellent, but it's hardly Paris."

"That sounds good," Fenella said. "I'll see you then."

"Excellent," the man replied. "I'll make our booking for half seven so I don't have to drive too fast to get there on time," he added as he took the necessary steps to the door.

"I'd appreciate that," Fenella told him. She reached for the doorknob, but he caught her hand.

"I'm really looking forward to having a chance to get to know you better," he said softly. When she looked up at him, he kissed her forehead. "I am terribly sorry about my mother's behavior."

"It's fine," Fenella muttered, feeling oddly touched by the gentle kiss. "I'll see you on Friday."

He nodded and then released her hand so that she could let him out. Fenella watched him walk down the corridor and onto the elevator before she shut the door behind him.

"He doesn't seem your type," Mona said as Fenella headed for the kitchen.

"I didn't like him at all until he was nice to Katie," Fenella admitted. "It's only one dinner, anyway. I won't have to see him again after that."

"I'm not sure he'll give up that easily," Mona told her. "But that's a problem for later. Tell me what Paulette said."

Fenella refilled Katie's bowls while she told her aunt what Paulette had said about her father.

"I can't imagine Paul Clucas writing his memoirs," Mona scoffed. "Nothing interesting ever happened to him, although he probably thought his sex life was fascinating." She yawned. "Quantity is no substitute for quality," she told Fenella. "And that man was all about quantity."

"Poor Phillipa."

"I always thought she'd have been much happier if she'd had an affair or two herself," Mona said. "But she was always busy with her children, especially little Paula."

"Until Paula died, anyway."

"That was tragic," Mona said solemnly.

"Paul was telling me about Maxwell Martin," Fenella said, trying to sound casual.

Mona laughed. "I did wonder how long it would be before his name came up. I must say, it has taken rather longer than I'd expected."

"He owned this building when it was a hotel?"

"Max owned a great many buildings," Mona replied. "The hotel here was his most elegant property. That terrible brightly lit lobby downstairs was once the entrance to another world."

"And you two were a couple for many years?"

Mona laughed again. "You could measure our relationship in days or weeks, never more than that. We fought constantly and made up gloriously. He was the only man who ever put a ring on my finger, and less than a fortnight later I threw the ring back in his face."

"Paul told me you threw it in the sea," Fenella countered.

Mona shrugged. "That sounds like me," she said. "The details don't really matter. Max and I were passionately in love some of the time, but we also couldn't stand one another."

"I don't think I understand."

"No one did," Mona replied. "I'm not sure Max and I understood it, really. Anyway, it didn't matter. We were together, off and on, from the time I was eighteen until Max's death just a few years ago."

"But you never married."

"Max wasn't the marrying kind," Mona told her. "Neither was I, when it came down to it. I suppose if either of us had pushed the issue the other may have gone along, but really we were both happy without the formal commitment."

A knock on the door interrupted Fenella's next question. "Shelly, hello," Fenella said brightly when she'd opened the door.

"I just thought I'd come over and ask how last night went," Shelly said. "Did you have fun?"

"It was interesting," Fenella replied. "But let me tell you all about it over a drink or two at the pub," she suggested.

"It's only five o'clock," Shelly said. "Let me get myself some dinner and then we can go."

"I don't think I can eat another bite," Fenella told her. "I ate far too many finger sandwiches and cream cakes at tea."

"I'll be back in an hour and we'll head to the pub," Shelly said. "You can tell me all about last night over a glass of white wine."

"Perfect," Fenella replied. She closed the door behind her friend and turned back around to ask Mona more about Max. The living room behind her was empty.

"Where did she go?" Fenella asked Katie.

The kitten looked up at her and shrugged before she bounced away into the spare bedroom. Fenella sighed. She had many more questions she'd wanted to ask and now she'd have to wait for another opportunity. She filled her hour with mindless television, watching a quiz show from several years earlier, all about news headlines that she didn't understand. By the time Shelly returned, Fenella was standing at the door with her handbag in her hand.

"You really need a drink tonight, don't you?" Shelly asked.

"I really need someone to talk to," Fenella replied. "I've had a very strange weekend."

The Tale and Tail pub was only a few steps away. They stopped right inside the door and Fenella took a moment to look around the huge room. She did that every time she arrived, and she didn't think she'd ever get tired of the incredible view.

The pub had once been the private library in the mansion of a very wealthy family. When the property was sold and turned into a luxury hotel, the library had been converted into a pub. A large bar had been installed in the center of the large lower-level room, but very little else had been changed. Most importantly for Fenella, bookshelves still covered nearly every inch of the walls and all of the books could be borrowed.

As the pair made their way to the bar, a large orange cat streaked past, nearly tripping Fenella. That was another thing that made the pub special. There were half a dozen or so cats that called the pub home. Large cat beds were scattered around the lower level. Sometimes they all seemed to be full of lounging animals, but tonight they mostly looked empty, as cats wandered around the room, getting pats and scratches from the various patrons.

Fenella and Shelly got glasses of wine and then headed up the spiral staircase to the upper level. There, amid even more bookcases, were tables with chairs and couches around them. The space was mostly empty, so the women had no difficulty finding seats in a quiet corner. As soon as they were seated, a large black and white cat jumped into Shelly's lap and settled in.

"I suppose I'll have to get the next round," Fenella laughed.

"I won't complain," Shelly replied. "But do tell me what's been going on that has you so frazzled."

Fenella told her friend all about her encounters the previous evening and then about her Sunday afternoon tea. After she'd told her friend about the ride home with Paul, she sighed and sat back in her seat. It had been a bit tricky telling the story without repeating anything that Mona had said. Now that she was done, she felt able to take a big drink of her wine.

"You have a much more interesting life than I do," Shelly said.

Fenella shook her head. "It was Mona who had all of the adventures," she countered. "Although I seem to have inherited a few enemies from her."

"And a few admirers," Shelly replied. "Paul sounds charming."

"I didn't like him until he started fussing over Katie," Fenella told her.

Shelly laughed. "Maybe you'll feel differently after Friday night," she said.

"Did you want a second round?" Fenella asked as they finished their drinks.

"Not really," Shelly replied. "I'd really like an early night. I was out with Gordon last night and we're going to have a late night on Tuesday as well. We can't come home before the fireworks."

They walked home together in companionable silence. Alone in her apartment, Fenella got ready for bed. She checked that Katie had fresh water, and then washed her face and combed her hair. Feeling slightly restless, she found herself a good mystery novel from Mona's extensive collection and curled up to read. She was startled when someone knocked on her door a short time later.

"Shelly?" she said in surprise.

"I was just heading to bed," Shelly said, glancing down at her pajamas and coloring slightly. "I switched the radio on to see if I could hear a weather forecast for Tuesday and I caught the end of the news."

"What's happened?" Fenella demanded.

"I'm not sure I have the name right," Shelly said. "But I thought one of the women you spoke to last night was Anne Marie Smathers."

"That's right."

"She's dead," Shelly said tersely.

Fenella pulled the other woman into her apartment. They sat together on the nearest couch. "What happened to her?" Fenella asked, her heart racing.

"They just said it was a road traffic accident," Shelly replied. "They didn't give any details. They said something like 'the body of the woman killed in the road traffic accident early this morning has been identified as Anne Marie Smathers, aged eighty-one, of Ramsey.' I think that's about right."

"So it was an accident," Fenella said, sitting back against the couch cushions.

"I suppose so. It just seems an awful coincidence that you were just talking to her last night and now she's gone."

"Just because I've stumbled into a few murder investigations since I've been on the island doesn't mean that everyone around me is being murdered," Fenella told her.

"I know," Shelly said quickly. "And I probably shouldn't have even come over to tell you, but it was just, well, odd."

"Life is full of coincidences," Fenella said. "She was at a large party last night. She would have spoken to a great many people. No doubt all of us will feel that it's a bit strange."

"I just thought you should know," Shelly said, getting to her feet. "I suppose it could have waited for morning, though."

"I'm glad you came over and told me right away," Fenella assured her. "I just wish I could call Daniel for more information."

Shelly made a face. "If it was murder, I'd feel much better if Daniel were the one investigating it."

Inspector Daniel Robinson was a Douglas-based member of the island's constabulary. He was currently in the UK on a training course that still had several weeks to run. Shelly and Fenella both liked the intelligent and handsome man. He and Fenella had taken a few tentative steps toward a romantic relationship, but he had pulled back abruptly when he'd found out he was going on the course.

Fenella missed him more than she wanted to admit to anyone, especially herself. The thought of being caught up in a murder investigation while he was away was especially unpleasant, though.

"They said it was an accident," Fenella reminded Shelly. "Anyway, she was from Ramsey. If there is a police investigation, someone from there would be in charge, even if Daniel were here."

"But he would be able to find out what was really going on and keep us informed."

"He isn't meant to do that," Fenella said. "And it really isn't any of our business this time, either. I only spoke to the woman for a few minutes and had no plans to ever see her again. I'm sorry to hear about her sudden death, but I'm not involved in any way."

Shelly nodded and headed for the door. "I probably should have waited to tell you until morning," she said again. "But I was too surprised to sleep."

"I hope you can sleep now," Fenella told her. "Thank you for telling me."

She let the other woman out. The book she had been reading had lost all of its appeal, so she crawled into bed next to Katie and tried to get comfortable. Her brain kept insisting on replaying her conversation with Anne Marie over and over again as Fenella tossed and turned. Eventually Katie jumped off the bed and took herself to the guest room to sleep. A short while later, Fenella managed to fall into a restless sleep.

"I'm not awake," she moaned as Katie began to pat her gently on the nose. "I only just fell asleep," she added as Katie began to accompany the taps with soft meows. When Katie didn't give up, Fenella sighed and climbed out of bed. She'd just get some breakfast for the animal and then try to get some more sleep, she promised herself.

"What did you do after I left last night?" Mona demanded as Fenella spilled cat food all over the floor. "You look as if you haven't slept at all."

"I went to the pub with Shelly for one drink and then came home and read a book," Fenella said testily. "And then Shelly came over and told me that Anne Marie Smathers was dead, which made sleeping nearly impossible."

"Anne Marie is dead?" Mona repeated. "What happened to her?"

Fenella shrugged. "Shelly heard it on the radio. Apparently she was in a car accident."

"Just like her husband," Mona said.

"Well, yes, I suppose so," Fenella replied. "But some sixty years later."

"I wonder what car she was driving."

"Maybe she was a passenger," Fenella suggested. "We don't know any more than what Shelly said last night."

"You should put on the local radio station. Maybe we'll hear more."

Fenella rarely listened to the radio, but now she switched on the one that was built into the expensive stereo equipment in the living room. Music she'd never heard before and didn't much like was playing, so she ignored it and started a pot of coffee.

"They'll do the news at half seven," Mona told her.

"I was thinking about going back to bed," Fenella replied.

"You can do, after the news."

While she waited for the coffee to brew, Fenella poured herself a bowl of cereal and added milk. She'd have preferred pancakes or maybe waffles, but she didn't have the energy or the ingredients to make either. The first sip of coffee helped wake her up and lift her spirits. She just managed a quick shower before the news began.

"Police are appealing for witnesses to the road traffic accident on the outskirts of Douglas yesterday morning. Anne Marie Smathers, aged eighty-one, of Ramsey, lost her life when she hit a garden wall at considerable speed," the news reported. It went on to give details as to where the accident had taken place, but Fenella didn't know enough about the island to be able to visualize it. At the end of the report, they asked again for witnesses.

"It sounds like it was an accident," Fenella said tentatively as she switched off the radio.

"Someone could have tampered with her brakes or the steering or anything," Mona replied. "You have to ring the police."

"The police? What am I supposed to tell them? That my dead aunt thinks there's something suspicious about a car accident that I know nothing about?"

"You should ring Daniel," Mona told her. "Ask him what's going on and mention that you'd just met the woman and thought it was odd that she died in the same way as her husband."

"I'm not calling Daniel," Fenella snapped.

"Has he texted you lately?" Mona asked.

Fenella frowned. She'd received a few texts from the man when he'd first gone away. They'd been casual, but at least they'd told her that he was thinking about her. She'd received the last one almost a week ago and the intervening silence was not something she wanted to be reminded of. "No," she said.

"Oh, dear, and I had such high hopes for that man. He seemed just right for you, really, as you don't like Donald."

"I do like Donald. He's lovely and he spoils me."

"Yes, dear, you keep telling yourself that. You and I both know that Donald is only a diversion, but at least he's keeping you from pining over Daniel while he's away."

Fenella opened her mouth to reply, but was interrupted by a knock on her door. "I hope that's Shelly," she muttered, glancing down at her hastily thrown-on T-shirt and jeans. She hadn't managed to put on any makeup yet and her hair was still damp from the shower.

"Ah, good morning," the man at the door said. "I'm looking for Fenella Woods."

"You've found her," Fenella said, wondering what the man was selling. The building had security that was meant to stop salesmen from bothering the residents, but clearly this man had managed to sneak in anyway.

The man gave her a bright smile. He reminded her of the car salesman that she'd bought her last car from. His hair was brown, with one lock that flopped over his green eyes. As he ran his hand through his hair, pushing the stray lock back into place, Fenella guessed that he was in his mid-thirties. He was wearing a dark suit with a pink shirt and tie. Fenella got ready to resist whatever hard-sell tactic he was about to try.

"I'm Mark Hammersmith," the man told her. "I'm a CID inspector and I'm looking into Anne Marie Smathers's accident."

Fenella gasped, as behind her, Mona clapped her hands.

"It was murder," Mona said. "I just knew it."

"I'm sorry," the inspector said. "I assumed you already knew that she'd passed away."

"Oh, I did," Fenella replied. "I, er, heard it on the news this morning. But I didn't expect a police inspector at my door. I can't imagine what her accident has to do with me."

"I was hoping you might be able to tell me that," the man replied. "I'd like to ask you a few questions, if you don't mind."

What if I do, Fenella thought to herself. She mentally shook her head. Taking an irrational dislike to the man because he looked like the car salesman who'd sold her the worst car she'd ever owned was completely unfair. "Please come in," she said, stepping backwards to let him do just that. "Would you like some coffee?"

"I'd love some," he replied. "I started early today and I haven't had my regular daily allowance yet."

Fenella smiled back at him as she handed him a mug of the hot drink. She refilled her own cup. "Sit down," she suggested, gesturing toward the bar stools at the kitchen counter. "We could sit in the living room, if you'd prefer," she offered.

"Oh, I would, if you don't mind," he said quickly. "The view is so incredible from there."

They took chairs next to one another in the living room and Mark stared out the window for a moment. "I would never get anything done if I lived here," he said. "I'd just sit and look out the window all day."

"It is tempting," Fenella told him.

"I understand you spent some time talking with Mrs. Smathers at a charity function on Saturday evening," the man said, pulling his phone from his pocket. "I'll be taking notes on my phone, if that's okay with you," he added.

"Whatever you like," Fenella said. "And yes, I did speak with her briefly at the party. She knew my aunt."

The man scrolled through his phone screen. "Yes, your aunt was the infamous Mona Kelly," he said. "I suspect everyone on the island knew your aunt."

Mona had taken a seat on the opposite side of the man. She raised an eyebrow. "I don't believe we'd ever met," she said to the inspector. "I'm sure I'd remember you if we had. I didn't often meet policemen."

Fenella sipped coffee to keep herself from laughing. "Was that all you wanted to know?" she asked the man after she'd swallowed.

"I'd like to know what you and Mrs. Smathers discussed," he replied.

"She introduced herself and mentioned that she'd been friends with Mona," Fenella said, trying to work out exactly how much she intended to tell the man. "She also mentioned that she was a widow and that her husband had died in a car crash."

"Good girl," Mona said approvingly. "Keep emphasizing that point."

Fenella rolled her eyes at the woman.

"And why was Mrs. Smathers coming to see you yesterday?" the man asked.

Fenella shook her head. "She wasn't," she replied.

"She told a friend that she was going into Douglas to see you," he told her.

"Well, that's news to me. We certainly didn't have any plans to see each other."

The man typed into his phone for a moment and then gave her the bright smile that she found so annoying. "Well, thank you for your time, then," he said, getting to his feet.

"That's it?" Mona asked.

"That's it?" Fenella echoed.

"We're doing our best to work out exactly what caused the tragic accident that killed Mrs. Smathers," he replied. "One piece of the puzzle is why she was in Douglas at all. She told a friend she was coming to see you, but you've told me that you didn't have plans. At the end of the day, it probably doesn't matter overly much. She may have lied to her friend or she may have wanted to surprise you. If we thought the death was anything other than an accident, I'd be more concerned, but thus far everything seems to suggest that it was simply that, an unfortunate accident."

Fenella walked him to the door, feeling slightly deflated. "I wish I could have been more help," she said.

"You can't tell me things you don't know," the man replied. "I appreciated your time, the coffee, and the chance to enjoy the view. Have a good day."

He was gone before Fenella managed a reply. She shut the door behind him and looked at Mona, who had followed them to the door. "It was just an accident," she said.

"Bah, that man is an idiot," Mona snapped. "He should have asked you to repeat the entire conversation you had with Anne Marie, not summarize, and he should have picked up on the fact that her husband died in a car crash, too. And why would she tell people she was coming to see you? What was that about?"

"I don't know," Fenella replied.

"And neither does he, but he should be trying to find out," Mona insisted. "There's something going on here that doesn't add up."

"Or maybe you just have an overactive imagination," Fenella suggested.

Mona waved a hand. "I might, but I'm also right."

"Who could have had a motive for killing an eighty-one-year-old woman?" Fenella asked.

"That's what Mark Hammersmith should be asking himself," Mona retorted. "She was coming to see you. Maybe that's significant."

"I can't see how. She probably just wanted to warn me again about Donald."

"She wouldn't have driven all the way into Douglas to repeat herself," Mona said. "Whatever she wanted to talk to you about, it wasn't something that you'd already discussed."

"Then I can't possibly guess what she wanted," Fenella said with a sigh. "And I have a driving lesson in half an hour. I need to do something with my hair and makeup."

"Your mind isn't on your driving today," Mel, her driving instructor, said as they made their way around the island.

"I'm sorry," Fenella told him. "An acquaintance of mine passed away yesterday and I can't stop thinking about her."

Mel nodded. "Why don't we stop so you can stretch your legs for a minute? Maybe you'll be able to get your focus back on the road if you take a short break."

Fenella was grateful for the break, as driving on the island was still stressful, but she didn't feel any more focused when she climbed back in the car a short while later. "I'm not doing very well, am I?" she asked as she swerved slightly to get back into the center of her lane.

"That's why we're taking back roads," the man told her. "We'll avoid traffic as much as we can for today."

They were heading back toward Douglas when they ran into a detour.

"I thought they'd have this cleared up by now," Mel muttered as Fenella was forced to turn left. "There was an accident there yesterday, you see."

"Is that where it happened?" Fenella asked, slowing down to see what she could see as they drove around the closed road.

"Yes, an elderly woman drove into a stone wall," the man replied. "She was driving an older car that didn't have airbags."

"I didn't think there were any cars still on the road without airbags."

"There aren't many, but this one was an old classic," Mel told her. "Apparently, she and her husband bought matching cars right after they were married some sixty years ago. He crashed his less than a year later."

Fenella shuddered. "And she crashed hers yesterday," she said sadly.

"It's sort of an odd coincidence, isn't it?" Mel asked. "Life's funny like that."

Fenella nodded, but didn't reply, and then did her best to focus on driving. She was even more grateful than normal to get home after her lesson.

"You're just about ready for your test," Mel told her. "You should get it booked. We can add in a few extra lessons just before the test, if you'd like."

"Oh, definitely," Fenella said. "I'll let you know." She walked back into her building trying not to think about Anne Marie or her driving test. It was time for some lunch, and she tried to work out what she wanted to eat as she walked.

"There's nothing here but cat food," she told Katie a few minutes later. The cupboards were all open, revealing mostly empty shelves.

"MMMeerreeww," Katie replied.

"Oh, sure, you're fine, but what I am to do?" Fenella shook her head. She needed to go grocery shopping, no matter how much she disliked it.

"This will be easier once you get your driving license," she muttered to herself as she pulled her little wheeled shopping cart out of the closet by the door. "Then you'll only have to shop once a week. Mel's right, you should schedule the test."

She stared at herself in the bedroom mirror as she brushed her hair and reapplied some lip gloss. Thinking about taking the driving test made her feel sick to her stomach. "Maybe you're just hungry," she said to her reflection.

The Fenella in the mirror didn't look convinced, so Fenella turned away and headed out. An hour later she was pulling a very full shopping cart, with a donut in her other hand. The world looks brighter when you have a donut, she thought to herself as she pushed her cart across her building's lobby.

"Fenella, I feel as if I haven't seen you in ages," a voice said from behind her.

"Peter, how are you?" Fenella asked, smiling at the man who'd followed her into the building.

"I'm fine," he assured her. "Just busy with work, as always."

They made their way to the elevator together. Peter Cannell lived next door to Fenella. When she'd first arrived, he'd taken her out once or twice, but now they seemed to have fallen into a friendship rather than a romance. While Fenella really liked the attractive man with salt-and-pepper hair and blue eyes, she didn't mind just being friends with him. Daniel and Donald were romantic complications enough for her.

"I've been so busy that I can't even remember the last time I made it to the pub," he told her as the elevator doors opened on the sixth floor. "But tomorrow is a national holiday, so I've given myself the afternoon off today as well."

"Good for you," Fenella said as they walked down the corridor together.

"Are you free for dinner tonight?" Peter asked. "I've nothing in my flat to eat, so I thought maybe I would go over to that little Italian place for spaghetti and garlic bread before the pub."

"That sounds wonderful," Fenella replied. She loved the food there and she hadn't bought anything for her evening meal that wouldn't keep.

"I'll collect you at six, if that's okay," Peter told her. "And I'll tell Shelly to meet us at the pub at half seven."

Fenella nodded and then let herself into her apartment. If Peter wasn't inviting Shelly to join them for dinner, did that mean he was thinking of the meal as a date, she wondered as she put her shopping away. She still hadn't had any lunch, aside from the donut, but now that she had plans for dinner, she didn't want to spoil her appetite, either. She ate a small bag of potato chips and washed them down with a cold soda. Still feeling hungry, she forced herself to sit down with a new biography of Anne Boleyn that she'd recently acquired.

When she'd moved to the island, she'd been excited that the move would give her the opportunity to finally write the book that she'd wanted to write for years. It was going to be a fictionalized autobiography of Anne Boleyn, the historical figure that most interested Fenella after a lifetime of studying and teaching history. Now that she had nothing to do but research and write, however, she found that her enthusiasm for the project had waned considerably. It was still an exciting idea in theory, but it was hard work actually doing the research and putting words on the page.

As she read, she took notes and added them to the large pile that she'd already taken. She was starting to suspect that the book was never going to get much further than that pile, but she wasn't ready to give up yet. What she really needed to do was to get to grips with what she actually had inherited from Mona. Thus far she'd been content with the monthly checks that kept arriving, and had been living cautiously off of the money. Now that she was settled, she needed to talk to the man who had been Mona's lawyer and now was hers.

"Doncan Quayle's office," a voice said when she rang.

"Ah, yes, this is Fenella Woods. I was just thinking that I probably need to meet with my lawyer to talk about Mona's estate," she said.

"Of course, my dear," the woman replied. "Mr. Quayle is quite busy at the moment, but he could see you one day in the second week of August, if that suits you?"

Fenella noted the date and time on her calendar and then hung up the phone. August seemed a long way off, but it was her own fault for not thinking about it sooner. She could always ask Mona about the matter, but it would feel awkward asking Mona exactly what she'd left her.

She changed into a skirt and light sweater and redid her hair and makeup just before six. Mona was strangely absent all afternoon. Fenella reminded herself not to worry about the dead woman as she gave Katie her dinner.

"I'll be back after dinner and the pub," she told the animal. "You behave."

Katie blinked at her and then padded away. She found a sunny spot near the windows and curled up. Moments later she appeared to be fast asleep.

Fenella still made sure to shut both bathroom doors before she left, though. Katie had already shredded a roll of toilet paper and a box of tissues. Fenella wasn't going to give her the chance to do it again.

Peter knocked at almost exactly six.

"All ready to go?" he asked.

"I am," Fenella agreed.

The man smiled at her. "You look lovely," he said.

"You look very nice yourself," Fenella replied, glad that she'd dressed up as he was still wearing his business suit from earlier.

"I'll take the jacket off once we sit down," he told her. "But I've been wearing a suit every day since I was eleven, so it feels quite natural, really."

"Who makes an eleven-year-old boy wear a suit every day?" Fenella asked.

"School uniform," the man replied. "They still wear jackets and ties in the schools here."

"It really is a different country," Fenella laughed.

It was only a short walk to the restaurant, which was moderately busy but still had a few free tables.

"Let's get a bottle of wine," Peter suggested. "We can drink it slowly, but neither of us has to be up too early tomorrow."

As he was right, Fenella didn't object. They enjoyed delicious food and wine and talked about local politics and their plans for Tynwald Day.

"I talked it over with Shelly," he told her. "I'm going to drive all three of us. There are several large car parks around the site, but it's best to take as few cars as possible."

"That sounds good to me," Fenella said. "I wasn't thinking of driving."

"How are the lessons coming?"

"Mel thinks I'm ready for my test," she replied.

"Mel knows what he's doing. He's been teaching people to drive for a long time now."

Fenella nodded. Peter and Mel had been childhood friends and it was Peter who had introduced her to the man. "I feel sick whenever I think about taking the test," she said quietly.

"You should plan on taking it twice, then," Peter suggested. "Treat the first test as a practice one, just so you can go through it and see exactly what it's like. Then you'll feel ready for the second one."

It was nearly eight o'clock by the time they left the restaurant. Fenella was full of garlic bread, spaghetti, chocolate mousse, and wine. Mostly she was feeling sleepy.

"Do you want to skip the pub?" Peter asked as he took her hand.

"Did you tell Shelly that we'd be there?" she asked.

"I did."

"Then we should go," Fenella said reluctantly. "But we'll have to walk slowly, as I'm very full."

Peter chuckled. "I won't complain. I'm enjoying the company."

Fenella flushed. She couldn't think of a suitable reply, so she kept quiet. The pub was nearly empty, and they'd only just walked in the door when Shelly joined them.

"There you are," she said, hugging Peter and then Fenella. "I was starting to get worried about you."

"We just ate very slowly," Fenella told her. "And we had dessert."

"I thought maybe you decided to have a long walk on the promenade and not bother with the pub tonight," she said.

"It was tempting," Peter said. "I don't often get Fenella all to myself."

Shelly laughed and took Fenella's arm. "Let's get drinks and then go upstairs," she said. "Once we're sitting down, you can tell me who that man was that was knocking on your door before eight o'clock this morning."

The upstairs was nearly empty, and the trio was soon settled in with two cats for company.

"So, who was he?" Shelly demanded. "I thought he looked like an American actor, but I can't work out which one."

"I thought he looked like a used car salesman," Fenella told her. "But he's a police inspector."

"A police inspector? Everything is okay with Daniel, isn't it?"

"I suppose so; why wouldn't it be?" Fenella asked.

"I don't know. When you said the police were at your door, he was the first thing that I thought of," Shelly replied.

"He didn't come to talk about Daniel. He came to ask me questions about Anne Marie Smathers," Fenella told her.

"She was murdered?" Shelly exclaimed.

"No, not at all," Fenella said quickly. "But she'd told someone that she was planning to visit me yesterday. He wanted to know why."

"You didn't mention that last night," Shelly said.

"Because I didn't know," Fenella replied. "She never said anything about it when we spoke and she never called to suggest a meeting."

"How odd," Shelly said.

"I knew her," Peter said. "She was friendly with my parents, although my mother didn't like her."

"Why not?" Shelly asked.

"My mother never said, but I can guess. Anne Marie was, well, she seemed to like other women's husbands. My mother wasn't really the jealous type, and my father never gave her any reason to be, but Anne Marie caused tension between them anyway."

"I met her last night," Fenella said. "But we only talked for a few minutes."

"I've no doubt she said something shocking or outrageous," Peter said with a chuckle. "She liked to do that."

"She told me far more about herself than I wanted to know," Fenella said. "And she didn't have very nice things to say about Mona, either."

"They were friends, at least on the surface," Peter told her. "Although I know she often accused Mona of having been involved with her husband before his death."

"It was all such a long time ago, I can't believe anyone still cares," Shelly said.

"Would you care, if you found out that your husband cheated on you many years ago?" Fenella asked.

Shelly flushed. "When you put it that way, yes, I would," she said. "But he didn't. He wasn't the sort of man who would have ever cheated."

They finished their drinks and headed for home. Fenella was still feeling rather full and as if she'd drunk a bit too much wine. It had been a nice evening, though, and she was looking forward to her first Tynwald Day as well.

Peter stopped outside her door and smiled down at her. "Thank you for joining me for dinner," he said softly.

"I'll see you both around nine," Shelly called as she let herself into her apartment.

"Thank you for dinner," Fenella replied. "I enjoyed it very much."

"I hope at least some of that enjoyment came from the company," Peter said.

"Of course it did," Fenella laughed nervously.

Peter bent down and gave her a gentle kiss. It was affectionate, but not passionate. When he lifted his head he sighed. "I really do enjoy your company," he said. "I'm looking forward to tomorrow."

Fenella nodded and then let herself into her apartment. Peter walked away as she shut her door behind her. Mona wasn't at home as Fenella got ready for bed.

6

Tuesday morning was bright and sunny, and for once Fenella didn't mind when Katie woke her. "It's Tynwald Day," she told the kitten as she bounced out of bed. She gave Katie her breakfast and started a pot of coffee before mixing up pancake batter. After a quick shower, she made herself pancakes and bacon, smothering the pancakes in a generous covering of maple syrup. As she ate, washing down each bite with coffee, she noticed Katie watching her.

"I know, I know. Pancakes are an indulgence, especially with this much syrup, but it's a special occasion. If I had a job, I wouldn't have to go to work today," she told Katie. "As it is, I'm going with Shelly and Peter to watch the ceremony and enjoy the festival."

Katie stared at her for a minute longer and then wandered off to find a place in the sun for a nap. Fenella wasn't sure what to wear, but as Shelly had told her that they were going to be sitting on the ground, she opted for jeans. If Shelly was dressed very differently, she could always change quickly, she decided. With her hair in a ponytail and a minimum of makeup on her face, she threw everything she thought she might need into her largest handbag and then paced around the living room for a short while.

"Where are you when I need you?" she asked Mona, who was nowhere to be found.

"Never mind," she said after a moment. "I'm sure you have important things to do." Try as she might, Fenella couldn't imagine what her aunt might be doing. "What do dead people do when they aren't haunting the living?" she muttered as she checked her hair in the bedroom mirror. Her reflection didn't have any answers for her, so she gave up and headed over to Shelly's apartment.

"I wasn't sure if jeans were going to be okay," she said once she and Shelly had hugged.

"Jeans are fine," Shelly told her. "My trousers are denim, too, they're just zebra print rather than blue."

Fenella nodded. Shelly loved colors and prints, and her outfit today celebrated both. The oversized sweater that she was wearing was bright pink, with large polka dots in green and yellow. Somehow on Shelly it just worked, though, at least as far as Fenella was concerned. Unable to imagine wearing zebra print denim pants, Fenella followed her friend to Peter's door.

"Good morning, ladies," he said, greeting them each with a hug. "You both look ready for a fun day." Peter was wearing dark grey pants and a navy blue polo shirt.

"Don't you have any jeans?" Fenella asked.

Peter shook his head. "I'm a bit too old for jeans," he told her. "And these are more comfortable, anyway."

He locked up his apartment and the trio rode the elevator down to the building's underground parking garage. When they arrived at Peter's car, Shelly quickly slid into the backseat.

"You sit up front with Peter," she told Fenella. "You'll be more interested in the scenery than I am."

The drive across the island didn't take long, although it seemed to Fenella as if everyone was heading to the same place. There was a long line of cars snaking along the twisting side road that led to the nearest parking area.

"Why don't you two get out here?" Peter suggested after they'd waited several minutes and moved only a few feet. "I'll park the car and find you."

"Nothing is going to happen for at least another hour," Shelly said. "We may as well enjoy your comfortable car for as long as possible. We won't be this comfortable on the grass."

After several more minutes where they did nothing more than inch forward, Fenella could see someone talking to the man who was directing traffic. A short while later, the line of cars began to move much more rapidly. They were parked and on their way to Tynwald Hill only a short while later.

Peter insisted on carrying Shelly's bag, which held the blanket for them to sit on and a few snacks. "I know there will be loads of food available," she told them as she handed the bag to Peter. "But the queues will be long, too. These are emergency rations to keep us from starving while we queue."

Fenella and Peter both laughed, but as Fenella surveyed the crowd, she began to think that Shelly had the right idea. It looked as if nearly every man, woman, and child on the island was there.

Food vendors were already hard at work and Fenella found her mouth watering as various smells wafted through the air around them. Glad that she'd had a substantial breakfast, she followed Shelly through the crowds.

"I think this is as close as we'll get," Shelly said as they crossed the large green space next to Tynwald Hill. "We may as well get settled in for the ceremony."

"I can't believe how many people are here," Fenella said as she sat down on the blanket.

"Nearly everyone on the island makes an appearance at some point," Peter told her. "Not everyone comes for the actual ceremony. Many people just come for the festival."

"I'm sure that will be more fun, but I'm really looking forward to the ceremony," Fenella told him. "I'm still surprised that we can just turn up and watch the island's government at work."

"They aren't really working today," Shelly said with a grin. "Today is ceremonial, really. There are some that would argue that our government is never really working."

"But today isn't a day for discussing island politics," Peter said. "I love the ceremony. I especially enjoy hearing the new laws read in

Manx. My first wife took some classes in Manx and every once in a while I manage to hear a word I recognize."

"I should try taking a class," Fenella said thoughtfully. "My mother spoke a little bit of Manx, but I never wanted to learn. I'm sorry now, of course."

"It's a very difficult language," Peter told her. "But I love the way it sounds."

All around them people were arriving and settling in on blankets or folding chairs. The ceremony itself started right on time, and everyone stood up as the official procession began. Fenella did her best to follow what was happening, but it was sometimes difficult to hear and understand things.

"Now the laws in Manx," Peter told her.

Peter was right; the language was beautiful to listen to, although it sounded incredibly foreign to Fenella's ear. "He's very good," Fenella whispered as the man finished speaking.

"I'm sure he's been learning the language for a great many years," Peter told her.

"I'm so glad we came," Fenella said as the ceremony finished and people began to stand up. "That was wonderful."

"It's the first time I've been to the ceremony in years," Shelly replied. "I'd forgotten how interesting it actually is. But now the fun can begin."

Fenella's phone buzzed as she stretched her legs. "It's a text from Donald," she said. "He can't get away from his business colleagues right now, but he'll try to catch up with us later," she told the others.

"So what would you like to do first?" Peter asked the women.

"What is there to do, exactly?" Fenella asked.

"One of the marquees will be full of Manx businesses, offering samples of their wares and the like, and the other contains representatives from different not-for-profit organizations around the island. They'll be passing out information about the work that they do. There are food vendors everywhere. Or we could take a walk through the arboretum, which isn't, strictly speaking, part of Tynwald Day, but is right next door," he replied.

"I'm hungry," Shelly said. "Although from the looks of the queues, so is everyone else."

Fenella looked around. "I think everyone got up from their seats and headed straight for the food," she said. "Maybe we should look around one of the tents and wait for the lines to get shorter."

"They may not get much shorter," Peter warned her. "But the tents are a good idea. We won't starve doing that, anyway."

Fenella wasn't sure what he meant, but she didn't have to wait long to find out. Right inside the first tent, the island's dairy farmers had a huge display. They were passing out small cups full of ice cream made from milk from the island's cows.

"So good," Fenella said as she scraped up the last bite of the sweet frozen treat.

The very next table was offering cheese samples, and all three friends were happy to indulge. The island's largest commercial bakery was next, passing out slices of their newest multigrain bread.

"I'm getting quite full," Shelly said with a laugh as they stepped back from the bakery table.

"It's all so delicious, though," Fenella said. "What's next?"

Several of the island's businesses had tables that followed. Instead of food, they were giving away pens and pencils with their company name on them and other similar items. Fenella was pleased when the local grocery store chain handed her a large empty shopping bag.

"You can put all your goodies in here," the woman behind the table told her with a smile.

"I didn't realize I'd need a bag," Fenella laughed. She'd already collected three pens, two pads of sticky notes and a large handful of brochures advertising a range of goods and services, many of which she hadn't known she needed.

"The bank is giving out refrigerator magnets," Shelly told her. "They've already run out of keychains."

"This is fun," Fenella said. "Although I'm starting to get hungry again."

"We should move on to the adult section," Peter suggested.

"What do they have there?" Fenella asked, slightly concerned.

Peter laughed. "Intoxicating beverages," he told her.

A small section of the tent had been roped off and a sign informed everyone that it was only open to those eighteen and older. The man guarding the doorway waved Fenella and her friends inside.

"Age does have its privileges," Shelly laughed.

A large local pub had the first table and was passing out small glasses of one of their home-brewed beers. Fenella took a sip and struggled not to make a face. It wasn't at all to her liking.

"Would you like the rest of mine?" she asked Peter in a low voice after he'd swallowed his sample in a single gulp.

"You didn't like it?" Peter asked as he took the drink from her.

"Not really," Fenella told him.

She was happier with the wine that was being poured at the next table. The man behind the table tried to sell her on the idea of holding her next big event at his venue as she sipped her drink. "I'll definitely keep you in mind if I ever have an event," she promised, taking the brochure he kept waving in front of her. "Thank you so much."

A short while later, the trio made their way back out into the open air. "That was fun," Fenella said. "I'm not sure what I'm going to do with all of these brochures, but it was interesting to see just how many local businesses there are on the island."

"The queues have died down a bit, if you want to get some food," Peter said, gesturing toward the line of food vendors. "Or we could walk over to the food tent across the way and see how busy it is there."

"I didn't know there was a food tent as well," Fenella exclaimed.

"They put it a short distance away to encourage people to use the food vendors and their trucks," Shelly told her. "The younger crowd usually do that, but us older folks like the marquee where we can sit down and have more proper food."

"Let's go," Fenella said. Although she'd spent most of the morning sitting down watching the ceremony, she was ready to sit again.

They were all pleased to find that the food tent was only about half full and the line at the counter was short. Having filled their trays with a variety of different items, they found an empty table near the open tent flap and sat down to enjoy their lunch.

"We should try some of the vendors for dinner," Shelly suggested.

"After I eat all of this, I won't want much dinner," Fenella replied.

"That makes the vendors the perfect choice," Peter said. "You can just get a snack. There are plenty of choices."

"Fenella? This is a pleasant surprise," a familiar voice said.

"Paul, hello," Fenella said, smiling at the man who was standing at her elbow. "I don't know if you know Peter Cannell and Shelly Quirk," she said. "This is Paul Clucas," she added.

"Of course I know Paul," Peter replied. "We've worked together on a project or two over the years."

Paul smiled. "I'd like to do more of that," he said. "Everything I've done with you has been hugely successful."

"It's nice to meet you," Shelly said.

"It's nice to meet you, as well," Paul replied. He glanced at the opening to the tent. "I'd love to stay and chat, but I'm meeting my mother and Paulette. My mother is, well, not having a very good day."

"I'm sorry to hear that," Fenella said.

"They'll be here in a minute to get something to eat. Please don't be offended if I try to keep my mother on the other side of the marquee," he replied. "I'd rather not see her any more upset than she already is."

"Oh, no, you worry about her, not me," Fenella told him. "I'm happy to pretend that I don't know any of you."

Paul nodded. "I appreciate that," he said. Some commotion behind him had him turning around. "And there they are," he muttered. He glanced back at Fenella and then hurried away.

"I told you I don't want anything," Phillipa Clucas shouted at her daughter. "I'm not hungry."

"Perhaps we should just go home," Paulette said in a strained voice.

"I want to watch the dancing," Phillipa replied. "You said we could watch the dancing."

"Yes, Mum, of course," Paulette said with a sigh.

"Let's get a table," Paul suggested as he joined the others. "Maybe in the back."

He took his mother's arm and began to lead her through the tent. Phillipa took a few steps and then stopped. "Peter, how are you?" she called across the small space. Before Paul could stop her, she turned and walked over to the table where Fenella and her friends were sitting.

"I haven't seen you in ages," Phillipa complained as Peter stood up and gave her a hug. "And you were so kind at Paul's funeral. If I'd known then what I know now, I wouldn't have been so upset."

"How are you?" Peter asked.

"Simply devastated," the woman replied. "I've only just discovered that Paul was unfaithful to me for nearly all of our married life." She narrowed her eyes at the man. "Did you know about all of his other women?" she demanded.

Peter patted her arm gently. "I was never privy to your husband's secrets," he said. "I don't think he ever stopped thinking of me as a child, really."

Phillipa laughed. "Of course, if anyone knew what Paul was doing, it would have been your father, wouldn't it?" She glanced around the room and then leaned in close to Peter. "Am I a bad person for being happy that someone is dead?" she asked in a low voice.

"I'm sure I don't know," Peter replied, looking rather desperately at Paul and Paulette.

"Mother, let's get that table, shall we?" Paul asked in a cheery voice.

"My husband had an affair with Anne Marie Smathers," Phillipa said, her voice suddenly far too loud. Fenella felt as if everyone in the room had stopped talking suddenly.

"I am sorry," Peter said after an awkward moment.

"She's dead, you know, and not a moment too soon. I wanted her dead as soon as I found out. I want them all dead, all of the women who were unfaithful with my husband." Phillipa was nearly shouting, and all around the tent, everyone was listening.

"Mother, that's quite enough," Paul said. He took the woman's arm and said something in her ear. She sighed and took a step backwards.

"I have to go now," she told Peter. "My son doesn't understand the depth of my betrayal. He thinks I should just forget it ever happened."

"Come on, Mum," Paulette said. "Paul is right. There's no point in making yourself miserable over things that happened such a long time ago."

Phillipa took another step and then turned back and stared at

Fenella for a moment. "I haven't forgotten who you are," she said softly.

Fenella felt a chill run down her spine as the woman turned and walked away with her children.

"That was creepy," Shelly said. "She's a scary old woman."

"She's a sad woman," Peter said softly. "I think she must be the last person on the island to learn about her husband's infidelity. It seems to have come as something of a shock to her."

They finished their lunch as quickly as they could. The atmosphere in the tent was subdued as they left. "What's next?" Fenella asked.

"There's still the marquee for the various organizations and also the arts and crafts area. And the entertainment will have started," Shelly said.

"So much to do," Fenella smiled. "Let's try that other marquee." She gave herself a mental high five for using the British term as they went.

They made their way to the other large tent, passing by the entertainment as they went. Fenella couldn't help but stop to watch the dancers for a short while as they made their way through a complicated dancing pattern.

"That was wonderful," Shelly said, as the crowd clapped when they'd finished.

"Like the language, Manx dance and music are experiencing a revival," Peter said.

"I'd love to try it," Shelly said. "But I have two left feet."

"You should try it anyway," Fenella told her.

"I'll take a beginners class if you will," Shelly challenged her.

Fenella laughed. "I'll think about it," she said. "But I think the language might be better. I'm not a very good dancer either."

The second tent was just as full as the first and the trio made their way around the space, chatting with volunteers and staff from children's charities, historical societies, wildlife protection organizations, and many others. Fenella collected even more pamphlets, which she added to her bag. Peter was stopped repeatedly by business associates and old friends. After a while, Fenella gave up on remembering everyone's names and simply smiled politely whenever Peter performed the necessary introductions.

"Peter Cannell, you get more handsome every time I see you," a woman's voice was only just audible over the crowd noise.

Fenella turned and smiled in anticipation of yet another introduction.

"Margaret, you look wonderful," Peter replied. He gave the woman a hug. "Fenella Woods and Shelly Quirk, meet Margaret Dolek," he said. "I worked with her husband some years ago."

Margaret laughed. "When my husband was on the island, anyway," she said. She shook hands with Shelly and then Fenella while Fenella tried to remember where she'd heard the woman's name before. It had to have been something that Mona said, she decided.

"My husband travelled a great deal," Margaret explained. "I think he spent more of our married life in London than on the island."

Of course, Fenella thought, this was the woman that Paul Clucas had begun flirting with after he'd ended things with Anne Marie, at least according to Mona. Mona had said that she didn't think it ever turned into an actual affair, which Fenella could believe as she studied the sweet-looking woman in front of her. Margaret was tiny, with short white hair.

"That must have been difficult for you," Shelly said.

"Oh, no, he was no fun at all. Life was considerably more enjoyable when he was away," the woman said, her brown eyes sparkling as if she relished shocking the others.

"Fenella is Mona's niece," Peter explained.

"Really? You don't look like her," Margaret said. "But you must meet Hannah. She was just here a minute ago, and we were talking about Mona. Don't move."

The woman walked away and then returned a moment later with another older woman in tow. "This is Hannah Jones," she introduced the new arrival. "She and Mona and I were all friends in our younger days."

Fenella shook hands with Hannah, another kindly-looking woman. Her hair was an odd shade of reddish orange that Fenella could only assume must have come from a bottle.

"Mona's niece, huh?" she laughed. "You're nothing like her, which is probably a good thing. I'm not sure the island is ready for another woman like Mona."

Margaret laughed. "She was one of a kind," she agreed. "Even my husband, who had the sex drive of a ninety-year-old monk, was crazy about Mona. He'd have left me for her in a heartbeat if she'd ever so much as let him hold her hand."

Hannah nodded. "Men always fell all over themselves for that woman, and I never could work out why. She wasn't even that attractive, but she had something special, something that made men crazy."

"I think you're more like your aunt than you realize," Peter said softly in Fenella's ear. Fenella blushed, something she was sure that Mona never did.

"No one else even came close when it came to attracting men," Margaret said. "I was quite jealous of whatever magic she possessed."

"Anne Marie tried," Hannah said.

"Yes, but Anne Marie simply threw herself at every man she met and then went to bed with them. Mona didn't have to sleep with a man to win his undying devotion. They were all crazy about her before they got anywhere near her," Margaret said.

"And men got tired of Anne Marie after a few weeks or months," Hannah added. "My husband fell for Mona the night they met and he was still mad about her when he died. The only reason I didn't mind was that I knew she'd never have touched him. He was simply enslaved from afar. Anne Marie, he slept with."

Margaret nodded. "Mine slept with Anne Marie, too, although I can't imagine either of them got anything out of it. Still, once he'd taken her to bed a few times, he quickly got tired of her and he bought me a diamond bracelet to make it up to me."

"I feel as if I missed a rather exciting time," Peter said.

The women laughed. "It was an exciting time," Hannah said after a moment. "We were all married off when we were far too young to know what we were doing and then thrown together at every social event on the island. It's such a small island that we all saw each other far too frequently."

"It wasn't nearly as exciting as it all sounds," Margaret interjected.

"Mostly, we all just flirted like mad and fantasized about running away with someone else's husband. I think Anne Marie was the only one who actually followed through on the innuendos that we all threw around."

"And then there was Mona," Hannah said. "She wasn't married, although I'm sure she didn't lack for offers. She was smart enough to remain single and let men spoil her, without having to deal with the tedious business of being a wife and mother. I was incredibly jealous of her, if I'm honest."

"She had the life we all wanted," Margaret agreed. "And she had Max."

Hannah smiled a bit dreamily. "I would have left my husband for Max," she said. "I probably would have murdered my husband for Max."

Margaret nodded. "He was perfect for Mona, of course. Gorgeous and sexy and brilliantly clever. I don't think there was a woman on the island who would have turned Max down if he'd propositioned her."

"And yet he was faithful to Mona," Hannah said. "Even when they weren't speaking."

"And the fights," Margaret said. "Do you remember the night Mona threw her engagement ring into the sea? That was the most spectacular fight I've ever seen."

"I never did know what they were fighting about," Hannah replied.

"No one ever knew what they were fighting about. I'm not sure they knew sometimes. I think they just liked to fight," Margaret suggested.

"My dear, we must have tea one day," Margaret said to Fenella. "I could tell you stories about Mona for hours."

"I'd really like that," Fenella replied.

"You should invite me to your flat," the woman suggested. "I've always wanted to see it. Max had it built for Mona, you know, after he decided to convert the hotel into flats."

"I'd heard that," Fenella said. "And you're more than welcome to come for tea any time."

The woman dug around in her handbag, eventually pulling out a small calendar. "How about tomorrow?" she asked after she'd opened the calendar to July.

Fenella checked her phone, but it was mostly for show. She knew she wasn't doing anything the next day. "Tomorrow sounds good," she said. "I won't promise anything elaborate, but I can make tea, at least. How about two o'clock?"

"That works for me. Hannah, you should come too," the other woman said.

"I might," Hannah replied. "If I can get away." She made a face at Fenella. "I live next door to my son and his wife," she explained. "And their two adorable little monsters. George is three and Anastasia is not quite one, and my darling son and daughter-in-law think that my job now should be providing as much free childminding as they can possibly take advantage of." She shook her head. "I love my grandchildren, but I raised my own children many years ago. It isn't my fault that my son didn't decide to settle down until he was in his late forties. And that wife of his wouldn't have been my choice, either."

Margaret patted her arm. "Tell your son that you're going out at midday tomorrow. I'll collect you and we'll go and get some lunch and do some shopping before we meet Fenella. If he argues, tell him he'll have to answer to me. I'm his godmother, after all, he ought to be afraid of me."

The two women walked away, still chatting about their plans for the next day. Shelly looked at Fenella and raised her eyebrows.

"Are you sure you want to have them over for tea?" she asked.

"I think they'll be fun," Fenella said, crossing her fingers for luck. "And I love hearing about Mona. I'm so sorry I never got to know her."

"Arts and crafts next?" Peter asked.

The trio spent the next hour happily exploring the many different tables and small tents that were showcasing local artists and crafters. Fenella bought a few little things and took business cards from many of the stalls, promising to check websites and visit stores as soon as she could.

"I want it all," she told Shelly. "Did you see the paintings in the little blue tent? That man is so talented. I can just imagine one of his paintings on the wall in my bedroom."

"But you don't want to buy it here today," Shelly said. "You'd have to carry it around all afternoon and hold it during the fireworks."

"Exactly," Fenella said.

Donald finally caught up with them as they were sizing up the various food vendors at dinner time.

"I'm so sorry," he told Fenella. "I kept trying to get away, but everyone wanted a word, and then there was a fancy catered lunch that I didn't know about." He shook his head. "I should have dragged you along with me for the day," he told her. "You would have been bored, but it would have improved my day no end."

Fenella laughed. "Sorry, but I've been having a wonderful time," she said. "I've found dozens of things I want to buy and I've collected half my body weight in brochures about the gorgeous foods and drinks that the island produces. It's all been rather splendid."

"I should buy you something wonderful to apologize for my tardiness," he replied.

"You've nothing to apologize for," Fenella said firmly. "I've been having fun with my friends. And we're just friends, as well. You're not obligated to spend your time with me."

Donald frowned. "I was rather hoping that we were working our way towards being something more than friends," he said. When Fenella frowned, he waved a hand. "I'm sorry. I'm acting like I'm trying to start a fight. It's only because I'm so annoyed with myself for getting roped into spending the day with people I don't particularly like rather than with you."

He slid an arm around her and pulled her close, kissing the top of her head. "At least I can enjoy the fireworks with you," he murmured in her ear.

7

Between them, the foursome got something from nearly every food vendor at the site. They found a bench that was just being vacated and everyone shared their snacks with everyone else.

"I ate too much," Fenella complained as she wiped her hands on a napkin.

"And I was going to suggest ice cream," Peter said.

"The fireworks aren't for hours yet," Shelly pointed out. "I'm sure we'll all have room for ice cream before it gets dark."

Feeling more than a little tired and very full, Fenella was happy to agree to find a quiet spot to watch some of the entertainment. Troupes of Manx dancers from the primary schools around the island were performing, and after a while, one group of school children made their way through the crowd, trying to find willing volunteers to join them for the next dance.

Shelly laughed and shook her head when one little girl approached her, but a voice in the crowd shouted out. "Go on, Mrs. Quirk. You can't say no to my daughter. Not after you taught me to read and write."

Shelly flushed and stood up to hug the man who had made his way over to her. "My goodness, but you've grown up, haven't you?" she laughed. "I didn't realize you were old enough to be married with children of your own now."

"I am, and my little girl is really keen on Manx dancing. Go ahead and see if she can't teach you a thing or two," he replied.

Shelly let the little girl lead her into the middle of the large green space. For several minutes it looked like chaos, as each child tried to teach an adult the steps to the dance. Finally a teacher clapped her hands.

"I hope you're all ready to begin," she announced. Several of the adults shook their heads and shouted "no," but she ignored them. Turning to the band that was accompanying the dancers, she grinned. "Whenever you're ready," she said.

The band started and the children did their best to lead the adults through the series of steps. The crowd clapped and cheered as everyone stumbled along, and after a few minutes it began to look as if the volunteers were getting the hang of it.

"Shall we try it at normal speed now, then?" the teacher asked with a wicked grin.

The band picked up the pace of the music and everyone laughed as the children danced happily while the adult volunteers began to trip over one another and themselves. When the band finished playing, everyone cheered wildly. Shelly sank back down on the blanket, breathing heavily.

"That was hard work," she said once she'd caught her breath.

"It looked like fun," Peter said. "But I'm really glad I didn't volunteer."

"There you are," Gordon said as he joined them. "I've been looking all over for you," he told Shelly. "I texted you over an hour ago, but you never replied."

Shelly gasped and dug around in her handbag for her phone. "I never heard it over all of the crowd noise," she said apologetically. "I'm so sorry."

"I was afraid you were having fun without me and didn't want me spoiling it," Gordon told her.

"I was having fun," Shelly replied. "But I'm very happy to have you join us."

Gordon sat down next to her and greeted the others. "I was meant to be here hours ago, but I got tied up with work and then I couldn't find anywhere to park. I think the entire island is here," he explained.

"It does seem busier than previous years," Donald agreed. "Which can only be a good thing."

As the evening wore on, Fenella enjoyed more dancing, a lot more music, and several different performances by various children's sports teams. A martial arts demonstration was particularly impressive, but Fenella enjoyed the school choirs the best, especially the ones with the smallest children.

At some point Gordon went and bought ice cream cones for everyone, and some time later Donald managed to find a bottle of wine and enough glasses for them all to enjoy a drink. The fireworks were the perfect climax to the day. As soon as they were over, everyone headed for their cars.

"Would you like a ride home?" Donald asked Fenella as they walked together.

"We all came in Peter's car," Fenella replied. "There's no point in you going out of your way. I can ride home with him and Shelly."

Donald looked like he wanted to argue, but after a moment he nodded and then stopped and pulled her close. "It was wonderful to see you," he told her. "Let's have dinner together on Friday."

"I'm sorry, but I already have plans," she replied, feeling oddly guilty about dinner with Paul.

"Peter?" Donald asked.

"No, I'm having dinner with someone I met recently. It's just friendly, though," she replied.

"Anyone I know?" Donald asked, his voice casual.

"Paul Clucas. I don't know if you know him."

Donald laughed. "He's a sweet kid," he told her. "But hardly in your league. He mooned after Mona for most of his life. I'm sure having dinner with you is the most exciting thing that's ever happened to him."

"He wants to apologize to me for his mother's behavior at the party the other night," Fenella explained.

"He should be apologizing for not supervising the woman properly," Donald said. "But whatever. I can't be jealous of Paul Clucas. What about Saturday?"

"I can do Saturday," Fenella replied.

"I'll ring you to confirm after I make a booking somewhere," Donald told her. He kissed her gently and then let her go. "Sleep well," he said softly as she turned away.

She rushed to catch up to the others, but she needn't have worried. Shelly and Gordon were having their own private chat only a few steps away. Peter had stopped to talk to yet another business colleague, and by now Fenella was too tired to even listen to the introductions. She nearly fell asleep in the car on the way back to Douglas, in part because they spent so much time sitting in traffic as the site cleared.

"I hope you both enjoyed the day," Peter said as the trio stumbled tiredly into the elevator in their building.

"It was wonderful," Fenella said. "But I'm glad it's only once a year. I'm exhausted."

"Next year maybe we should skip the ceremony and just go for the fun parts," Shelly suggested.

"I liked the ceremony," Fenella told her. "Maybe we should go to the ceremony and then come home for a nap in the middle of the day. We could go back later for the fireworks."

"If only parking weren't so tricky," Peter said. "But we have a year to think about it."

"And forget how tired we are," Shelly laughed. "I'm sure by next year we'll want to do the whole day again."

"As long as it doesn't rain," Peter suggested.

Fenella had left extra food out for Katie, but she wasn't surprised to find that both of her regular bowls and the extra water bowl she'd left out were all empty. She refilled everything and then fell into bed, falling asleep as soon as her head hit the pillow.

"Merroww," Katie said in her ear.

"Not yet," Fenella said sleepily.

"Meeerrrrooooooowwwww," Katie replied.

Fenella opened one eye and looked at the clock. It was seven, and far too early for her to be awake after her late night the previous evening. "I'll give you extra treats if you let me sleep for one more hour," she told the animal.

Katie tilted her head and studied her for a moment, and then jumped down and disappeared. Fenella waited to hear the complaints from the kitchen, but she was back asleep before she heard a sound.

"MMMeeeeeoooowwww," Katie said insistently.

Fenella sighed and opened one eye again. It was exactly eight o'clock. "How did you do that?" she asked the animal.

Katie shook her head and jumped down. This time when she started shouting from the kitchen Fenella heard her.

"Yes, yes, all right," Fenella called as she crawled out of bed. "I'm coming and I haven't forgotten your extra treats, either."

She gave Katie the treats and then started coffee before refilling the animal's bowls. Her head was pounding and she felt much worse than she should have, considering she'd only had one glass of wine before the fireworks display.

"I'm getting too old for late nights," she said as she hunted around in the cupboard for her bottle of headache pills.

"But did you enjoy the day out?" Mona asked from behind her.

Fenella shrieked and dropped the bottle of pills that she'd just found. She spun around and sighed. "I didn't know you were there," she said.

"So I gathered," Mona replied. "Next time I'll make more noise as I come in."

Fenella didn't believe her, but she nodded anyway. She washed the pills down with coffee and then poured cereal into a bowl. While she'd have preferred pancakes, she didn't have the energy to make them.

"What did you think of Tynwald Day?" Mona asked as Fenella slid onto a stool at the counter.

"It was better than I expected," Fenella said. "The ceremony itself was fascinating, and the fair was fabulous. I hadn't expected there to be so much to do. I must have hundreds of brochures for local businesses and charities now, and I've been introduced to dozens of amazing artists and crafters that I want to buy things from."

"Didn't Donald buy you anything nice?" Mona asked.

"He offered, but I wouldn't let him," Fenella replied.

Mona shook her head. "You should never turn down a gift from a man," she told her. "Donald can afford it and it would have made him happy to give you something."

"I don't want him to think that I'm for sale," Fenella countered.

"He should be smart enough to know better than that," Mona scoffed.

"Anyway, I met some friends of yours," Fenella changed the subject.

"Did you?"

"Margaret Dolek and Hannah Jones," Fenella told her.

Mona smiled. "I hope they're both well," she said. "As we grew older, we saw less and less of one another, but I still have very fond memories of both of them. Neither had a particularly happy marriage. We used to get together and complain about men on a regular basis."

"The way they tell it, you didn't have anything to complain about," Fenella told her. "They both said they were crazy about Max."

Mona gave her a smug smile. "Max was irresistible to women," she said. "But he never looked at another woman in all of our years together."

"But you fought all the time?" Fenella made the statement a question.

Mona shrugged. "We both had passionate personalities. Conflict was inevitable, and only added to our relationship."

"Well, Margaret is coming for tea this afternoon, so get ready to see her again. Hannah may be coming as well, if she can get away from her grandchildren."

Mona laughed. "I couldn't believe it when I heard that her son had finally married," she said. "He's very stupid and not at all attractive. I've never met his wife, but I do wonder what sort of woman would marry that man. I can't even imagine what their offspring will be like."

"Apparently they use Hannah as a babysitting service. She didn't seem too happy about it, either."

"Hopefully she'll be able to get away today, then," Mona said. "It will be nice to see them both, although I know they're only coming over so that they can get a look at my flat."

"Oh, thanks," Fenella said sarcastically. "Maybe they found me fascinating and wanted a chance to get to know me better," she suggested.

Mona laughed. "I rarely had visitors here," she said. "It wouldn't have been proper when the building was a hotel, even though I had two rooms and used one as a sitting room. By the time I moved into this flat, I was too old to change my ways. Shelly and Peter used to visit, and Max, of course, but I rarely invited anyone else here." She looked around the beautiful kitchen. "Maybe I should have made more of an effort."

"It's such a wonderful apartment," Fenella said. "I can't imagine not wanting to show it off."

"By the time it was finished, Max was unwell," Mona told her, frowning at the memory. "He loved to come and sit here and watch the sea. I couldn't have guests. He wouldn't have been comfortable here with other people around."

"I'm sorry," Fenella said, surprised at the amount of pain she could hear in the other woman's words.

Mona nodded. "Thank you," she murmured.

Fenella finished her cereal and dumped the bowl into the dishwasher. "My guests are supposed to be here at two. What do you think I should feed them?"

"You've invited them for tea," Mona replied. "You must have a proper tea for them."

"You don't mean like what I had on Sunday at the Seaview," Fenella protested. "Sandwiches and cakes and cookies and fruit and piles and piles of lovely food."

"That's exactly what I mean," Mona said. "Margaret and Hannah will be expecting it. Why, when I hosted tea parties, they were magnificent affairs. You mustn't let me down."

"I thought you said you never entertained here," Fenella argued.

"Oh, I didn't. I used to have tea parties in the dining room of the restaurant when this was a hotel. Max would have the chef prepare dozens of trays of food for me. We always tried to outdo the previous event, with even more variety each time. The chef would fly in all manner of exotic fruits and salad leaves from all over the world for the sandwiches. It was wonderful."

"I can't possibly compete with that," Fenella said. "And I don't really see the point in trying. I'll make tea and put out a plate of cookies. Your friends will have to be happy with that."

"No," Mona said sternly. "You don't have to compete with what I did, but you do have to put some effort into the affair. My tea parties were legendary. You haven't the time to manage that, but you can at least try for [illegible]."

Fenella sighed. "I should have asked them to come to lunch," she said.

"Some day I'll tell you about the fabulous luncheons that I used to host," Mona said, winking at her.

"What do I need and where can I get it, then?" she asked.

An hour later she had a long grocery list and a headache. "I don't know if I can afford all of this," she complained. "And I hardly think it's worth it for one little old lady, anyway."

"Hannah will come," Mona assured her. "She won't want to miss the chance to see what Max did for me."

"Even so, this is far too much food for three people."

"You can have Shelly over later to help you eat the leftovers. Invite Peter as well, if you think he won't get the wrong idea."

"There's no way I can get all of this into my little shopping cart," Fenella said. "I'll have to make two or three trips to the grocery store."

"You'd better get started, then," Mona suggested.

"Tell me again why I have to do this," Fenella demanded.

Mona sighed. "In my heyday, my tea parties were the highlight of many women's social calendars. Women like Hannah and Margaret and Anne Marie would spend hours deciding what to wear and having their hair and nails done. We always started at two o'clock with tea and food, oh, the most delicious food. The parties often went on into the small hours of the morning, though. Wine would start flowing around six and the chef would make us more and more food as we drank and talked and laughed about life and men and anything and everything."

"And did Phillipa Clucas come to your tea parties?" Fenella wondered.

"Sometimes," Mona told her. "She never stayed for very long, but she would come and have a cup of tea and tell us all about her children." She frowned. "Actually, she'd talk about Paulette and Paul. She never really talked about Paula, although after about half an hour she'd look at the clock and announce that she needed to get home to Paula. She'd rush away and we'd all carry on having a wonderful time. The men would begin arriving around six, and Paul Clucas was always among them. He was never in a rush to get home to Paula, or Phillipa for that matter."

"How sad," Fenella said. She looked at her shopping list again. While there was no way she was going to buy everything that Mona had insisted on, even if she only bought half of the items on the list she'd need to make two trips with her small wheeled cart. She hated asking her friends for favors, but she felt like she didn't have much choice.

"Shelly? It's Fenella. I was wondering if you might have time to run me to the grocery store. I want to put on a proper tea for my guests this afternoon and I can't do that without a trip to the store," she said when Shelly answered her phone.

"Of course I can," Shelly said. "If we leave in the next five minutes, we should be able to get there and back before I have to worry about meeting Gordon for lunch."

"I don't want to get in the way of your lunch plans," Fenella exclaimed.

"You won't," Shelly assured her. "We have plenty of time."

Fenella ran into her bedroom and threw on clothes. She'd have to shower later, before her guests arrived. Pulling her hair into a messy ponytail, she put on the barest minimum of makeup and grabbed her handbag. She was at the door when Shelly knocked.

"Ready?" Shelly asked.

"I just need my list," Fenella told her. She grabbed the sheet of paper off the counter and followed Shelly down the corridor. "I'm hugely grateful," she said as they boarded the elevator. "You should come to tea, too, once you've finished lunch with Gordon."

"I might," Shelly said. "But the last time I had lunch with Gordon we ended up talking until dinner time. He's, well, he's rather special. I just wish I knew what he thought of me."

"He obviously likes you or he wouldn't keep making plans to see you again and again," Fenella pointed out.

"Yes, but are we just friends or is there something more there?" Shelly asked.

"You need to ask Gordon that question," Fenella said as she slid into the passenger seat of Shelly's car.

"I can't bring myself to ask that," Shelly replied, blushing.

"So kiss him," Fenella said, feeling as if she were channeling Mona as the words came out

Shelly laughed. "Well, that's one way to find out how we both feel, isn't it? I'm not sure I'm brave enough for that, though."

"Take him to the pub, sit next to him on one of the couches and split a bottle of wine," Fenella suggested. "After each glass, slide a little closer to him and see what he does."

"You sound like Mona," Shelly said. "That's exactly the sort of advice I'd have expected from her."

"Maybe living in her apartment is wearing off on me," Fenella said.

They went their separate ways at the large grocery store. Fenella felt a little overwhelmed as she filled her shopping cart with cream cakes and biscuits along with the ingredients for several different types of sandwiches.

"How many people did you say were coming?" Shelly asked as Fenella loaded her bags into the trunk of Shelly's car.

"Just two," Fenella replied. "But after my tea at the Seaview the other day, I felt like I had to put some effort in."

"Mona used to host fabulous tea parties," Shelly told her as they headed toward home. "I remember hearing about them when I was younger. Only the very wealthiest women were invited, and even having lots of money was no guarantee of an invitation. As I understand it, there was a subsection of high society that didn't approve of Mona and her lifestyle. They did their best to snub her and she returned the favor."

Fenella laughed. "That sounds like her," she said. "I mean, from what I've heard about her," she added quickly.

"I didn't move in the same social circles as Mona in those days, of course," Shelly said. "Or I should say my parents didn't, as I was only a child when Mona was in her prime. From the stories I've heard, though, it was all terribly glamorous and wonderful."

"Just looking at the clothes in Mona's wardrobe suggests that she had a very glamorous life," Fenella said. "I'm sure my tea party will pale by comparison."

Shelly helped Fenella carry all of her shopping bags up to her apartment. It took them two trips and left Shelly shaking her head.

"It does seem like rather a lot of food," she said as she put the last bag on the kitchen counter.

"So you'll come over when you finish your lunch, right? I don't care what time it is, just come hungry," Fenella said.

"If I come right after lunch, I probably won't be very hungry," Shelly replied. "Maybe I should come over for dinner."

"You'll be more than welcome," Fenella told her. "I'll probably invite Peter, as well. As you say, I've bought far too much food." Although she'd only intended to buy half of the things on Mona's list, once she'd started shopping, she'd become overenthusiastic and bought nearly everything. She blushed as she realized that she'd even purchased a few extra items that Mona hadn't mentioned. She was going to be eating cream cakes and cookies for weeks.

"I'll see you later," Shelly promised as Fenella let her out. "I'll ring first to see if your guests are still here or not, though."

"You should bring Gordon back with you," Fenella suggested. "And any other random people you come across."

Shelly laughed and then disappeared into her own apartment. Fenella walked back into the kitchen and stared at the food that was piled everywhere. She didn't even know where to begin.

"There are tiered trays in the cupboard next to the refrigerator," Mona told her. "You've probably never even looked in those cupboards, have you?"

Fenella shrugged. When she'd first moved in, she'd glanced inside every cupboard and wardrobe in the apartment. She would have sworn the cupboard in question had been nearly empty when she'd looked, but now she opened it to find several beautiful sets of silver trays. She took two out and set them on the counter.

"It's too soon to start putting the food out," Mona said. "But you can make the sandwiches and then put them in the refrigerator until later."

Under Mona's watchful tutelage, Fenella made dozens of fancy finger sandwiches, carefully cutting off the crusts before wrapping them in plastic and storing them in the refrigerator.

"I'm starving," Fenella commented as she put the last of the sandwiches away."

"You'll have plenty to eat soon," Mona told her. "And you'll need to be hungry. You'll want to try everything, won't you?"

Fenella glanced at the various packages that she'd spread across the counter. Every single thing looked delicious. "Yes, I will," she said eagerly.

"Remember to offer everything to your guests first," Mona said sternly. "You may fill your plate only after they've filled theirs."

"Yes, Aunty Mona," Fenella said.

"You should use my silver tea service," Mona instructed her. "It's in the same cupboard where you found the trays."

Fenella couldn't believe she hadn't noticed the beautiful silver tea set when she'd taken out the trays. "This is beautiful," she said.

"Max had it made for me," Mona said casually. "You can see our initials in the design work."

Fenella looked at the elaborate engraved design on the teapot. If you knew what you were looking at, you could just see the "MM" and "MK" intertwined throughout the design.

Mona gave her very specific instructions on how to make tea properly while Fenella paced around the kitchen and living room, watching the clock. Katie had her lunch and then took herself off to the guest bedroom, clearly unnerved by all of Fenella's rushing about. After a while, Fenella remembered that she hadn't had a shower yet and rushed to take one. She threw on one of Mona's lovely summery dresses before going back to pacing for a short while.

At half past one, Fenella got to work. She opened packets of cookies and arranged them on plates, sliced cakes into bite-sized pieces and arranged them in between the cookies, and then decorated the plates with fresh strawberries and raspberries.

The sandwiches came out of storage and were carefully stacked and restacked until they met with Mona's approval. Grapes and blueberries were carefully dotted around the trays, adding color.

"What do you think?" Fenella asked her aunt after she'd dropped the last blueberry into place.

"I think it all looks wonderful," Mona replied.

"You sound surprised," Fenella said.

Mona chuckled. "I wasn't sure that you'd manage it," she admitted. "But you've done a splendid job."

"I just hope Margaret and Hannah appreciate the effort," Fenella said.

"But they won't," Mona told her. "They'll be expecting all of this. You are my niece."

"And if you weren't here, they'd have been given a mug of tea and a few cookies, and I wouldn't have given it a moment's thought," Fenella replied.

"Thank goodness I'm here, then," Mona laughed.

With everything ready to go, Fenella found herself pacing again. Mona watched her for a moment and then sighed. "Do calm down," she suggested. "You're getting yourself into such a state. Have a glass of wine or something."

"I haven't eaten since breakfast. A glass of wine on an empty stomach would be dangerous."

"You mustn't touch your lovely trays," Mona said. "But you can nibble on whatever you didn't put out."

"Why didn't I think of that?" Fenella asked. She dug out the last plate of sandwiches that hadn't fit on the serving trays. She'd munched her way through three of the delicacies before she looked at the clock. "It's two," she said. "Is Margaret usually late?"

"Perhaps," Mona shrugged. "I never worried much about being on time for things myself. It was much more important to make an entrance."

Fenella ate a few more sandwiches and a few bites of cake and then resumed pacing. She was still feeling oddly nervous, but at least she wasn't hungry. It was quarter past two when the knock finally came on her door.

Mona was right on her heels as she crossed the room.

"You are eager to see your old friends, aren't you?" Fenella asked as she reached for the doorknob.

Mona stopped and took a step backwards as Fenella swung the door open, a bright smile in place. The smile faltered when she recognized the man on the doorstep.

"Inspector Hammersmith? But what are you doing here?" she asked.

"I'm sure I told you to call me Mark," he said, smiling brightly at her. "I hope I haven't come at a bad time?"

Fenella flushed. "No, of course not," she said. "It's just that I'm expecting some friends for tea. I thought you were my friends."

"Friends for tea," he repeated. "How lovely. I won't stay for long, then." He raised his eyebrows and Fenella took a step backwards.

"Do come in," she said reluctantly.

The man walked into the apartment and crossed to the open kitchen. "This is quite a spread," he said. "How many friends are you expecting?"

"Only two," Fenella muttered.

"I would have guessed a lot more from the amount of food on offer," he said, his tone conversational.

"I had tea at the Seaview on Sunday," Fenella felt obliged to explain. "I wanted to try to do my best to recreate that for my guests."

"Your guests must be important," Mark suggested. "Do you mind telling me who you are expecting?"

"Friends of my Aunt Mona's," Fenella replied. "Two women whom I met yesterday at the Tynwald Day fair. Margaret Dolek and Hannah Jones were telling me stories about my aunt. In the end, I invited them for tea today so that they could tell me more."

"You never met your aunt?"

"She visited the US a few times when I was a child, but I hadn't seen her for a great many years before she died," Fenella replied.

The man nodded. "So Mrs. Dolek and Mrs. Jones were meant to be coming for tea today."

"Are meant to be coming," Fenella corrected him.

"At least this time you really were expecting someone," he said. "And your story matches Mrs. Jones's version perfectly."

Fenella's heart sank. "What's happened?" she demanded.

"Just another unfortunate accident," the man said blandly. "Mrs. Dolek fell down the stairs in her home last night and broke her neck. The only thing that I find curious about the whole affair is the fact that she was meant to be meeting you this afternoon."

Fenella felt the color drain from her face. Mark must have noticed, because he took her arm and led her to the nearest chair.

"Just take a few deep breaths," he told her. "I shouldn't have just sprung that on you like that. I am sorry."

Fenella shook her head. "I'm okay," she said. "I was just surprised, that's all. I just spoke to the woman yesterday."

"And she was coming here for tea today."

Fenella nodded and then looked over at the kitchen counter. Looking at the piles and piles of food made her feel slightly ill. "You're sure it was an accident?" she blurted out.

Mark raised an eyebrow. "Do you know of any reason why it wouldn't have been?" he asked.

"No, no, not at all," Fenella replied quickly. "I think I've just been caught up in too many murder investigations lately, that's all."

Mark studied her for a moment. "What exactly were you and Mrs. Dolek going to talk about today?" he asked.

"She was going to share some memories of my aunt with me, that's all. I don't really remember Mona very well. Margaret and Hannah were going to tell me about her."

"Mona led a rather adventurous life," Mark said.

Fenella shrugged. "I've heard a few stories, but I don't know how true any of them are."

"But you were happy to find out more?"

"I'm eager to find out more," Fenella replied. "I'm fascinated by what I've learned thus far."

"Can you think of any reason why anyone would want to keep you from hearing more about Mona's past?" the man asked.

Fenella sat back in her chair and tried to think. "I can't imagine that anyone on the island cares what I do or don't know about Mona," she said eventually.

Mark nodded. "As I said, both deaths appear to have been unfortunate accidents. The only link between them, aside from the fact that they both knew each other, is that they both had plans to talk to you on the day they died. It's probably just one of life's odd coincidences."

"Unless something happened in the past that has motivated someone to kill them now," Fenella suggested.

"It's hard to imagine what that something could be," he replied. "If you have any ideas, I'd love to hear them."

"Someone is killing all of the women who knew Paul Clucas," Mona said. She'd been sitting on the couch, staring out the window, since Mark had announced Margaret's death. Now she came and stood next to Fenella. "Phillipa's lost her mind and she's going around killing all of the women in Paul's memoirs. That has to be it."

"As I understand it, there was some infidelity in that social circle, back in the day," Fenella said, trying to work how best to word her comments. "Maybe someone is just now getting their revenge."

Mark stared at her for a minute and then chuckled. "I don't know anything about that social circle, but I find it hard to believe that anyone would wait this long to extract revenge if they felt wronged."

"Paulette told me that her father left notes for his memoirs detailing his affairs," Fenella said. "According to her, her mother had no idea he'd cheated until she read his notes."

"And she just found these notes recently?"

"Yes, the man just passed away a few months ago."

"So you're suggesting that Phillipa Clucas is now systematically killing the women her husband slept with some forty or fifty years ago?" Mark asked, his voice incredulous.

"You asked me if I had any ideas of what the something could be," Fenella replied, working to keep her voice steady.

"I suppose I did," Mark said. "More fool me," he added under his breath.

Fenella pretended not to hear him. She stood up and walked to the kitchen counter. "Would you like some cake or sandwiches?" she asked. "Everything will be going stale sitting out like this."

The man joined her. She handed him a plate and he helped himself to a few sandwiches, some cake, and a handful of cookies.

"Thank you for this," he said after a few bites. "I didn't get lunch."

"You're very welcome. Would you like tea?"

"Sure, that would be great," he replied, eating steadily.

Fenella made a pot of tea, ignoring the fancy silver tea set. After she'd handed Mark a mug, she took a slow sip of her own drink. She was surprised to find tears in her eyes as she did so.

"Are you okay?" Mark asked.

"I'm fine," she said. "I think I'm just a bit overwhelmed by it all. First Anne Marie and now Margaret."

"We're going to conduct thorough investigations into both deaths, but at this point we've no reason to believe that either was anything other than a sad accident," he said. "As I said before, I believe your involvement is merely an odd coincidence."

"He's an idiot," Mona said. She sat down next to the man at the counter and made a face at him. "They were both murdered. I'm sure of it."

Fenella looked at her aunt and shook her head slightly. Mark didn't seem to notice. He was finishing off the last of his pile of cookies.

"There is another possibility," he said as he stood up.

"Is there?"

"It's possible one or even both of the women committed suicide," he told her.

Fenella shivered. "What a horrible thought," she said. "Neither seemed at all suicidal when I spoke to them."

"But you didn't really know either of them," he reminded her. "You don't know what they were normally like."

"Driving your car into a stone wall seems an odd way to kill yourself," Fenella said. "And I can't even begin to imagine throwing yourself down a flight of stairs."

"It does happen," Mark told her. "It was a steep and straight flight of stairs. She may have simply jumped."

Fenella shook her head. "The woman I talked to yesterday was not thinking about going home and jumping from a great height. She was looking forward to coming here and seeing Mona's apartment."

Mark nodded and tapped a few times on his phone. "All evidence thus far points to her tripping at the top of the stairs and falling to her death. There was a piece of loose carpet on the upstairs landing, which could easily have caused her to stumble."

"The question is, was that piece of carpet loose before Margaret fell down the stairs, or did her killer pull it up to try to hide the fact that she'd been murdered?" Mona said.

"Was there anything wrong with Anne Marie's car?" Fenella asked, trying to ignore Mona.

"It's still being examined," the man replied. "It was an old car. It's not outside the realm of possibility that the brakes failed or that something happened to the steering."

"How awful for Anne Marie," Fenella said softly.

"Whatever happened, it happened quickly," Mark said. "She probably didn't have time to panic."

Fenella nodded, but didn't feel reassured.

"Anne Marie took meticulous care of that car," Mona said. "If something went wrong with it, someone tampered with it."

"One last question before I go," Mark said, smiling at Fenella. "Can I just ask what your plans are for the next few days? I'm especially interested in who might be coming to see you."

Fenella flushed. "I hardly think..." she began, but Mark held up a hand.

"I'm only joking," he said. "As I said, I'm sure your involvement in all of this is merely coincidental. And I'm sure both deaths were accidents. I only came to see you today to make sure that I covered every possible angle."

"I don't mean to be rude, but I hope I don't see you again," Fenella said.

The man nodded and then headed for the door. "If someone else with plans to see you dies, we might have to have a more serious conversation," he said. "Life is full of strange coincidences, but a third death would be a coincidence too far."

Fenella let the man out and then leaned against the door after she'd shut it. Mark's last words had almost sounded like a warning. It was pointless to warn her, though. She'd had nothing to do with the two deaths, after all.

"I can't believe Margaret is dead," Mona said, moving restlessly around the living room. "Anne Marie's death was less of a shock, for some reason. Perhaps that's because I was really looking forward to seeing Margaret today."

"I'm sorry," Fenella told her. "Do you really think both women were murdered?" she asked tentatively.

Mona shrugged. "That was my first instinct, but I don't know. It seems impossible that Phillipa would kill anyone, let alone women who used to be her friends, but it seems impossible that both Anne Marie and Margaret had accidents within days of one another."

"Maybe it isn't Phillipa, then," Fenella suggested.

"Paulette is too timid to do anything as outrageous as murder, and I can't see Paul caring in the slightest what his father did. I'm sure he knew what the man was up to years ago. His father's notes won't have shocked him at all."

"Can you think of any other reason why someone would want Anne Marie and Margaret dead?" Fenella asked.

"Not both of them," Mona said after thinking for a minute. "They both have children who might be eager to inherit, but that's about all I can think of for a motive."

"You don't think the two of them were keeping some secret for years and now it's been found out?" Fenella asked.

"I still think Anne Marie might have had a hand in her husband's death, but I can't imagine who would want to murder her over that, especially not after all this time."

"Do you think Margaret knew anything about Herbert's death?"

"I'm sure she had the same suspicions that I did, but Anne Marie was too smart to use an accomplice or anything like that."

"What about secrets relating to money or one of the men's businesses?"

"I have no idea," Mona said. "But Mark Hammersmith should be doing everything he can to find out."

"He thinks they were both accidents," Fenella reminded her. "And I'm inclined to agree with him," she added, earning a frown from Mona.

"Why was Anne Marie coming to see you?" Mona asked. "That may well be the key."

"I've no idea," Fenella said. "Maybe she was lying about coming here because she was really meeting up with someone she shouldn't have been."

"Like who?"

"A married man? She seemed to have had a thing for married men."

"That was a long time ago," Mona told her. "There weren't any married men left that were her age."

"And if there had been, they probably would have wanted a younger woman," Fenella added.

Mona nodded. She opened her mouth to reply, but the phone interrupted.

"Is that Fenella Woods?" the voice quavered slightly.

"It is, yes."

"This is Hannah Jones. I was just ringing to apologize for not coming for tea as planned. Margaret was going to collect me, you see. Anyway, at two o'clock I was still talking to the police."

"I'm very sorry for your loss," Fenella said. "I know you were friends for many years."

"Yes, well, thank you for that. We were friends, but not great friends. There was too much competition between all of us; that prevented us from becoming close. We were actually becoming better friends in just the last few months. Now that all the men we used to fight over are dead, we were able to enjoy one another's company."

"How sad," Fenella murmured, unsure of what else to say.

"Yes, well, I hope you didn't go to too much trouble for the tea party," Hannah said. "I'd hate to think that you wasted a lot of time and money."

"Oh, no, no trouble at all," Fenella lied brightly, looking sadly at the kitchen counter. Mark had left only a small dent in the vast amount of food on offer.

"I would really like a chance to sit down and talk with you about Mona," the woman added. "Maybe we could try again? I'm free tomorrow."

Fenella looked at her nearly empty calendar and shrugged. "I can do tomorrow," she said. But there was no way she was going to try to recreate today's tea party, she decided. "Why don't we meet for lunch somewhere, my treat?"

"Ooh, I'd like that," Hannah replied. She named a restaurant. "It's close to home, so I don't have to drive," she added. "I know I'm being silly, but driving worries me since Anne Marie's accident."

"I'll meet you there at noon," Fenella said.

"Midday is perfect," the woman told her. "I'm looking forward to it."

Fenella put down the phone and then sighed. Maybe she ought to put some effort into learning to speak British English, but saying flat for apartment or midday for noon still felt odd to her. Maybe they'd become more natural over time.

"You should ring Mark and tell him you're meeting Hannah tomorrow," Mona said. "He should offer her police protection."

"Don't say that," Fenella snapped. "I'm sure she'll be fine. Anyway, Mark didn't take anything I said seriously. He'd just laugh if I suggested that Hannah needed police protection."

"I wish Daniel was here," Mona said.

"Me, too," Fenella agreed. For all sorts of reasons that have nothing to do with Anne Marie and Margaret, she added to herself.

She was staring at the food again when her mobile phone buzzed.

"I hope this is Shelly and she's texting to let me know that she and

Gordon are on their way to eat everything," she said as she picked up the phone.

It wasn't Shelly. "What is going on over there?" the message from Daniel Robinson read.

"Nothing much," Fenella texted back.

"Why did Mark Hammersmith pull me out of a class to ask me questions about you, then?"

Fenella sighed deeply.

"Who is it?" Mona asked.

"It's Daniel. Inspector Hammersmith pulled him out of a class to ask him about me."

"Oh, dear," Mona said. "But at least now you can share our theory with Daniel. Tell him everything."

"He's busy," Fenella replied. She thought for a minute, and then texted again. "Sorry about that. Just a few unfortunate accidents that have a tenuous link to me."

"I have to get back to my class. I'll ring you later," was the message that came back.

"He's going to ring me later," Fenella told Mona.

"Excellent. You can tell him everything and insist that Hannah get some protection."

"I'm sure Hannah doesn't need protection," Fenella protested. "Inspector Hammersmith is a professional. If he thinks both deaths were accidents, well, he should know."

"You were calling him Mark before," Mona said.

"That was before he dragged Daniel into this," Fenella snapped. "As if I don't have enough problems right now."

A knock on the door cut short the discussion. Fenella was thrilled to see Shelly and Gordon on her doorstep.

"I hope you're hungry," she said as she pulled Shelly into the apartment.

"It doesn't look like your guests ate very much," Shelly said as Fenella handed her a plate.

"They didn't come," Fenella replied.

"Oh, dear. I hope nothing serious came up," Shelly exclaimed.

"Margaret Dolek fell down her stairs last night and broke her neck," Fenella said. As soon as the words were out of her mouth, she felt tears forming.

Shelly put her plate down on the counter and pulled Fenella into a hug. "You poor thing," she said. "Are you okay?"

"I barely knew the woman," Fenella said, angrily wiping away a tear that managed to trickle down her face. "I've no reason to be this upset."

"You were looking forward to talking with her about Mona," Shelly said, patting her back. "And this is the second person that you'd only just met who died suddenly. With all the other horrid things you've been tangled up in lately, it's hardly surprising that you're upset."

Fenella swallowed hard and tried to get her emotions under control. Shelly's kind sympathy made her feel even worse.

A plate clattered behind her, causing both women to look at Gordon. "Sorry," he said sheepishly. "I nearly dropped a biscuit and I did drop my plate trying to catch the stupid thing."

Fenella managed a small smile. "I hope nothing's broken," she said.

"The biscuit snapped in half, but the plate is fine," he assured her.

Shelly laughed and shook her head. "Quick, hide the evidence," she told the man. He obligingly stuck half of the offending treat into his mouth.

The distraction had been enough of a diversion to allow Fenella to pull herself together. "I was hoping you'd bring a dozen friends with you," she said as Shelly patted her back one more time and then picked up her plate again.

"I'm not sure I know a dozen people," Gordon said.

"But Shelly does," Fenella laughed. Shelly was one of the most outgoing and friendly people that Fenella had ever met. There was no doubt in her mind that Shelly could have found twelve or even twenty people to come to an impromptu tea party that afternoon if she'd tried.

"You should ring Peter. Leave a message on his answering machine and tell him to come over when he gets home from work," Shelly suggested. "It will save him the bother of making himself dinner."

Fenella followed her friend's advice and then made tea for everyone.

"How did you find out what happened to Margaret?" Shelly asked as they all sat down to eat.

"The police inspector who came to ask me about Anne Marie told me," Fenella replied. "He found it interesting that both women were planning to visit me right before they died."

"Life is full of odd coincidences," Gordon remarked.

"Margaret's death was just an accident, wasn't it?" Shelly asked.

"He seemed to think so, although I don't think there's been enough time for any official verdict," Fenella replied.

"What else could it have been?" Gordon asked around a mouthful of cake.

"Murder," Shelly said dramatically. She looked at Gordon's shocked face and laughed. "I know it sounds farfetched, but Fenella's been caught up in several murder investigations in the past. Look at what happened last month with Harvey and Mortimer Morrison."

Gordon frowned. "But this was an accident, right?"

"As I said, the police seem to think so," Fenella repeated herself.

"They're wrong," Mona said from her seat in the living room.

"And they know what they're doing," Fenella added, mostly for Mona's benefit.

"No one could possibly have any motive for killing a little old lady like Margaret," Shelly said.

"Of course not," Gordon agreed. "It must have been an accident."

"Inspector Hammersmith also suggested it could have been suicide," Fenella told the others.

"That's almost as impossible to believe as murder," Gordon said. "At her age she must take a cocktail of tablets every day. I'm sure if she wanted to kill herself she could have simply taken an overdose of something and died peacefully in her bed. Deliberately falling down a flight of stairs would take considerable nerve, I think."

"As would purposefully driving into a stone wall," Fenella said.

"You talked to both women the day before they died," Shelly said. "Did either of them seem depressed or unhappy?"

"No, not at all," Fenella replied. She sighed and rubbed her forehead. The whole conversation was giving her a headache.

"Let's talk about more pleasant things," Shelly said quickly. "These little cakes are delicious, and I love the sandwiches."

The trio talked about food for another hour while the overfull trays gradually began to empty. By the time Peter arrived, just after five, Fenella was starting to think they might actually manage to eat the lot.

"Come and eat," she told Peter after she'd answered his tentative knock.

He smiled when he saw the now half-empty trays. "Did your tea party go well?" he asked as he began to fill a plate.

"It never happened," Fenella replied.

"We can talk about that later," Shelly said brightly. "But you just arrived in the middle of a discussion about Christmas cookies, which sound wonderful. Tell me more," she said to Fenella.

Shelly kept the conversation inconsequential and abundant for several hours as the foursome finished off as much as they could of the feast.

"That's it," Fenella said eventually. "I can't eat another bite, and even if I wasn't full up, I can't stand the thought of one more sandwich or cake. I've even gone off the idea of cookies. I'm going to throw the last of this stuff out."

"Usually I'd object," Shelly said. "I hate to see food going to waste. But we've been nibbling on this stuff for hours. I'll be happy to see it all gone."

"I'll take any biscuits you don't want," Gordon offered. He shrugged when Fenella looked at him. "I never think to buy them," he explained. "My wife always did the grocery shopping, and now that I'm on my own, I tend to buy what I know I need and never give a thought to little treats that I might want."

"We should do our shopping together," Shelly offered. "I'd remind you to buy biscuits for sure."

Gordon smiled at her. "I'd like that," he said. Fenella hid a smile as the man reached over and gave Shelly's hand a squeeze.

"They're awfully cute together," Mona said from her seat. "Tell Shelly that she needs to make the first move, though. Gordon doesn't have enough confidence to try to kiss her without some encouragement."

Fenella nodded and then caught herself before she could reply. "I'll just put all of the cookies, er, biscuits into a bag for you," she told Gordon.

A few minutes later she had the trays cleared. Gordon had a bag of treats to take home with him and Shelly was running hot water to help with the dishes.

"These are such beautiful silver plates," she said as Fenella cleared the table. "Mona had such gorgeous things."

"I'm feeling incredibly spoiled," Fenella admitted. "I'm sure one of the reasons I did so much food was because I wanted to use the fabulous trays."

"I don't blame you," Shelly told her. "If I had Mona's things, I'd want to use them all the time."

A short while later the trays were washed, dried, and put away, and Fenella had the kitchen back to normal. Katie had been given her dinner and was now busy chasing a piece of string that Gordon was waving while Peter watched.

"I think we could all do with a drink," Shelly announced as she walked out of the kitchen. "I'll even buy the first round."

"I'm only staying for one round," Fenella said quickly. "I feel as if I've been drinking far too much lately."

"We all have," Shelly agreed happily. "So we'll all stick to one drink tonight."

The Tale and Tail was quiet, just the way they all liked it. Shelly insisted on buying the drinks and they took them to a quiet table on the upper level.

"To Anne Marie and Margaret," Shelly said softly, clinking glasses with Fenella.

"To Anne Marie and Margaret," Fenella echoed. She sipped her drink and let the conversation wash over her as Shelly explained to Peter what had happened to Margaret.

Mona has an overactive imagination, Fenella told herself, but was it possible that Mona was right? Had someone murdered both Anne Marie and Margaret? It seemed impossible, but the thought still worried Fenella. Did Phillipa have a credible motive? Or Paulette? Or

Paul? Or was there something else in the women's shared past that had driven someone to murder at this late date?

"You're very quiet," Peter murmured in her ear.

"I'm sorry," she replied. "Margaret's death came as a huge shock, especially on the heels of Anne Marie's."

"I am sorry," he told her. He slid an arm around her shoulders and pulled her close. "Maybe you need to get away for a few days," he suggested. "I'm swamped at work and can't go with you, but I have a cottage in Cornwall that's sitting empty right now. You're more than welcome to borrow it for a week or more."

"Thank you," Fenella said, feeling deeply touched by the man's thoughtfulness. "I might like a short vacation, but I don't really want to leave the island while the police are still investigating. I would hate for Inspector Hammersmith to think I'm trying to get away."

Peter chuckled. "He can't possibly suspect you of anything," he said firmly. "If he does, Daniel will soon set him straight."

"Daniel," Fenella gasped. "He was going to call me tonight." She pulled out her mobile phone, expecting to see a missed call or a text, but found neither.

"You should get home, if he's going to ring," Shelly said. "Maybe he can set your mind at rest about what happened to Anne Marie and Margaret."

"I hope so," Fenella said.

They carried their empty glasses back down to the bar to save the staff from having to clear their table and then made their way outside.

"It's the perfect night for a long walk on the promenade," Peter said. "Too bad you need to get back."

Fenella sighed. "Let's at least cross over and walk on that side," she suggested. "I'm sure the air is fresher over there."

Away from the bars, restaurants, and hotels, the air did feel fresher, at least to Fenella. They walked a short distance past their building before she began to worry again about missing Daniel's call. When they turned around, she was nearly knocked over by a huge dog who had run up behind her.

"My goodness," she exclaimed. "It's good to see you again, too, Winston." The dog barked excitedly and then ran back to his owner before racing back to Fenella's side. Fenella gave him an affectionate embrace, rubbing his head and scratching behind his ears.

In June, Fenella had looked after Winston for several days when his owner had disappeared. She'd been both relieved and disappointed when the man had returned. Now she looked forward to bumping into them on the promenade on occasion so that she could get her fill of doggy devotion.

"He spotted you as soon as you left the pub," Harvey Garus told her when he caught up his dog. "I was hoping you might cross over and take a walk, but I thought you'd go on a lot further."

"I have to get home for a phone call," Fenella explained. She gave the man a hug and then fussed over Winston again. "He looks great. You must have just had him groomed," she guessed.

"Aye, he got away from me yesterday and spent ages splashing in the sea," the man laughed. "I swear he and Fiona worked it out between themselves. They ran around in circles and got me tangled up in their leads, and then they took off in opposite directions. I ran after Fiona, but she only went a few feet and then dashed back and followed Winston into the sea. They've both been at the groomer's today."

Fiona was a much smaller dog, and she'd almost escaped Fenella's notice. Now Fenella gave the tiny animal her share of attention. Fiona, too, had spent some time living with Fenella in the previous month. When her owner turned up dead, Harvey had agreed to keep the shy and timid animal who had developed a devotion to Winston.

"She's not as timid as she used to be," Fenella remarked as the little dog raced around, demanding to be petted by everyone in turn.

"No, I think Winston is teaching her all of his bad habits," Harvey agreed.

Fenella gave both dogs another quick body rub and then gave Harvey a hug. "I really need to get home," she said apologetically.

"Come and visit any time," he told her. "You know you're more than welcome."

Gordon and Shelly decided to continue their stroll, but Peter was quick to offer to escort Fenella home.

"It's only a few steps," she protested. "You enjoy the beautiful evening."

"I think I might be in the way," Peter said very softly, nodding toward Shelly and Gordon, who were talking with their heads together.

Fenella gave Shelly a quick hug and then she and Peter crossed the road together. Outside her apartment, she turned and smiled at the man. "Thank you for walking me home," she said.

"Thank you for dinner," he replied, bowing slightly. "Any night I don't have to cook is a good night. Maybe you'd like to have dinner with me one evening soon, so that I can repay your kindness?"

"I'd like that," Fenella replied.

"I have business associates here this weekend," the man said with a frown. "I'll be entertaining them both Friday and Saturday evenings. Sunday seems a long way off, but it's probably the best I can do."

"I'll put it on my calendar," Fenella said.

"I'll collect you here at six," he told her. "I'm not sure what all is open on a Sunday evening, but I'll find somewhere nice to take you."

"It doesn't have to be nice," she replied.

He laughed. "Of course it does," he told her. He took a step closer to her and then pulled her into his arms. The kiss was short, but very sweet.

Fenella let herself into her apartment and shut the door. Without turning on any lights, she crossed the room and sank down on the couch. It was getting dark outside. She watched people strolling up and down the promenade, but she couldn't be sure which ones were Shelly and Gordon.

"Are you okay?" Mona asked softly.

"I'm just feeling a bit overwhelmed," Fenella admitted. "And a little bit scared that you might be right."

"Tell Daniel everything," Mona suggested.

"If I do that, I'll have to tell him about you."

The phone began to ring before Mona could reply.

9

"Hello?"

"Fenella, are you okay?" Daniel asked.

"I'm fine," she replied, settling back on the couch and switching the phone to speaker mode. That way, Mona could hear the conversation, too.

"Mark said that two different people with plans to visit you have died in the past three days."

"That's about right," Fenella said with a sigh. "Although I didn't know the first woman was planning to visit me. She didn't tell me she was coming."

"If there was any way I could, I'd come back for the weekend." Daniel sounded frustrated. "But we're all going to Edinburgh this weekend to tour some of their crime lab facilities. I can't get away."

"It's fine. Really it is," Fenella said, working hard to sound like she meant it. "Inspector Hammersmith is sure that both deaths were accidents and that my involvement is purely coincidental."

Daniel sighed. "Would you mind starting at the beginning? Pretend I know nothing and walk me through everything that's happened in the past week or so."

"I'll start with last Saturday evening," Fenella said. "That's where I met Anne Marie Smathers." Feeling very conscious that she hadn't given Mark the same full accounting of her conversation with the dead woman, Fenella started slowly.

"I'll start when we arrived at the party, and tell you everything that I can remember," she said. She wanted to tell him about her conversation with Phillipa Clucas, but she didn't want to make it obvious that she thought it might be relevant. By the time she'd finished recounting her evening at the charity auction, she needed a drink.

"When you spoke to Mrs. Smathers, did you get the feeling that she was planning on seeing you again?" Daniel asked as Fenella filled a glass from her tap.

"No, not at all. I didn't like the woman. If I'd thought she was planning to see me again, I probably would have tried to discourage her."

"So what happened next?"

Fenella told him all about tea the next day with Paulette and Paul, and then hearing the news that Anne Marie had died. "Someone told me that the car she was driving was the same model as the one that her husband crashed sixty years ago," she added.

"Yes, apparently she enjoyed driving it but didn't use it very often. As I understand it, she took very good care of it and only drove it on special occasions."

"It seems macabre, having the same car as the one that crashed and killed your husband," Fenella said.

"People are odd," Daniel said.

Fenella chuckled. "They are, at that."

"So what happened next? How did you happen to make plans to see Mrs. Dolek?"

"I met her at the Tynwald Day fair," Fenella explained.

"I was sorry to miss that. Maybe we can go together next year and you can explain everything to me."

"I'd like that." Fenella frowned at Mona, who'd made a face. Mona was always telling her to keep the men in her life guessing as to how she felt, but Fenella wasn't good at playing those kinds of games. She really liked Daniel, and his suggestion that they might spend time together in the distant future had lifted her spirits immensely.

"So tell me all about Tynwald Day," he said. "Not the actual event, but who you spoke to and what was said."

Fenella did her best to comply. She glossed over most of the day and focused on the conversation with Phillipa and her children and the later chat with Margaret and Hannah. When she was done, she felt sad again.

"She seemed like a nice woman," she told Daniel. "And I was looking forward to talking with her about Mona."

"So you were planning for tea today but she never arrived?"

"Inspector Hammersmith turned up instead. At least he ate some of the food that I'd prepared. Otherwise it would have gone to waste."

"Mark was kind enough to email me copies of his reports. It really does look, at least at this initial stage, as if both deaths were accidental. What do you think?"

"I think if the experts think they were accidents, they were accidents," Fenella said firmly. "It's just a little odd that I met both women the day before they died."

"But I'm sure you met a great many people at the party and also at Tynwald Day," Daniel pointed out.

"Tell him your theory about Phillipa," Mona hissed.

Fenella rolled her eyes. She didn't have a theory about Phillipa. That was all Mona's idea. "I am a little worried about Phillipa Clucas," she said slowly. "Her finding out that her husband cheated is the only thing that I can possibly imagine would give anyone a motive to kill those two women."

"If they were murdered, I might agree," Daniel said. "Mark made a note that you mentioned that very thing to him. How can you be sure that both women had affairs with the man?"

Fenella frowned. "Anne Marie told me as much," she said. "And I'm sure someone said something about Margaret, as well."

"It was a long time ago," Daniel reminded her. "I shouldn't tell you this, but Mark talked to Phillipa and Paulette. Neither of them mentioned any memoirs."

"What excuse did they give for Phillipa shouting at me at the party, then?" Fenella demanded.

"According to Paulette, her mother got upset when you mentioned

Mona's name because they were such good friends many years ago. She gave Mark an account of your conversation over tea as well. In it she never once mentioned her father, except in passing."

"She's lying, which must mean she had something to do with the two deaths," Mona said.

"Why would she lie?" Fenella asked.

"How much did you drink at the charity auction?"

Fenella stared at the phone for a minute before answering. "I had a few glasses of wine, but I only drank tea the next day, which is when Paulette told me about her father's memoirs," she said. "And I only went to tea with Paulette because she insisted that she needed to apologize for her mother's behavior."

Daniel sighed. "As both deaths appear to have been accidents, I don't think it matters whose memory is more accurate," he said. "I wouldn't have bothered you at all, except, well, after your recent track record, I can't help but worry when you're involved in any deaths, accidental or not."

"When will you know for sure if the two deaths were accidents?"

"I don't know that we will ever be certain," he replied. "Anne Marie's car is still being inspected and the lab is still testing samples to see if she had any drugs in her system, but even if we find something wrong with the car or drugs in her system, that won't necessarily prove anything."

"And Margaret?"

"Again, they are looking for evidence that she might have been drugged, but that may or may not prove anything."

"Is there a chance that the carpet was torn up on purpose?"

"That seems quite a stretch," Daniel said. "Are you suggesting that someone broke into Mrs. Dolek's house and tore up a patch of carpet, hoping that the woman would then trip over it and fall to her death?"

"When you put it like that, it sounds crazy," Fenella admitted. "But what if someone pushed her down the stairs and then tore up the carpeting to make it look like an accident?"

"People do crazy things, but again, that's something of a stretch," Daniel replied. "I have suggested to Mark that he talk to a few of her friends to see if he can find out how long the carpet has been like that. It won't prove anything, but it's another piece of the puzzle."

"I know you have a lot going on there," Fenella said. "I'm sorry that you've been dragged into this as well."

"You should have rung me when Anne Marie Smathers died," Daniel said. "Or at least sent me a text. I was caught by surprised when Mark rang."

"I told you so," Mona hissed.

"I didn't think it was a big deal," Fenella said defensively. "Inspector Hammersmith said it was an accident."

"And both deaths probably were, but when my friends are mixed up in unexpected deaths, I like to hear about it, preferably from them directly."

"If anyone else dies, I'll ring you," Fenella promised.

"If anyone else dies, Mark will ring me, and I suspect he'll also have a very long conversation with you."

"None of this has anything to do with me," Fenella exclaimed.

"I have to go," Daniel said. "There's a late lecture on body decomposition that I can't miss."

"That sounds like such fun," Fenella said sarcastically.

Daniel chuckled. "Yes, I'd rather be at the Tale and Tail with you and Shelly, but that isn't an option right now. This training course is costing the Isle of Man Constabulary a lot of money. I owe it to them to go to every single class."

"Well, I hope you learn lots of interesting things. And I hope what you learn doesn't interfere with your sleep."

"Oh, I don't have any trouble sleeping," Daniel said. "I hope you sleep well, too."

He disconnected and Fenella sat back, feeling oddly like crying.

"You're already growing too attached to that man," Mona said sharply.

"He's very kind," Fenella countered. "And gorgeous."

Mona nodded. "He is both of those things, but he's also the settling-down type. If you get serious, he's going to want to get married."

"What's wrong with that?"

"Yawn," Mona said, shaking her head. "I can't imagine why you'd want to tie yourself down to just one man for any length of time. Not when there are so many lovely men out there vying for your affections."

"Yes, well, we'll see," Fenella said. "He isn't even going to be back on the island for over a month. Maybe I'll be in love with Donald by the time Daniel gets back."

Mona laughed. "Is Daniel really insisting that the deaths were accidents?" she asked after a moment.

"He is, but he did say that he'd let me know if they found any evidence to suggest otherwise."

"Whoever is behind the killings is very clever," Mona said. "So maybe it isn't Phillipa. She's never seemed overly clever to me."

"Paulette didn't seem particularly bright when we spoke," Fenella said. "But maybe she has hidden depths."

"She's always been a rather odd girl. I often wondered if there was something slightly wrong about her, too, some sort of genetic flaw that runs in the family. Obviously it was worse for Paula, but that doesn't mean that Paulette doesn't have her own issues."

"She didn't seem that odd to me, just rather sad," Fenella argued.

"And then there's Paul, Junior," Mona said. "He was always somewhat strange, as well. Neither he nor his sister ever married. I wonder why."

"Perhaps they simply share your opinion on the matter," Fenella suggested.

"I hardly think Paulette has had many men to choose from over the years," Mona said. "I don't think she's ever so much as looked at a man, though. She was thoroughly devoted to her parents and idolized her father. Perhaps no one else ever measured up."

"Which is why she's so upset to find out that he cheated on her mother."

"Yes, but is she upset enough to start killing the women who were involved?" Mona asked.

"I certainly hope not." Fenella yawned and then got to her feet.

"Of course, I'm fairly sure that Paul didn't have an affair with Margaret. We need to get a look at those notes. If he claimed he'd slept with me, he probably made up all sorts of lies about many different women."

"It's horrible to think that someone killed Margaret because they thought she'd had an affair that she never actually had," Fenella exclaimed.

"I suppose I should be glad I'm already dead," Mona said.

Fenella shook her head. "I'm worn out. I'm going to get some sleep. Tomorrow I'm having lunch with Hannah. I can't wait to hear what she has to say about you."

"Just remember to ask her about the carpet at the top of Margaret's stairs," Mona told her. "And warn her that she might be next on the killer's hit list."

"I'll try to find a way to work both of those things into the conversation. In the meantime, I think you should start trying to work out whether anyone else had a motive for killing either or both women," Fenella instructed her aunt. "You knew both of them for a long time. What other secrets were they hiding?"

Mona looked thoughtful. "I shall give the idea some thought while you are sleeping," she said, as Fenella refilled Katie's bowls. "Maybe there's something I've overlooked."

When Fenella went into the master bedroom a short while later, Mona was sitting on one of the couches staring out at the sea. Fenella's "good night" went unanswered.

Katie had Fenella up at seven yet again. She gave the kitten breakfast before making her own. Mona was still sitting on the same couch, staring at the sea.

"Are you okay?" Fenella asked.

"I'm fine," Mona replied. "It's difficult thinking about the past. I didn't like Paul Clucas and I didn't approve of his behavior, but I also don't think that anyone deserves to die because of it." She sighed. "I've been thinking about how badly we all behaved in those days. We felt young and wild and carefree, but not everyone was able to enjoy life the way that we did. I wish I'd made more of an effort to befriend

Phillipa. At the time I was barely aware of her existence, but she had a difficult life."

"Have you thought of any other reason why anyone might have wanted to kill Anne Marie and Margaret?" Fenella asked.

Mona shook her head. "There could have been something in either of their husbands' businesses that was an issue, but I don't recall hearing anything. Not that I would have, necessarily. Men didn't discuss business with me, unless it was to brag about how successful a deal had been. I doubt they discussed it with their wives, either, though, so I can't see why anyone would want to take revenge on them."

The pair chatted for a while longer, but it was clear that Mona was distracted. Fenella cleared away her breakfast dishes and then did some more reading and note-taking for her book, while Mona continued to sit and stare out the window for much of the morning. When Fenella started getting ready for lunch, Mona finally stirred.

"Enough of this woolgathering," she said. "I'm going to treat myself to something special. Maybe it's time for a new look. Maybe I should try being ten or twelve for a change."

"Oh, please don't," Fenella exclaimed. It was strange enough sharing her apartment with the woman; she couldn't imagine how odd it would be having a young child living with her.

"I didn't really enjoy childhood, anyway," Mona told her. "Your mother was always so much better behaved than I was. I gave up trying to be good by the time I reached my teens. I could never compete with my younger sister."

"Mum would be very sad to hear you say that," Fenella said.

"I know. That's part of what was so annoying. She was always good, but she didn't even have to work at it. After she fell in love with your father, she never so much as looked at another man. All that time when they were apart, she stayed faithful and was confident that it would all work out in the end."

"And she was right."

"She was always right," Mona snapped. "Oh, I'm sorry. I'm out of sorts and I'm taking it out on you," she added quickly. "I've spent too much time thinking about my past and some of the unpleasant things I lived through. Maybe I need to go and visit Max. That would cheer me up, I'm sure."

"If you can go and visit people whenever you want, you should go and visit Margaret and Anne Marie and ask them both whether they were murdered or not," Fenella suggested.

"It isn't that simple," Mona told her. "I haven't any idea where to look for either of them, but Max is here."

"Here?"

"In the building," Mona explained. "He usually spends his time in the back, in what used to be the ballroom. It's just offices now, but I'm not sure Max sees it that way. Anyway, I'll see you later. I'll want to hear all about your lunch with Hannah when I get back."

Fenella watched as the woman faded from view. She wasn't sure if Mona was telling the truth about visiting Max or not, but for her aunt's sake, she hoped it was true. She liked the idea of Mona being able to visit old and dear friends who were also dead.

She changed into a dress and low heels and then took a taxi to the restaurant that Hannah had suggested. There were only a handful of people scattered around the room when Fenella arrived. Her heart sank when she realized that Hannah wasn't one of them.

"Just you today, love?" the middle-aged woman who was waiting tables called as Fenella hesitated in the doorway.

"I'm meeting a friend," she replied.

"Oh, aye? Is it a blind date? Will he recognize you or did you send him a doctored photo?"

Fenella flushed. "I'm meeting a female friend who I will certainly recognize," she said firmly.

The woman shrugged. "Sorry, but we get a lot of blind dates out here. We're just far enough away from Douglas city center so that people think they can meet here and no one will know. This Internet dating thing has been good for my business, I can tell you that."

"Good for you," Fenella said.

"It's quite fun for me, too," the woman said confidingly. "You would be amazed at what some people put in their dating profiles. The truth comes out here, though, let me tell you."

"Really?" Fenella was intrigued.

"Mostly, people just touch up their photos so that they look better than they really do," the woman shrugged. "But we did have a man come in once and his date took one look at him and started shouting. When I went to see what was wrong, she showed me the picture he'd sent her. It was some guy off the telly. Even I recognized him and I don't watch much telly."

"I take it the man didn't look much like the photo, then?"

"He was about five feet tall, bald and nearly round," the woman replied. "He was missing a few teeth, didn't look like he'd bathed in a week, and he was wearing cowboy boots with shorts."

Fenella burst out laughing. "And he thought the woman would be okay with all of that?"

"He said he thought she would overlook his slight deception, and those were his words, not mine, because they'd made such a strong connection in their emails."

"Presumably, she didn't agree."

"According to her, they'd only barely spoken via email," the woman replied. "She said she only agreed to meet him because he was so gorgeous. She thought he was really boring in the few emails they had shared, but she was willing to overlook it because he had great abs."

Fenella and the woman both laughed, and then the woman showed Fenella to a table in the corner. "Can I bring you a drink while you wait for your friend?"

Because it was a warm day, Fenella ordered a soft drink, and then looked over the menu. There were several salads that looked good, but she was having trouble focusing on food. Every minute that went by made her more worried about Hannah.

When the bell on the door rang a few minutes later, Fenella was hugely relieved to see Hannah making her way into the café.

"I'm sorry I'm late," she told Fenella. "It takes me longer to walk places now than it used to."

"No problem," Fenella said, trying to keep her tone light.

Hannah slid into the seat opposite her and sighed. "I almost cancelled," she said softly. "I didn't sleep much. I can't stop thinking about Margaret."

"I'm sorry," Fenella said, patting the woman's hand.

"She shouldn't have been going up and down stairs, not at her age. I told her to move into a bungalow, but she loved that old house. She lived there for fifty years or more. Her son wanted her to move, too, but that only made her more determined to stay at home. They didn't agree on anything, those two."

"Someone told me that the carpet at the top of the stairs was torn," Fenella said. "That sounds dangerous."

"There were a lot of things in her house that needed repairing," Margaret told her. "Like I said, she'd lived there for a long time. She did her best, but she'd just about outlived her resources. Putting in new carpeting was out of the question."

The waitress came over and took their orders, and the two women chatted about the weather and local news for a short while.

"But you wanted to hear about Mona," Hannah said eventually. "What can I tell you about her? She was the woman we all secretly wanted to be. She was pretty, but more than that, she was sexy and glamorous. We all thought she could have been a Hollywood star if she wanted to be, but she seemed happy enough here. I always thought she stayed because of Max."

"What was he like?"

"So beautiful and so sexy," Hannah said, giggling. "We were all crazy about him. He used to say the most wonderful things, just a long stream of compliments every time he saw you. That probably sounds weird, but he always sounded so sincere that I never questioned it. He would look at you as if you were the only woman in the world and then tell you how beautiful you were and how perfect your dress was. It was mesmerizing, I can't think of another word for it."

"I've been told that everyone in your social circle used to flirt with everyone else," Fenella said, choosing her words carefully.

"There was a lot of flirting," Hannah agreed. "And some infidelity as well, although not as much as everyone pretended. Most of the men were more interested in their bank accounts than in their sex lives and most of the women were too busy with their children to manage secret rendezvous."

"So Max was just flirting?"

Hannah shook her head. "It wasn't even flirting with Max. It was just his personality. We all knew he only had eyes for Mona, even if we wanted to believe otherwise."

"I understand they fought a lot, though."

Hannah laughed. "Mona lived for drama," she said. "I swear that woman would start a fight with Max about anything. The thing is, though, Max always bought her extravagant things to apologise, even though the fights were never his fault. They would have a screaming row and then, a week later, Mona would turn up at a party with a huge emerald ring on her finger and a smug smile on her face. Max had to know what she was doing, of course, but he went along for some reason."

"Do you think they loved each other?" Fenella had to ask.

"Oh, I suppose so," Hannah replied. "Although I don't know much about love, myself. My parents picked out my husband for me and we were never particularly close."

"How awful," Fenella exclaimed.

"He treated me well," Hannah said. "We had three wonderful children together, he was a good provider, and he kindly dropped dead of a heart attack three months before he was due to retire. I'm not sure we would have stayed together if he'd retired and been at home all day, every day. As it is, I inherited a small fortune in life insurance and I finally got my freedom, aged sixty-four."

"I can't even imagine," Fenella told her.

"That was over ten years ago," Hannah said. "And there are days when I miss the man, which I never thought would happen. Maybe I did love him, in my own way. But Mona and Max? They were crazy about each other. Even when they were fighting, they couldn't stay away from one another. And even when they were fighting, they stayed faithful. I know Mona had something of a reputation for being wild, but I think Max was the only man she ever actually slept with."

While they'd been talking, the pair had worked their way through their salads. "Did you want pudding?" the waitress asked as she cleared their plates.

"Oh, I shouldn't," Hannah said.

"Why not?" Fenella demanded. "What are our choices?" she asked the waitress.

The woman rattled off at least a dozen different options. Fenella laughed.

"You had me at chocolate sponge," she told her. "I didn't hear anything you said after that."

"I'll have the sticky toffee pudding," Hannah said. "It's my favorite and I haven't had it in ages."

"This has been nice," Hannah said as they waited for their sweet course. "I hope you'll come to Margaret's memorial service once we work out the details."

"I'd like that," Fenella said. "Will you let me know where and when it's being held?"

"Of course," the woman promised. "I'm helping her children make the arrangements. They all live across now."

"Hannah? I thought that was you," a voice said. Fenella was sure she recognized the posh accent, but she couldn't quite remember where she'd heard it before.

She turned in her seat and smiled as she recognized Patricia Anderson walking toward her from a table on the other side of the room.

"Oh, it's Fenella, isn't it? You're Mona's niece."

Fenella nodded. "It's nice to see you again," she told Patricia.

"I didn't expect to see you having lunch with Hannah," the woman said, her tone questioning.

Hannah looked at Fenella and winked. "How are you, my dear?" she asked, ignoring the unasked question.

"I'm very well, thank you," Patricia said. "I was so sorry to hear about Margaret. I was going to ring you, actually, to see how you were doing. I know you two were great friends."

"We were," Hannah agreed.

"I was always on the outside, just a little bit, in that crowd," Patricia told Fenella. "I'm somewhat younger."

"Patricia was a trophy wife," Hannah said.

"Hannah!" Patricia gasped. "I was no such thing."

"Patricia was eighteen when she married her husband," Hannah explained. "He'd just divorced his first wife and was about to celebrate his fortieth birthday."

Patricia frowned. "There are two sides to every story," she said tightly.

"I'm just sharing the facts," Hannah replied.

"But, Fenella, I was hoping I might bump into you somewhere," Patricia said, turning away from Hannah. "It was so good of you to come with Donald to our little auction the other night. Melanie and I were talking afterwards and we both agreed that you could be invaluable to our efforts. We're always desperate for new volunteers, and with your background, you could bring a whole new perspective to our work."

"Did Mona do much volunteer work with you?" Fenella asked, wondering if the woman would lie.

"No, er, I mean, Mona had her own pet projects. I was always sad that our charity wasn't one of them, because we do such wonderful work, but then all of the island's charities do great things. There are just so many of them and such a limited supply of volunteers. I told Melanie that we'd have to track you down and get you signed up quickly, before all of the other groups start asking. You'll be in huge demand once word gets out that you're here."

"I am rather busy," Fenella said. "I'm writing a book."

"Really? What sort of book?" Patricia asked.

Fenella hesitated. "It's going to be about Anne Boleyn," she said finally. "I'm a historian." Both statements were true. It wouldn't be her fault if Patricia put them together and decided that Fenella was writing a traditional biography, she thought.

"How exciting," Patricia said. "I'll look forward to reading it one day. But in the meantime, surely you can spare an hour or two a week? That's all we would need, I promise. Give me your number and I'll ring you in a few days. Melanie and I can take you to lunch and tell you all about the wonderful things we do."

Fenella wrote her home phone number on the card that Patricia produced from her handbag. She would have to try to remember to let the answering machine screen her calls from now on, she thought.

"Excellent," the woman beamed as Fenella handed the card back.

"And now I must be off. We're having a coffee morning next week and the woman who was meant to be organizing it dropped the ball. Of course, I've had to step in yet again." She sighed and then swept out of the restaurant, leaving Hannah shaking her head.

"It was lovely to see you, too," she called after Patricia. The other woman was long gone.

"She's a bit overwhelming," Fenella said.

"She's a bit horrible," Hannah replied. "Do yourself a favor and don't have lunch with her. She'll talk you into organizing something and then complain about every single thing you do until you end up quitting out of sheer frustration."

"Oh, dear. That sounds like bitter experience."

"It is. I worked with her in the early days, before she got this bad. Now I just sit back and watch as she begs people to help and then refuses to actually let them do anything. Melanie is the only one who can work with her, and that's only because they're family."

"Perhaps Mona was smart to not get involved, then."

"Mona would have, though, if Patricia would have let her. But Patricia didn't approve of Mona, at least in part because her husband thought Mona was wonderful. I understand that Mona volunteered for a couple of things and was always politely told that they didn't need her help. If you ask me, Mona was lucky."

It didn't take the women long to eat their desserts once they were delivered.

"I'll ring you when I know what's happening for Margaret," Hannah said as she got to her feet once Fenella had paid the bill. "Thank you again for lunch. I didn't mean for you to pay."

"It was my pleasure," Fenella insisted. The older woman took a few steps and then stopped, resting her hand on the back of a chair. "Are you okay?" Fenella asked.

"Just a bit stiff from sitting for so long," the woman replied. "I'll be fine once I get going."

"Take my arm," Fenella suggested.

Hannah slid her hand around Fenella's arm and the pair slowly made their way across the room. Outside the sun was shining on a beautiful summer afternoon.

"I haven't far to go," Hannah said as they crossed the parking lot. "I'll be fine from here."

"If it isn't far, then I'll walk you home," Fenella replied.

They both jumped as a car door slammed behind them. Fenella looked back and was surprised to see Paul and Paulette Clucas heading toward them.

10

"Fenella, wait," Paulette called.

Hannah smiled as the pair reached them. "Paul and Paulette, look at you," she said. "You're both all grown-up now, aren't you? I remember when you were both tiny babies."

"How are you, Mrs. Jones?" Paul asked.

"I can't complain," Hannah replied. "I don't get around as well as I used to, but otherwise, I'm doing all right."

"I just need a quick word with Fenella," Paulette said. "I hope you don't mind."

"I was going to walk Hannah home," Fenella explained. "Are you getting something to eat? I can walk her home and then meet you in the café."

"Paul can walk her home," Paulette said. "He won't mind."

Fenella looked at Paul, who seemed surprised. "Sure," he said after a moment. "I'm happy to do that."

"I don't want to be any bother," Hannah said.

"It's no bother," Paul assured her. "Paulette wants to talk to Fenella, anyway. You're only just up the road, if I remember correctly."

"I am. Still in the same house I've lived in since I got married," Hannah confirmed.

Paul nodded. "I'd quite like a word with you as well," he told Fenella as he took Hannah's arm. "Please don't rush off if you and my sister finish before I get back."

Feeling oddly popular, Fenella nodded. She and Paulette watched as Paul and Hannah walked slowly away, Hannah leaning on Paul's arm.

"I just wanted to apologize," Paulette said once the pair was out of earshot.

"For what?" Fenella asked.

"My mother has had trouble sleeping since my father passed away," the woman replied. "Her doctor gave her some tablets to help her sleep, but they give her very odd dreams."

"I've heard that some sleeping pills can do that."

"Well, these definitely do. The worst part is that she can't always tell what was a dream. I'm afraid everything she told me about my father's memoirs was untrue."

Fenella thought for a minute. "I thought you told me that you found them on his computer?"

Paulette flushed and shook her head. "I don't recall exactly what I told you, but it hardly matters. When Paul came to check the computer, I told him what Mum had said about our father's note, and he searched the machine. He couldn't find any trace of anything like what Mum had said she'd found."

"How odd."

"I don't really know much about computers," Paulette told her. "Even my mother is better with them than I am. Paul is the real expert and he did everything he could to find the files that Mum said were there. You can imagine that my mother was terribly upset when we told her that she'd imagined the whole thing."

"Yes, I'm sure that would be upsetting."

"She's hugely embarrassed that she said such horrible things to you at the charity auction and on Tynwald Day. I, well, I'm sorry, but I told her that she dreamed that as well. I couldn't stand seeing her so upset."

"That's fine," Fenella said quickly. "I would probably have done the same in your shoes."

"Thank you for being so understanding. I can't tell you how difficult this has been. I've always loved my father dearly. I was devastated when my mother told me what she'd seen, and furious with my father. To learn now that it wasn't true, that my father didn't cheat on my mother, well, that's been almost as difficult. My emotions are all over the place."

"Where is your mother today?"

"We have a woman who comes over twice a week to sit with her for a few hours so that I can have a break," Paulette told her. "I usually stay close to home, but Paul persuaded me to come out here for lunch today. This used to be one of our favorite places when we were small children."

"The food is excellent," Fenella told her.

Paulette smiled. "It didn't used to be. It used to be quite ordinary, but the puddings were wonderful. Obviously, as a small child, that was much more important."

"It's much more important to me even now," Fenella laughed.

"You should have come along, Paulette," Paul said as he rejoined them. "Her house looks exactly the same as I remember it. I don't think she's changed a thing in the last thirty years."

"She probably can't afford to," Paulette suggested.

"Maybe, or maybe she just likes it the way it is," Paul said with a shrug. "Anyway, I'm starving. Let's get lunch. I do have to get back to work, as well."

"You wanted to talk to me about something?" Fenella asked.

"Oh, I just wanted to double-check that we're still good for tomorrow night," the man said. "I was going to ring you later today."

"We're still good," Fenella confirmed. "I'm looking forward to it."

"Me, too," Paul said. He smiled brightly at her and then turned to his sister. "But for now, lunch?"

"Yes, let's," Paulette said. "Thank you for being so understanding," she told Fenella. "Again, I am sorry."

"Please don't apologize anymore," Fenella said firmly. "Your mother is lucky to have you looking after her."

"Yes, well, we're trying to find something else to help her sleep," Paulette said. "It's unfortunate, because the tablets she was taking were very effective."

Fenella watched as the siblings walked into the café. It was only then that she remembered that she needed a taxi to get home. All those years of driving herself everywhere she wanted to go had obviously spoiled her. She dug her mobile phone out of the bottom of her bag and rang the taxi service she had at the top of her contacts list. They had a car there only a few minutes later.

"Promenade View Apartments," she told the driver.

"Those are meant to be really nice," the man said. "My daughter and son-in-law were looking at flats a while back, and they looked at one in that building. It was tiny and very [illegible], but it did have wonderful views."

"Yes, the views are amazing," Fenella agreed.

She sat back in her seat and listened as the man complained about property prices on the island. When she didn't argue back, he switched to local politics, a subject that Fenella knew very little about.

"They're all criminals, really," he concluded as he pulled up in front of her building. "That's why they've built such a fancy new prison, you know. They all reckon they're going to end up in there at some point."

Fenella bit her tongue to stop herself from laughing as she paid the man. No matter how nice the prison in Jurby was, she didn't think any of the island's politicians would be happy to spend time there.

Mona was pacing around the apartment when Fenella let herself in.

"Was Hannah there? Was she okay?" she demanded as soon as Fenella shut the door behind herself.

"She was there and she was fine," Fenella said. "And on my way out, I bumped into Paulette."

"How did she look? Did she look like a murderer?"

"She looked perfectly normal. And she apologized for her mother's behavior again. It seems that the notes that Phillipa found don't actually exist."

Mona narrowed her eyes. "What do you mean?"

"Paulette told me that her mother has been taking some strong sleeping pills that cause her to have nightmares. Apparently, she only dreamt that she'd found her husband's notes on the computer."

"I don't believe it," Mona said flatly.

"Why not?"

"It's too convenient. Paulette is trying to hide the fact that she and her mother have motives for murdering Anne Marie and Margaret."

"If she were planning to murder all of the women named in the memoirs, why would she tell me about it in the first place?" Fenella demanded. "Anne Marie died on Sunday morning, and I didn't have tea with Paulette until that afternoon. Surely if she'd already started killing people, she wouldn't have told me about the notes."

Mona frowned. "It's odd, but maybe she didn't realize the significance of what she told you until later."

Fenella shook her head. "The police are happy that both deaths were accidents. Maybe they really were."

"Maybe Phillipa is the murderer," Mona said. "But Paulette didn't know she'd done it until after your brunch. Now she's trying to protect her mother."

"I got the impression that Phillipa needs more looking after than that. They have a woman who comes and sits with her twice a week so that Paulette can get away for a short while."

"So, maybe it's Paul who is behind the deaths," Mona said. "He wouldn't even need to read any notes. I'm sure he has a pretty good idea of which women his father was involved with over the years."

"I thought you said that Margaret didn't really have an affair with the man?" Fenella asked.

"But Paul might think she did. They did spend a lot of time together after he and Anne Marie stopped seeing each other," Mona argued.

"I'm going to work on my book," Fenella told her. "Maybe, just maybe, you're overreacting to a couple of accidents."

"If the killer comes after you, don't complain to me," Mona said.

"Why would he or she come after me? I didn't have an affair with Paul Clucas."

"Guilt by association. You said Phillipa thinks I slept with the man."

"I have work to do," Fenella said firmly. Mona had always loved a good murder mystery, a passion she shared with Fenella. It seemed now, though, that perhaps the woman had read one too many books on the subject. If the police were sure the deaths were both accidents, Fenella wasn't going to argue with them.

She spent a few hours taking notes on Anne's years living in France. When she got bored with the process, she sat back and closed her eyes. It was hard to imagine what Anne's life would have been like, living in France as an attendant to a French queen. She must have missed her family, and England as well. There was frustratingly little known about Anne's childhood and teenaged years. Shaping the little information that she had into the beginning of her book was going to be a huge challenge.

"Merrow," Katie interrupted her.

"Is that the time?" Fenella exclaimed as she glanced at the clock. "You're right. It's time for dinner."

After filling Katie's food and water bowls, Fenella opened her refrigerator and studied the contents. Nothing tempting, she thought as she tried the freezer. A frozen pizza was the only thing that appealed to her.

"That's far too much for one person to eat," Mona remarked as she settled in at the kitchen counter.

"But it's what sounds good," Fenella replied. "I won't eat it all. I'll save half for tomorrow or something."

She unwrapped the pizza and added a generous handful of shredded cheese to the top of it. While the oven was preheating, she poured herself a small glass of wine.

"And don't tell me that drinking alone is a bad sign," she told Mona after her first sip. "It's only one glass of wine."

"I wasn't going to say a word," Mona protested. "I used to have a glass of wine every evening, sometimes two. I wasn't often alone, but when I was, I didn't worry about it."

Fenella took another sip and then almost dropped the glass when the phone startled her.

"It's Shelly. I was meant to be having dinner with Gordon, but something has come up with work and he can't make it. Would you like to go out somewhere?"

"I just unwrapped a frozen pizza," Fenella told her. "But you're more than welcome to share it with me. It's just cheese, although I've added some extra. I have some garlic bread that I can throw in with it, as well."

"Are you sure you don't mind?"

"Of course I don't mind," Fenella said. "Come on over."

A moment later, Shelly was at the door. "Thank you," she said as she followed Fenella into the kitchen. "I really didn't feel like cooking tonight."

"Neither did I. That's why we're having frozen pizza," Fenella told her.

She slid the pizza and a frozen loaf of garlic bread into the oven and then poured Shelly a glass of wine.

"I think it's a good night to head to the pub after dinner," Shelly said.

"That sounds good to me," Fenella agreed.

"I do miss the Tale and Tail," Mona sighed.

"I hope everything is okay with Gordon's work," Fenella told her friend.

"I don't know," Shelly said unhappily. "I mean, I don't even know if it really is work. I'm starting to feel as if Gordon is trying to avoid me."

"What happened?" Fenella and Mona asked at the same time.

"Nothing, at least nothing that I know of," Shelly sighed. "We had a nice walk on the promenade the other night, but then when he walked me home he seemed, I don't know, odd."

"Odd how?"

Shelly shook her head. "I don't know. Odd. I kept thinking about what you said about trying to kiss him. I was actually thinking I might try it when we got to my door, but I didn't get the chance. He actually only walked part of the way down the corridor and sort of just waved to me before dashing back to the lift and jumping on."

"Oh, dear," Fenella said.

"He's afraid he's falling in love," Mona said. "Men are so stupid sometimes."

"Anyway, I haven't seen him since. We were going to have lunch together yesterday, but he had to cancel because a meeting ran late. Then we were going to have dinner tonight, but he cancelled again. I don't know, maybe I'm reading too much into all of this, but I feel as if he's avoiding me."

"Maybe he's afraid he's falling for you," Fenella suggested.

"Or maybe he's afraid that I'm falling for him and he isn't interested," Shelly said sullenly.

"Maybe he's just really busy with work," Fenella said.

"He might be," Shelly said with a shrug. "I know he's working on two different projects at the moment and they're both keeping him busy but I can't help but worry. I really like him, and if he just wants to be friends, I'm okay with that. I don't want to drive him away if he isn't looking for anything more serious."

"Do you have plans to see him again?" was Fenella's next question.

"He said something about trying again tomorrow, but we didn't make firm plans, in case he's busy again."

"I'm meant to be having dinner with Paul Clucas tomorrow, and then with Donald on Saturday."

"Aren't you popular," Shelly laughed. "What's Paul like? Is this going to be a great romance or just a one-off dinner?"

"I suspect it's much more likely to be a single date," Fenella replied. "He seems very nice, but I don't know that he's my type."

"You can do much better," Mona interjected.

The oven timer buzzed and Fenella dragged the pizza out onto a large platter. About the only thing Mona's gourmet kitchen had been missing when Fenella moved in was a pizza cutter. Now Fenella dug the one she'd recently purchased out of the drawer and sliced the pizza. While she worked, Shelly pulled the garlic bread out of the oven and chopped it into pieces.

"This isn't bad," Shelly said after a few minutes. "It's better than I was expecting."

"I added some extra cheese," Fenella told her. "But I think it would have been pretty good anyway."

The pair chatted about television and movies while they ate. Mona sat and listened, but it seemed to Fenella that her mind was elsewhere. With the dishes in the dishwasher and the kitchen tidied up, it was time for the pub.

"Let me pop back and feed Smokey," Shelly said. "She likes her meals on time."

"Don't we all?" Fenella laughed. She gave Katie a few extra treats and some fresh water, and then headed into the bathroom to touch up her makeup.

"Put on something nicer," Mona suggested from the doorway. "A skirt would be good, but even trousers are better than jeans."

"Jeans are comfortable," Fenella argued. "We're only going for one drink, and it's a Thursday night. No one will be there."

"You don't know that," Mona countered. "I know you haven't ever gone through everything in my wardrobe, but if you ever do, you won't find a single pair of jeans in there. I never wore them."

"I'd feel silly getting all dressed up to go the pub," Fenella told her. "Everyone else in the place will be wearing jeans."

"Shelly won't. You've never seen her in jeans, have you?"

"Not really, although she did wear denim trousers to Tynwald Day. They were zebra print, though, so they didn't look like jeans," Fenella replied. She looked over at her aunt and sighed. "I won't wear fancy trousers for a quick pub visit, but I will put on something nicer on top. How's that?"

"If that's the best I can get, it will do," Mona replied. "Try the right side of my wardrobe. There are some lovely shirts there, including a blue one that should bring out the blue in your eyes."

Fenella quickly found the top in question and pulled it on. It was incredibly soft, and Mona was right. The color did make her eyes look bluer. "What do you think?" she asked, twirling slowly in front of the mirror.

"It suits you," Mona said. "It would look better with the grey trousers in the drawer underneath the shirts, but it works with jeans as well."

"It looks great with jeans," Fenella said firmly. Shelly knocked before Mona could argue any further. As she locked up her apartment behind her, Fenella couldn't help but think about Shelly's outfit. The other woman had changed as well, into a pair of bright pink trousers and a white top. The top was covered in large irregularly shaped spots in neon colors, including a few spots that matched the trousers. Her shoes were neon green.

"Do you ever wear jeans?" Fenella asked as they walked onto the elevator.

"Not really," Shelly said. "Aside from the zebra print ones, I've only had a pair or two over the years, but I couldn't wear them for work and my husband didn't really like them. He preferred me in skirts or dresses, and I was always happy to oblige him. It was only a small thing and it made him happy."

The pub was busier than Fenella had been expecting for a Thursday night. "Why is it so busy tonight?" she asked Shelly as they waited in line to get drinks.

"I've no idea," Shelly replied. "You can never tell with this place. I understood when it got busy after the local paper ran that article, but I don't know what's going on tonight."

They finally got their drinks and made their way up the stairs. Clusters of people seemed to be everywhere, but Shelly finally spotted a table that had a few empty chairs around it.

"We'll have to invite ourselves to join that couple," she told Fenella. "I hope they don't mind."

The couple in question seemed to be having a very intense conversation. "I'm sorry, but do you mind if we sit here?" Shelly asked, when they reached them.

The man and woman stared at Shelly for a minute before the woman sighed deeply. "I suppose not," she said, clearly reluctantly.

"Thanks," Shelly said, sliding into a chair.

Fenella sat down opposite her, trying to remember where she'd seen the woman before. The couple went back to their conversation after little more than glancing at Fenella.

"Isn't this nice?" Shelly said quietly.

"That's one word for it," Fenella whispered back.

Shelly laughed. "Maybe they'll decide to get a room," she said, tilting her head toward the couple who had slid their chairs closer together.

"It doesn't seem like that sort of conversation," Fenella replied. She couldn't make out any words, but it felt to her as if the pair were arguing.

Unusually for the Tale and Tail, there weren't any books within easy reach of where the women were sitting. Fenella felt disappointed as she sat back in her chair. One of the things she liked best about the place was the chance to pull out random books and flip through them whenever conversation lagged. As it was busy and noisy, conversation with Shelly seemed like far too much work. A book to look through was exactly what she needed.

"You're Donald's friend, aren't you?" the woman sitting next to her suddenly demanded.

Fenella looked over at her. "Melanie Anderson-Stuart," she exclaimed. "I knew you looked familiar, but I couldn't place you."

"I'm afraid I don't remember your name," the woman said, sounding as if she didn't care in the slightest.

"I'm Fenella Woods and this is my friend, Shelly Quirk," Fenella said. "Shelly, this is Melanie Anderson-Stuart. She and her mother, Patricia, run the Manx Fund for Children, which was behind the charity auction that Donald and I went to last weekend."

"It's very nice to meet you," Shelly said, nodding at the woman. She looked at the man sitting next to Melanie. He was sitting back, looking around the room with a bored expression on his face.

"But where's Donald tonight?" Melanie asked.

"I've no idea," Fenella told her.

"My dear, that's unwise," Melanie said. "Donald is the sort of man that needs to be kept track of. If he isn't with you, he's probably out with another woman."

Fenella shrugged. "We aren't serious. I see other men as well."

"You're more like your aunt than I realized," Melanie said. "But don't make the mistake of thinking that Donald will be your Max. He isn't the type to buy a woman cars and flats."

"I'm quite capable of buying my own cars and flats," Fenella said, feeling her cheeks burning.

Melanie shrugged. "I'm just trying to help," she said. "I'd hate to see you get your heart broken, and you seem like the type who might.

Donald loves to romance a woman and shower her with gifts, but once he wins her heart, he loses interest."

"That sounds like personal experience," Shelly said.

"A friend of mine thought she was going to be his fourth wife," Melanie said. "It didn't work out that way."

"Mel?" the man said.

She looked at him and sighed. "Yes, dear, we should go," she said in a long-suffering tone

"We didn't get introduced," Shelly said. "I'm Shelly Quirk." She held out a hand and the man took it almost instinctively.

"Oh, I'm Matthew Stuart," he said. "I'm Melanie's husband."

"It's a pleasure to meet you," Shelly told him. "This is our local pub and we're here nearly every night. I don't think I've seen either of you in here before."

"No, we wanted to go somewhere quiet and away from all of our friends," Melanie said. "We only got the second half right, it seems."

"It isn't usually this busy on a weeknight," Shelly told her.

"I can't see why it's ever busy," Matthew said. "There are cats and cat hair everywhere and the whole place smells like old books."

Fenella and Shelly exchanged glances. That was exactly why they loved it there.

"I don't suppose you've seen my mother lately," Melanie said in a casual tone.

"I saw her today, actually," Fenella said. She told the other woman where she'd had lunch.

"And my mother was there?" Melanie asked.

"Yes. She came over to chat with me while we were waiting for our desserts," Fenella explained.

"Interesting," Melanie said.

"Why?" Fenella had to ask.

"She was meant to be at a meeting across today," the woman replied, waving a hand. "I'm sure she rang to tell me that it was cancelled, but I've been having trouble with my phone all day."

"I see," Fenella said, not understanding at all.

"Darling, as fun as this is, we should go," Matthew said. He got to his feet and held out a hand to Melanie.

She smiled tightly and then, ignoring the hand, stood up. "Yes, let's do that," she muttered.

"It was nice to see you again," Fenella told her as Melanie picked up her handbag.

"Oh, likewise. I'm sure my mother told you that we'd love for you to get more involved in our little endeavors. My mother got the impression that you and Donald were somewhat more serious than you suggest, though."

"So you won't be wanting my help after all?" Fenella asked.

Melanie laughed lightly. "We're always happy to have more help," she said. "I'll have someone ring you the next time we're planning an event. I'm sure there will be loads you can do to help out."

With that, she turned and walked briskly toward the elevator at the back of the room. Her husband followed on her heels.

"Well, that was interesting," Shelly said. "She more or less told you that they don't want your help because you aren't involved enough with Donald."

"If I'd known that was all it was going to take to get me out of being asked to help, I'd have told Patricia that this afternoon," Fenella laughed.

"It was still odd," Shelly told her.

"You know what else was odd?" Fenella asked.

"What?"

"When I met Melanie, she told Donald that she and Matthew had split up."

"They didn't look split up."

"No, but they didn't look happy, either," Fenella mused.

The pub didn't get any less busy. When a large and noisy group came up the stairs a short while later, Fenella and Shelly agreed to that it was time to go home. Several people in the group cheered as they got up to go, and before they'd gone more than a few steps, their chairs and the ones that Matthew and Melanie had vacated were already being claimed.

"Maybe we need to find a new favorite pub," Shelly said as they stepped outside.

"I can't imagine finding anywhere else I'd like as much," Fenella replied. "But the next time it's that busy, maybe we should go somewhere else."

"The pub next door to us is actually quite nice," Shelly told her. "It just doesn't have cats or books."

"That doesn't sound nice at all," Fenella teased.

"It does have some good wines," Shelly assured her. "And it's never busy."

"At least not so far. Maybe if we start going there, it will get busy, like the Tale and Tail did."

"You make it sound like we're trendsetters," Shelly laughed. "But if it does get busy, we can just go back to the Tale and Tail, which should be quiet by then."

Katie was fast asleep in the center of Fenella's bed when she let herself back into her apartment. Mona wasn't around, so Fenella watched some television and then took herself off to bed. As usual, Katie woke her the next morning.

"I think you're getting old enough now that you could survive until eight," Fenella told the animal, who was bouncing in the center of Fenella's chest.

"Meeowoowww," Katie replied.

After she'd fed Katie, Fenella had some cereal and then showered and got dressed. Mindful of her aunt's words from the night before, she pulled on a pair of grey cotton trousers instead of her usual jeans. She hadn't worn jeans for work in all the years she'd taught, but she'd been living in them since she'd arrived on the island. Maybe Mona was right. Maybe she should make more of an effort now and again. She was still thinking about jeans and how the trousers she was wearing weren't any less comfortable than jeans, really, when someone knocked on her door.

"Inspector Hammersmith? This is a surprise," Fenella said, her heart sinking as she recognized the man. Whatever he wanted, she was sure it wouldn't be good.

"I have one simple question for you," the man said. "Were you planning on seeing Hannah Jones today?"

Fenella gasped. "Has something happened to Hannah?" she demanded.

"If you could just answer the question, please," the man said.

Fenella shook her head. "I didn't have plans to see her today," she said.

"Thank you," he replied. He turned and took a step away.

"I did have lunch with her yesterday, though," Fenella added.

The man's back stiffened. He slowly turned back around and frowned at her. "We'd better talk inside," he said eventually.

11

Fenella poured them each a cup of coffee and then sat down next to the man in the living room. He was staring out the window watching the sea or the people on the promenade when she joined him. Mona was sitting on the other side of the room, her face even paler than normal.

"Hannah had the first appointment at her doctor's surgery this morning. When she didn't turn up, they rang her house but no one answered. Because of her age and mobility issues, they rang the police and asked for a welfare check. The constable on duty went around and had her neighbor let him in." He paused to take a sip of his coffee while Fenella braced herself for what was next.

"Oh, get on with it," Mona snapped from her seat.

"She was in the bathtub. It appears that she slipped somehow, probably while climbing in, and hit her head on the bath. She must have been having a bath before going to bed. The water was cold and she'd been dead for at least eight hours when she was found."

Fenella put her coffee mug down on the table in front of her and drew a deep and shaky breath.

"Are you okay?" the inspector asked.

"No, I'm not," Fenella told him. "Something weird is going on and it's terrifying. I understand that accidents happen and that sometimes coincidences seem strange, but this is one accident too many. Someone is killing these women and I don't know why."

"You're suggesting that the three women were all murdered? And by the same person?"

"Yes, that's exactly what I'm suggesting," Fenella snapped.

"Can you provide me with any possible motive for such a thing?" was the man's next question.

"It must be tied to something in their pasts," Fenella said thoughtfully. "I told you about Phillipa Clucas and her upset when she found her husband's memoirs."

"Paulette Clucas rang the station yesterday to tell me about that very thing," the man told her. "She was concerned that you might have mentioned it when you told me about your tea with her and she wanted to make sure that I understood the situation."

"She told you that her mother dreamed up the whole thing," Fenella said flatly.

"She did. Do you have any reason to doubt her?" he asked.

"Just three dead bodies," Fenella muttered.

"With all due respect, even if some or all of the dead women were murdered, I'm not sure that qualifies as a particularly good motive. We're talking about affairs that allegedly happened some thirty years ago. Do you really think anyone still cares?"

"Phillipa cares very deeply," Fenella argued. "She shouted at me merely because I'm related to a woman that she thought had had an affair with her husband. And Paulette cares, too. She told me she was devastated when she thought that her father had cheated on her mother."

"The coroner will be conducting a thorough investigation into Mrs. Jones's death," he told her. "Right now it looks very much like another tragic accident. The only thing that keeps me from filing it away is the one common denominator."

"Which is?"

"You," the man said.

"He'll be accusing you of murder soon," Mona scoffed.

"They were all friends for many years," Fenella argued. "There must be a great deal in their shared past that people might want to keep hidden."

"Because of the third accident, we'll be looking more closely into the women's lives," the inspector conceded. "I don't suppose your aunt left any diaries or memoirs herself that might help?"

"Tell him you'll check," Mona said excitedly. "And I'll write them this afternoon."

"I don't think so," Fenella said. "You should talk to Phillipa and to Patricia Anderson. They were both part of the same crowd."

"I think I can manage to do my job," the man said testily. "I'll also be talking to the families of the dead women. I'd really like to believe that this is a wild goose chase, but, well, we'll see."

"Paulette and Paul talked to Hannah yesterday, too," Fenella said. "In fact, Paul walked Hannah home after our lunch meeting. And Patricia was at the café while Hannah and I were there."

"I know this is a small island, but you do seem to run into everyone you know all the time, don't you?" the man asked.

"Last night, in the Tale and Tail, I saw Melanie Anderson-Stuart and her husband," Fenella told him.

"You're making yourself look even more suspicious," Mona cautioned her. "Like you're going around seeking out suspects."

Mona was probably right, but Fenella was determined to tell Inspector Hammersmith everything she'd done and everyone she'd seen.

"Anyone else?" the man asked, having typed several things into his phone.

Fenella sat back and stared out at the waves that were gently splashing onto the sand below them. She hadn't been kidding when she'd said she was terrified. "I can't think of anything else," she said eventually.

"Can you take me through everything that you and Hannah talked about yesterday, please?" the man asked.

Swallowing a sigh, Fenella did her best to remember the conversation. When she was done, the man shook his head. "I should have done this from the very beginning. Can you start back on the night you met Phillipa Clucas and take me through the entire party?"

"He's finally starting to take you seriously," Mona said. "Too bad it's too late to save Hannah."

Feeling as if she'd already told this story several times, Fenella walked the man through the evening at the charity auction.

"I may have to ring Donald Donaldson and ask him to confirm your statement," the man said when she was finished.

"By all means," Fenella replied. "We're having dinner together tomorrow night. You'll want to talk to him before that, so that I don't have a chance to influence his statement."

The man frowned. "I don't appreciate your attitude," he said sharply. "You're the one who keeps insisting that there's something suspicious going on. You should be happy that I'm taking the matter seriously."

Fenella opened her mouth to reply and then shut it again. It wasn't like her to argue with the police, especially not when they were doing exactly what she wanted. There was just something about Inspector Mark Hammersmith that was rubbing her the wrong way. She picked up her mug and drank the rest of her coffee while he was busy on his phone.

"Tell me again about tea with Paulette Clucas," he said.

"He's just humoring you," Mona said grumpily. "Or trying to find a way to put the blame on you. I don't like him."

"Now tell me everything that was said yesterday between you and the Clucas siblings," the man said after she'd finished recounting the Sunday tea.

"We ran into each other in the parking lot," Fenella began. By the time she'd finished, she was starting to resent the man's ever-present mobile phone. He'd typed on it continually while she'd talked, no doubt taking notes. For some reason she found this far more annoying than when Daniel took notes on paper.

"Are you having dinner with Paul tonight?" the man asked after she'd finished.

"I'm meant to be," Fenella replied. "Although I don't really feel like it right now."

"Because you think he might be behind the murders?"

"Because I'm sad that someone else I'd only just met is dead," Fenella replied.

The inspector nodded. "As I said before, all three deaths appear to have been nothing but accidents. If any were murder, I assume you'd suggest one of the Clucas family as the most likely suspect?"

"I don't know," Fenella replied. "I don't know what secrets those three women might have shared. As you said, it seems odd to suggest that they were murdered because they may have had an affair with a married man thirty years ago, but I also know that people have been killed for far stupider reasons."

"That is true," the man acknowledged. "I think that's all I have for today. I may be back once I've had a chance to start looking into the women's backgrounds. If you do find any diaries or anything from Mona, please let me know."

"I will do," Fenella told him. She stood up as he did and then followed him to the door.

"Thank you for your time," he said as he exited her apartment.

She shut the door behind him and then sank down on the nearest sofa. Looking over at Mona, she saw a single tear trickling down the woman's face. "I can't give you a tissue, can I?" she asked her.

Mona shook her head. "I don't need one," she said, her voice quavering. She cleared her throat and then spoke again. "Being dead isn't all that bad, but I still feel sorry for people when I hear that they've died, especially when they've been murdered."

"We aren't sure that anyone has been murdered," Fenella felt obliged to remind the other woman.

"But we know they were," Mona said. "Now, I still think Phillipa or Paulette is behind this, or maybe Paul, although he would be third on my list, but I'm prepared to consider other options. I've been trying to remember anything that might have happened in the past that could be behind this, but it was so long ago. I have a very vague recollection of Paul Clucas being angry with Herbert Smathers at one point, just before Herbert died, but I don't even know if I ever knew what they'd disagreed about."

"Did Hannah have an affair with Paul?" Fenella had to ask.

Mona shook her head. "I don't think so, and I think I would have known. Paul's list must include just about every woman he ever met, though."

"Surely there must be something else going on. What about Herbert's death?" Fenella asked. "Do you really think that it wasn't an accident?"

"I always thought Anne Marie killed him," Mona said. "If she did, maybe someone killed her for revenge, but why kill Margaret and Hannah?"

"Maybe they were all in on it," Fenella suggested. "And maybe Herbert had a relative that no one knew about. Maybe that relative has come back to avenge Herbert's death."

"Now you're thinking," Mona said, clapping lightly. "It's entirely possible that Herbert had relatives across. There was even a rumor at one point that he left a wife and possibly even children to pursue Anne Marie. Maybe his son or daughter is on the island, seeking out and killing anyone who might have had a hand in Herbert's death."

"It seems farfetched," Fenella said with a sigh.

"But it's worth considering," Mona argued. "Especially as Anne Marie was the first to die and she was killed the same way Herbert was."

Fenella nodded and then jumped when the phone rang.

"I only have about two minutes, but I wanted to ring to make sure you're okay," Daniel's voice came down the line.

"I'm fine, just very sad," Fenella told him. "And a little bit worried that someone very clever is murdering people for some reason we don't understand."

"All three cases look very much like accidents," Daniel told her. "Aside from the fact that the victims all knew one another, there's nothing to link them."

"Except for me," Fenella said glumly.

"Yes, well, Mark is keen on pointing that out for some reason, even though he knows you didn't have anything to do with any of the deaths."

Fenella bit her tongue. Daniel may have been convinced of her innocence, but she wasn't sure that Mark Hammersmith was.

"Anyway, Mark is going to send me a copy of his notes. I understand he talked to you this morning about the latest death?"

"Yeah, I had lunch with the woman yesterday."

Daniel sighed. "How do you keep getting mixed up in these things?" he asked. "I mean, I've never..." he trailed off and took a deep breath. "I'm sorry. I know you don't want to be in the middle of this any more than I want you there. I really do have to go, but I'll ring you later, after I've read Mark's report."

"I have plans for dinner tonight," Fenella said, wishing she didn't have to tell him about Paul.

"So maybe you should ring me when you get home from your evening out," Daniel suggested. "Or better yet, text me. If I'm still up, we can talk then."

"That sounds great," she replied. She opened her mouth to add something, she wasn't sure what, but she heard a loud click before she could speak.

"And he hung up on me," she muttered.

"He's jealous," Mona said. "He did tell you to date other men while he was away. He shouldn't be surprised that you're doing just that."

"We're just friends," Fenella said. "He needed to get back to work, anyway."

It was nearly time for lunch, so Fenella flipped through a magazine for a short while before feeding herself and Katie. Her mind was racing around too much for her to settle into her research, so after lunch she took a walk into the center of Douglas. There wasn't anything she needed, but she enjoyed looking through the shops and even tried on a few pairs of shoes before returning home.

"What should I wear tonight?" she asked Mona as she stood in front of the woman's wardrobe with both doors open.

"Don't waste anything too nice on young Paul," Mona said. "You're only having dinner with him because you miss Daniel."

"That's not true," Fenella protested. "I'm having dinner with him because he seems very nice. He's also quite attractive."

"Yes, well, in that case, maybe you should wear the little red dress in the corner," Mona suggested.

Fenella pulled the dress out and held it up. "It's a bit short," she said. "And rather low-cut at the front."

"It's very sexy," Mona agreed. "But you do find the man attractive. You should want to look sexy."

"There's a difference between finding him attractive and wanting to make him see me as a sex object," Fenella told her. "I don't think this is at all appropriate."

"What about the blue one?" Mona asked as Fenella pushed the red dress back into place.

Fenella pulled out the next dress along the rack. It was much more modest, with a knee-length skirt and a pretty draped neckline. The color seemed to flatter Fenella. "I like this," she exclaimed. "I'll try it on."

"The matching shoes are in the bottom drawer," Mona told her.

Fenella pulled out shoes that matched the blue in the dress perfectly. "You must have spent a fortune on shoes," she said as she slipped the dress over her head.

"Max liked me to look good," Mona replied. "He never once complained about buying matching shoes or handbags for my dresses."

"Is there a matching handbag?" Fenella asked as she studied herself in the mirror. The dress fit beautifully, showcasing her curves without looking the least little bit racy.

"Of course there's a matching handbag," Mona said. "In the drawer under the shoes."

Fenella found the bag. It was a perfect color match. "It's gorgeous," she told Mona.

"Yes, it was always one of my favorites," Mona said. "Timothy, who made so many of my most wonderful clothes for me, had a friend called Samuel who worked with leather. He made the most exquisite bags and shoes for me to match whatever Timothy dreamt up."

"I can't believe how closely the colors match," Fenella remarked.

"He could do anything with dyes," Mona told her. "You should put your hair up," she added as Fenella sat down to apply her makeup. "There's a clip in the bottom drawer that goes with the dress."

Fenella found the clip and twisted it into her hair. After she'd redone her makeup she put everything she thought she might need into the matching handbag. “I’m ready,” she said to Mona. “But I’m not looking forward to this.”

“Why not?” Mona asked.

“Do you think Paul could be behind everything?”

“You mean, do I think he killed Anne Marie, Margaret, and Hannah? No, I don’t,” Mona said. “If he wanted to kill his father’s former lovers, he could have done so years ago. I’m sure he knew about them.”

“Maybe he was just waiting until his father died,” Fenella suggested.

Mona frowned. “I hadn’t thought of that,” she said. “Maybe you should cancel dinner.”

A knock on the door made both women jump. “Too late,” Fenella said nervously.

Paul looked very handsome in a dark grey suit. “You look wonderful,” he told Fenella. “That dress looks as if it were made for you.”

Fenella opened her mouth to tell him that it was Mona’s, but stopped herself. If the man really had been slightly obsessed with her aunt, she wasn’t sure she wanted him to know.

“I hope it’s okay with you if this is a fairly quick dinner,” he said as he escorted her out of the apartment and down the corridor.

“Of course,” Fenella said. “I hope nothing is wrong.”

“My mother is in hospital,” the man replied. “I told her I’d come back to see her later tonight.”

“We can forget about dinner,” Fenella said quickly. “Or rather, reschedule for when your mother is well again.”

“I have to eat, and selfishly, I’d rather eat in the company of a beautiful woman than on my own.”

Fenella blushed. “Only if you’re sure,” she said.

“I had planned on taking you to one of my favorite restaurants for five courses and wine, but I’m afraid that’s a bit too ambitious under the circumstances. I hope you don’t mind if we just go somewhere nearby?”

“We can go anywhere you want.”

“You look far too lovely to take to a pub, even one that does good food,” he said. “But in the interest of time, how about the Chinese place down the street? They’re usually very fast.”

"That sounds great," Fenella said.

As the restaurant in question was only a short distance away, they walked. It was about half full when they arrived and they were seated, at Paul's request, at a quiet table in the back.

"I hope your mother is okay," Fenella said after they'd ordered drinks and food.

"I think she'll be fine," Paul said. "My father's death has hit her incredibly hard. I know Paulette told you about the dreams she's been having about him leaving behind memoirs that detailed his infidelities. I'm afraid my mother is having trouble telling her dreams from reality. Paulette has been doing her best, but Mother can't seem to sleep without the tablets now and Paulette is afraid to give them to her. Mother's doctor thought a night or two in hospital might help."

"So you're sure the memoirs were all just a bad dream?" Fenella asked.

Paul shrugged. "I'm in an awkward position," he admitted. "I can't find any trace of anything like that on my father's computer, but, well, the thing is, I wasn't surprised when Paulette told me what she'd found."

"You knew your father was writing his memoirs?"

"No, not at all," Paul replied. He stopped as the waiter delivered their soft drinks. "Sorry about this," he said to Fenella, nodding toward the drinks. "I wanted to wine and dine you, but I'm driving."

"It's fine," Fenella told him. "I don't need wine to have a good time."

Paul grinned. "It certainly helps, though," he laughed. "But where was I? Oh, yes, my father and his memoirs. No, I didn't know he was planning to write them, but then, he wasn't, was he? That was just my mother's fancy. No, I knew he'd been unfaithful, or I should say, I suspected that he'd been unfaithful."

"I see."

Paul sighed. "My father didn't spend much time at home with us," he explained. "Paula was, well, difficult, and my mother was devoted to her. Paulette did everything she could to help with Paula's care, but I was rather in the way. As soon as I was old enough, I started spending as much time as I could with my father. Mostly I just sat around his office, doing my schoolwork. Sometimes my father would give me little jobs to do around the office, but mostly I just wanted to be there so I wouldn't have to be at home."

"I'm sorry. That sounds like an unhappy way to spend your childhood."

"In some ways, but in other ways it was quite good. I learned a lot about running the business and I was able to get to know my father better than I would have otherwise. By the time I was sixteen, my father started taking me with him to parties, which felt like a huge privilege. All my school friends were jealous, that was for sure."

"And that's how you found out your father was cheating?"

"At first I didn't understand it. I was still pretty naïve at sixteen, but it gradually dawned on me that some of the women in the crowd were a little too friendly with him. A lot of it was just for show; some of the women seemed to take great delight in flirting with other men in front of their husbands, but over time, and I'm talking years here, I began to realize that there was more than just flirting going on, at least with some of the women."

"Were you tempted to tell your mother?" Fenella asked. As soon as the words were out of her mouth, she flushed. "I'm sorry. That's an incredibly rude question," she said quickly.

"Rude, maybe, but understandable," he replied.

"Here we are," the waiter said. He put plates full of steaming hot food in front of each of them. "Do you need anything else right now?"

"We're good," Paul said, waving the man away.

"It looks delicious," Fenella said, ignoring the chopsticks she'd been given and picking up her fork. They ate silently for a few minutes before Paul cleared his throat.

"I did think about telling my mother, but it felt as if that would have broken some sort of unspoken bond between my father and me," he said. "He included me in his parties and let me see what he was doing, but I couldn't tell anyone what I saw. That was the unspoken agreement."

Fenella nodded. "That makes sense," she said.

"Later, when I was old enough to really understand what was happening, I made the conscious decision not to tell my mother. Their marriage wasn't a happy one, but I don't think she ever knew that he was unfaithful. It wasn't my place to destroy any illusions she held about my father."

"How is everything?" the waiter asked.

"Fine," Fenella said quickly, although she hadn't really tasted anything that she'd eaten. She'd been too caught up in Paul's story to notice the food.

"I have to believe that she knew," Paul said as the waiter walked away.

"Why?"

"Because of her dream," Paul explained. "Maybe she didn't know, but I'm sure she must have suspected. Otherwise, why would she dream that she'd found proof of his infidelity?"

Fenella nodded slowly. She still wasn't convinced that the story about the memoirs was just a dream, but if it was, then what Paul was saying made sense. "So you think she suspected, but never said anything until the story finally came out in her dream?"

"It certainly seems that way," Paul said. "But of course the whole thing has put me in an awkward position. When Paulette first told me what Mother had found, I tried to sound shocked, but I don't think I really carried it off. When I couldn't find the files on the computer, I got the impression that Paulette thought I'd hidden them to try to protect our father's reputation."

"Would you have done that, given the opportunity?"

"I don't know," Paul said, shrugging. "I might have been tempted to, because both my mother and sister were so upset. If anything, I think Paulette was more upset than my mother. As I said, I believe she must have suspected, but I'm pretty sure that Paulette had no idea."

"And now some of the women from that social circle have died suddenly," Fenella said, trying to sound casual.

"That's not helping my mother's state of mind either," Paul said. "She had a very strange reaction to Anne Marie's death."

"Strange?"

"I didn't see her until the next day, but when I offered my sympathies, she told me not to bother, that Anne Marie was no friend of hers. Of course, at that point she still thought that Anne Marie had had an affair with my father."

"And did Anne Marie have an affair with your father?" Fenella knew the answer, but she wondered if Paul did.

"I think so," he replied. "Anyway, Margaret's death was a shock, but she's taken Hannah's very badly. That's part of the reason why she's in hospital, really. Paulette couldn't calm her down after she told her about Hannah."

"I am sorry."

Paul shrugged. "I just hope there aren't any more accidents," he said. "It's strange that they're all happening at once, so soon after my father's death, but I suppose the women in question are all at an age where they're more prone to such things, aren't they? My mother nearly took a tumble down the stairs at my house a week or so ago, and Paulette told me that she slipped in the bath the other day as well. We don't let her drive anymore, so at least that's one thing we don't have to worry about."

"How about pudding?" the waiter asked.

"You want to get to Noble's," Fenella said to Paul.

"We have time for pudding, if you'd like," Paul told her. "I think I need some bread and butter pudding if I'm going to be spending hours with my mother and sister after this." Fenella opted for the chocolate sponge with warm chocolate sauce.

"The police have been asking me a lot of questions about the three women," Fenella said, choosing her words carefully. "I spent time with all of them not long before they died. I've been wondering if all three deaths really were accidents."

"What else could they have been? No one commits suicide by falling down a flight of stairs, surely?"

"But maybe Anne Marie killed herself," Fenella suggested. "The only other option, I suppose, is murder."

Paul frowned at her. The waiter delivered their desserts before he spoke again. "That's why your name was familiar," he said after he'd taken a bite. "You found Alan Collins's body and that body on the ferry as well. I knew I'd heard the name before."

Fenella flushed. "I was hoping people would have forgotten about all of that by now," she said.

"But just because you've stumbled across a few murder victims doesn't mean that everyone who dies unexpectedly has been murdered. Accidents do happen."

"Of course they do. I was just telling you how I felt after talking to the police," Fenella said. "They asked me a lot of questions, just like in a murder investigation."

"I'm sure they were just being thorough," Paul said dismissively. "There hasn't been anything in the local paper about any of the deaths being suspicious, and the local paper would be all over the story if they had any hint of anything. They love murder cases. Murder sells a lot of papers."

Fenella finished her cake before she replied. "As I said, it was just an impression I got. I hope you're right. While accidents are sad, they aren't nearly as worrying as murders."

"And on that rather odd note, I think we'd better call it a night," Paul said. He waved to their waiter and handed him his credit card. A moment later the waiter was back and Paul signed the receipt.

"That was very good," Fenella said as they walked out of the building. "I'm going to have to come back here again soon."

"It was good, even if the conversation wasn't exactly what I'd hoped for," Paul said.

"I am sorry," Fenella told him.

"Next time, I want to hear all about you," he said. "We won't talk about my family and our little difficulties at all."

"My life story won't take long," Fenella laughed. "We'll have plenty of time to talk about yours as well."

The walk back to Fenella's door was a short one. She opened the door and then turned. "Thank you for dinner," she said.

"It was my pleasure. I'll ring you in a few days, once I know for sure what's happening with my mother. I'd really like to do this again without all the talk about death and murder."

"That sounds good," Fenella said.

The man bent down and gave her a quick kiss. "I really do have to get to Noble's," he said softly. "Otherwise, I'd be finding ways to prolong the evening."

"Go and see your mother," Fenella told him. "She needs to be your first priority at the moment."

Paul nodded and then turned and walked away. He waved to her as the elevator doors shut in front of him. Fenella sighed and pushed her door shut.

"That was quick," Mona said. "Don't tell me you ran out of things to talk about."

"His mother is in the hospital. He probably should have just cancelled altogether."

"What's wrong with Phillipa?" Mona sounded concerned.

"Her doctor wants to see what he can do about the sleeping pills and her reaction to them, I gathered."

"Perhaps she should just stop taking them."

"Apparently she's still upset about her husband's death. The recent accidents also have her unsettled and she's having trouble separating reality from the dreams she's been having. All in all, her doctor thought she could do with being under his care for a few days."

"Now you need to ring Daniel," Mona reminded her.

"I don't want to talk to him," Fenella replied. "He makes me nervous."

"If you don't ring, he'll be even more cross."

"I know," Fenella sighed. She pulled out her mobile phone and sent the man a text, letting him know that she was home. "Maybe he'll be busy and won't be able to call back," she said as she dropped the phone onto a table. A moment later her landline began to ring.

12

"I wasn't expecting you home for hours yet," Daniel said.

"I had dinner with Paul Clucas, but his mother is in the hospital, so we didn't dawdle."

"Why do you insist on spending time with suspects?" Fenella could hear exasperation in the man's voice.

"I wasn't aware that he was suspected of anything," she countered. "The last I knew, all three deaths were tragic accidents."

"I suppose it all depends on how you feel about coincidences," Daniel replied. "I don't like them."

"I don't like them either," Fenella said. "I wish you were here, handling the investigation."

"Mark's a good investigator. If there is something going on, he'll discover it."

"I feel so awful about Hannah," Fenella admitted. "I feel as if I should have warned her."

"Hindsight is a wonderful and terrible thing. The last thing you wanted to do was worry an elderly woman who was already upset about losing two friends in a short space of time. It's highly unlikely that anything you could have said to her would have made a difference. If she was murdered, all of the evidence suggests that it was by someone she trusted."

"That just makes me feel worse," Fenella complained.

"I'm sorry," Daniel said. "And I'm sorry to ask, but can you take me through your entire day yesterday? I want to hear all about your lunch with Hannah and the conversation afterwards with Paulette and Paul."

Fenella made a face and then sank down into the nearest chair and tapped the speakerphone button. Mona seemed to be listening intently as Fenella recounted everything she could remember from the previous day.

"And now, if you don't mind too much, can you take me through your dinner tonight?"

Fenella obliged, feeling as if she were betraying Paul by repeating what he'd said over their meal.

"So he knew that his father cheated, but he couldn't find the memoirs that his mother claimed to have read," Daniel said thoughtfully when she'd finished.

"That's what he told me."

"It seems as if his mother and his sister have the best motives for killing the three victims," Daniel said.

"Unless their deaths don't have anything to do with Paul Clucas," Fenella said. "I've been thinking about Herbert Smathers a lot. He died in a car accident, the same as his wife. I wonder if there was more to his death than meets the eye."

"I've read the police report on his death. Mark included it when he sent the report on Mrs. Smathers. It was investigated, but not in the same way we would do it now, of course. All those years ago, they didn't have the technology that we have now when it comes to investigating accidents."

"So it could have been murder?"

"It could have been, but as I said, it was a long time ago. Are you suggesting that someone is just now, all these years later, avenging the man's death?"

"I don't know," Fenella said with a sigh. "It's just another instance of odd coincidence, Herbert and Anne Marie dying in the same manner in identical cars, that's all."

"I'm not sure I can imagine Anne Marie, Margaret, and Hannah all being involved in the man's death," Daniel said. "Even if they were very close friends, murder has a way of getting between people."

"They weren't friends," Mona said. "Especially not when Herbert was alive. Anne Marie hated all of the women that he tried to take to bed, and that was pretty much every woman he met."

"They were little old women who used to drink and party together fifty years ago," Fenella said. "Why would anyone start killing them now?"

"We're checking into as much of their pasts as we can," Daniel told her. "None of the women ever worked, but they were all involved with various charities. It's just remotely possible that there's something there."

"That's not a bad idea," Mona said. "I can see Patricia being angry enough to murder someone if they didn't appreciate the importance of the Manx Fund for Children. It is her life's work."

"Charities? Maybe Patricia Anderson is killing them all because they didn't donate enough to her pet project," Fenella said.

"That isn't really funny," Daniel said. "But hers is one of the charities that we're looking into. Thus far we have no reason to suspect that we're going to find anything, though."

"So where does that leave us?" Fenella demanded. "You suspect that someone is murdering a group of women, but you don't know why they're being targeted so it's virtually impossible to work out who is behind it. Can't you at least warn other potential victims?"

"Can you suggest other potential victims?" Daniel asked. "As we don't know what's behind the murders, or even if all three women were murdered, it's very hard to work out who else might be a potential victim."

"Patricia Anderson," Mona said. "If the killer is targeting women who were involved with Paul Clucas, she could be next."

Fenella opened her mouth to reply, but remembered just in time that Daniel couldn't hear Mona. "What about Patricia Anderson?" she asked. "She's another woman from that social circle. She may be the only one left, actually."

"Mark was going to talk to her today," Daniel replied. "He was hoping she might be able to suggest why her group of friends is being targeted and he was going to suggest that she be extra careful, as well. I haven't spoken to him tonight to hear how it went."

"This is awful," Fenella sighed. "I don't suppose the police can keep a close watch on Phillipa and Paulette Clucas?"

"You really think one of them is behind this?"

"It seems like the most obvious answer," Fenella told him.

"You don't think that you might be biased because Phillipa was so horrible to you when you met her?" he asked.

Fenella stared at the phone for a moment. "I, no, I mean, I didn't think," she stammered.

"Take a deep breath, and then tell him he's an idiot," Mona suggested.

"She's a confused elderly woman," Fenella said. "The experience was uncomfortable, but it certainly didn't make me hate her enough to start throwing unfounded accusations at her. Paulette has been nothing but nice to me, but I'm still suggesting she might be behind all of the deaths."

"I'm sorry, but I had to ask," Daniel said. He sighed deeply. "Mark is doing his best, but he doesn't have any reason to doubt what Paulette has told him. If the memoirs don't exist, then neither does any motive for Phillipa or Paulette."

"Paul told me that his father did cheat," Fenella reminded him. "The motive remains, whether they found proof on the computer or not."

"I'll suggest to Mark that he keep an eye on both women and also on Paul," Daniel said. "But he won't be able to have someone watching them all the time. At least he'll be able to keep tabs on Phillipa while she's in hospital."

"If the deaths don't have anything to do with Paul Clucas, then Phillipa may well be another potential victim," Fenella said as the thought occurred to her. "Maybe Mark should warn her as well as Patricia."

"I'll suggest it to him," Daniel said. "Aside from the unexplained deaths, how are you?"

Fenella sighed. "I'm okay, I suppose," she said. "I'm picking at my research and trying to start thinking about writing, but there are so many other things that seem to fill my days."

"Like what?"

"Like reading fiction and watching television and taking long walks through Douglas," Fenella replied. "It's terrible because none of it is productive, but I can't seem to work up any real enthusiasm for my writing at the moment."

"How is the driving coming?"

"I'm dragging my feet on taking my test," Fenella admitted. "Every time I think about it, I feel like I might throw up."

"It isn't that bad," Daniel chuckled. "If you haven't taken it by the time I get back, I'll take you out for a practice run. I know enough about how the test works to give you a similar experience."

"That's just giving me more incentive to get the test over with," Fenella said.

"That's good, too," he replied.

"How is your course?"

"Fascinating, but challenging. It's been a while since I was in a classroom for this length of time. It's a little bit frustrating, if I'm honest, being stuck here dealing with lectures and exams when I'd rather be there, trying to work out what's going on with these three deaths."

"Are you sure there are only three?" Fenella asked as an idea popped into her head.

"What do you mean?"

"I mean, I'm sure that there have been other accidents on the island in the past week or so. Is it possible that some of them weren't accidents, but we don't know it yet because we haven't spotted the common link?"

"I believe Mark thinks you are the common link," Daniel said. "But I understand what you're saying. I'll suggest to Mark that he have another look at all of the island's accidents over the past seven days. Maybe there's something else going on and we just haven't worked it out yet."

"What are you learning about at the moment?" Fenella asked, not wanting to talk anymore about the local deaths.

"We're still doing body decomposition," he said. "Although tomorrow, if there's time, we're going to start talking about defensive wounds."

"I think I'll stick to Anne Boleyn," Fenella said.

"At least you know exactly how she died."

"Yes, and there wasn't any question of it being an accident, either."

"I'd better go and get some sleep," Daniel said after they'd chatted a while longer about nothing much. "If I'm not up by six, I'll miss my turn in the showers."

"That's one thing I don't miss about my college days," Fenella laughed.

"At least once I'm through the shower, someone has breakfast ready for me," he replied. "Every cloud, you know."

"He misses you," Mona said after Fenella put the phone down. "And he's worried about you."

"I miss him, too. But I'm worried about Patricia."

"Yes, maybe you should ring her. Make an excuse to see her and warn her yourself."

"I can't do that," Fenella said. "There's no way to tell a woman that you think she might be murdered because she had an affair fifty years ago."

"It wouldn't have been that long ago for Patricia," Mona said thoughtfully. "She was very young when she married into our little group. Her husband left his first wife for her. She couldn't have been much more than eighteen."

"Hannah said as much yesterday," Fenella recalled.

"Some of the other women in the group were rather horrible to her, at least at first. She was seen as a threat or maybe a reminder of how men could behave."

"But none of the other men decided to trade in their old wives for newer models," Fenella pointed out.

"I suspect they learned from George's mistake. He and Patricia were miserable for the most part."

"Why?"

"She was too young to settle down, really. She flirted outrageously with every man she came into contact with. It wasn't until she fell pregnant that she finally settled down, at least a little bit."

"How old is Melanie?" Fenella asked.

"Oh, maybe thirty or a bit older, but she wasn't Patricia's first child. She and George had a son only a few years after they married. Patricia was devoted to him, but he was born with some sort of problems and passed away when he was eight or nine."

"How awful," Fenella exclaimed.

"Patricia went crazy with grief. I'm sure that's when she had her affair with Paul Clucas. It wasn't long after that that she started her charity, and then after a while she fell pregnant with Melanie. She's always smothered Melanie just a bit. I thought that might get better when Melanie got married, but I suspect Patricia runs her daughter's life for her."

"Melanie told Donald that she and Matthew had split up, but I saw them together at the Tale and Tail," Fenella said. "They didn't look very happy together, but they were definitely together."

"Did Melanie say anything about why they'd separated?"

Fenella tried to remember the conversation. So much had happened since then and she'd worked so hard to remember so many of the conversations that had come later in the evening that she had to struggle. "She said he wanted children and she didn't," Fenella said, giving herself a mental pat on the back.

"I wonder if she's concerned that her children might have the same issues that her older brother had," Mona said thoughtfully. "Such things may be hereditary."

"She said something about working with abused and mistreated children, which made her not interested in having any of her own."

"I suppose that's also a possibility. Still, it's odd that you saw her and Matthew together only a few days later. Maybe they're still working things out."

"Or maybe she was just flirting with Donald," Fenella muttered.

Mona laughed. "My dear, if you're going to date a handsome and very wealthy man, you must expect other women to flirt with him, behind your back at least, but probably right in front of your face as well."

"Did other women flirt with Max in front of you?"

"Of course they did," Mona replied. "But Max had a way of pretending that he hadn't noticed. He was very good at acting as if he didn't understand the innuendos and whispered suggestions that came his way."

"Really?"

"One night Anne Marie whispered a naughty suggestion in his ear. He turned around and asked me, in a very loud voice, what one of the words meant. Anne Marie only just laughed, of course, but it made it clear to her and everyone else that he wasn't interested."

"What was the word?" Fenella had to ask.

Mona shrugged. "I'll tell you when you're older," she said.

Fenella was surprised to see how late it was. She got ready for bed as quickly as she could. "I should have known it was past bedtime," she told Katie. "You've been in bed for hours, haven't you?" Katie, who was fast asleep, didn't reply.

She'd done it. She'd finally arranged for her driving test and today was the day. Shelly gave her a ride to the test center, where a large and angry-looking man in a black suit was waiting for her. He led her to a small parking lot and motioned to a tiny black car that was parked in the middle of it.

"You'll be taking your test in this," he told her gruffly.

Fenella climbed behind the steering wheel and immediately tried to work out how to adjust the seat. It was far too close to the pedals. There was no way she could drive like this. While she was struggling, the man climbed in the passenger seat. Fenella felt the entire car sink on his side.

"Let's go," he barked.

"I need to adjust the seat," she replied.

"That's as good as it gets," he snapped. "Let's go."

Fenella took the keys from the man and started the engine. With all of Mel's instructions ringing in her head, she stepped on the clutch and the gas and slowly released the handbrake. After a slow start, she was soon following the man's instructions as he had her drive around the island.

"Now we're going over the mountain," he told her.

"I didn't think the mountain was part of the test," she protested.

"Turn left," he said. A short while later she was driving faster than felt comfortable along the twists and turns of the mountain road. "You need to drive faster," the man said. "I need to know that you can use all of the gears."

Fenella sped up as much as she could, but the little car didn't seem to be able to go much faster. Suddenly, a sheep stepped into the road in front of her. She screamed and slammed on the brakes as the passenger door flew open and her examiner either fell or jumped out of the car. The car didn't seem to be slowing down as she hit the brakes again and again. Just before she was about to hit the sheep, she turned the steering wheel to the left, desperate not to hit either the sheep or the mountain. The car skidded off the road and began to sail through the air. Fenella screamed again and then gasped as something landed on her chest. When she felt her cheeks being licked, she realized that her eyes were closed.

Forcing them open, she gasped for air as she looked around her bedroom. Katie was sitting on her chest, looking at her with concern.

"Merroowww?" she asked.

"I'm okay," Fenella said shakily. "It was just a bad dream."

Her heart was pounding too hard for her to even consider trying to go right back to sleep. The clock in the kitchen told her it was four as she got herself a drink of water and sipped it, watching the cars that were slowly driving up and down the promenade. It was half an hour before she felt ready to try to sleep again. Katie curled up with her, which helped, but her sleep was still uneasy and she wasn't at all sorry when Katie woke her for breakfast.

"It's a pancakes kind of morning," she told the kitten as she poured dry cat food into a bowl. "With extra butter and syrup. But first, coffee."

While the coffee bubbled away, she mixed up pancake batter and then let it rest on the counter while she waited for the coffee. "I'm not doing anything with flames until I've had coffee," she told the kitten, who was munching contentedly on her food.

"Are you okay?" Mona asked as Fenella was taking her first sip of coffee.

"Better now," she replied, taking another sip.

"You don't look as if you slept very well," Mona said.

"I had a nightmare. But I'll be fine after some pancakes and a hot shower."

"Did the nightmare have anything to do with all of the unexplained deaths that have happened lately?"

"No, it was my driving test," Fenella told her. "I think I'm more afraid of that than I am of any murderer."

"It isn't that bad," Mona said. "I'll come along if you'd like."

"No!" Fenella exclaimed. "It will be bad enough doing it at all. It would be horrible trying to concentrate with you in the backseat. You'd probably start talking to me and I'd end up replying and the examiner would think I'd lost my mind."

"I'd sit quietly and not make a sound," Mona told her. "I'd just be moral support."

"Thank you, but I think I'll do better on my own," Fenella said. She heated a pan and melted butter in it, and then smiled happily as she poured in the first pancake and it began to sizzle softly. Two cups of coffee and six pancakes with maple syrup later, she was starting to feel better.

"What are you going to do today?" Mona asked as Fenella cleared up the kitchen.

"I don't know. I'm having dinner with Donald tonight. I thought maybe I'd try to get to the Manx Museum finally, or maybe just curl up with a good book. It's Saturday, so I don't have to work on my book."

"You're taking weekends off?" Mona asked, sounding amused.

"Yeah, why not?"

"Why not, indeed," Mona grinned.

"Anyway, I'm going to get a shower before I do anything else."

"When you're done with that, you should ring Patricia. You should warn her."

"I can't just call her out of the blue and tell her that I think someone is tracking down and killing all of the women who might have slept with Paul Clucas," Fenella protested. "Anyway, warning her is Mark Hammersmith's job. Daniel said he was going to take care of it."

"So just make an excuse to see her," Mona suggested. "Then you can work the conversation around to the deaths and make sure that Inspector Hammersmith really has warned her."

"Maybe after my shower," was as far as Fenella was willing to go. She took her time in the shower, conditioning her hair and shaving her legs, postponing what was feeling like an inevitable phone call. By the time she was dressed and had her hair and makeup done, she'd accepted that she was going to have to call Patricia Anderson, even though she didn't want to do it.

"Just tell her you want to help with the Manx Fund for Children," Mona suggested as Fenella stood next to the telephone. "Maybe you could meet her for lunch today to talk about it."

"I don't want to get roped into actually helping, though," Fenella complained. "I just want to make sure she's been warned, that's all."

The phone rang, interrupting the debate. "Hello?"

"Ah, Fenella, it's Patricia Anderson. Melanie and I were just talking about you and we've agreed that we simply must get you on board for our next big event. We're having a dinner at Castle Rushen, which will be the island's most sought-after charity fundraiser of the year."

"That sounds great," Fenella said with as much enthusiasm as she could muster.

"I knew you'd think so," Patricia said. "Anyway, Melanie and I are having tea at the Seaview tomorrow at two. Please meet us there so we can work out how best to use you in our planning."

"Tomorrrow? I'm not sure..." Fenella said.

"We'll see you then," Patricia interrupted. "I'm sorry, but I really must dash."

Fenella stared at the phone. "She hung up," she said to Mona.

"What did she want?"

"We're to have tea tomorrow at the Seaview," Fenella told her. "She wants me to get involved in planning for a dinner at Castle Rushen."

"That sounds very nice," Mona said. "But do your best to get out of getting involved. Patricia will dump all of the work on you and then blame you when it all goes wrong."

"I'm not sure I want to talk about all of the deaths in front of Melanie," Fenella mused.

"She'll be late," Mona predicted. "She was overdue by a fortnight when Patricia was expecting and she's never been on time for anything since. You'll have plenty of time to talk to Patricia, who's never late for anything, before Melanie gets there."

While Fenella had been in the shower, a steady rain had begun to fall outside her windows. Walking to the Manx Museum held little appeal as the skies continued to darken as the morning wore on. Fenella curled up with a few Agatha Christie books from Mona's shelves and relaxed. She was just thinking about lunch when someone knocked on the door.

"If that's Inspector Hammersmith, I'm shutting the door in his face," Fenella told Mona as she crossed the room. "If he's here to tell me that something has happened to Patricia, I don't want to know."

"Smokey was wondering if Katie would like a play date," Shelly said, holding up the cat, when Fenella opened the door.

"Of course, do come in, both of you," Fenella said.

Shelly set Smokey down and both women watched as she raced toward Katie. The smaller animal waited until Smokey had nearly reached her before springing up from the ground and streaking away with Smokey on her heels.

"I'm tired out just watching that," Fenella laughed.

"Have you had lunch yet?" Shelly asked. "I have some potato and leek soup in my refrigerator that needs eating up. Would you like to share it with me?"

"That sounds delicious," Fenella said. "How would it be with garlic bread? I have another loaf of that frozen kind we had the other night with our pizza."

"I think it would be wonderful," Shelly said. "I'll just go and get the soup."

Fenella switched on the oven while Shelly was gone. It didn't take long, once the oven was hot, to heat the garlic bread. Shelly's soup was already in a pot, so she simply heated it on the stove while the bread was in the oven.

"That smells wonderful," Fenella said as the soup heated.

"Thanks. It's one of my favorites. I made a big batch of it because Gordon was meant to be coming over, but he had to cancel again. There's no way I can eat all of this by myself."

Fenella gave Shelly a measured look. "Are you okay?" she asked, pretty sure she'd detected repressed tears in the other woman's tone.

"I'm fine," Shelly said, waving a hand. "Let's eat."

Fenella found large soup bowls and let Shelly ladle soup into them while she sliced the garlic bread and piled it onto a serving plate. There was still enough coffee left in the pot for them each to have a cup with their meal.

"This is delicious," Fenella said after her first bite. She managed to empty her bowl twice while Shelly had a much smaller second helping. The talk over lunch had been general, but as Fenella tidied up the dishes, she tried again.

"So you haven't seen Gordon since our evening at the pub?" she asked, trying to sound casual.

"No, I haven't. He's very busy with work," Shelly said. After a moment she sighed deeply. "At least that's what he keeps telling me. He's even working today, or so he claims. I don't know. Maybe he's found another woman."

"Surely, if he had, he would have told you," Fenella said. "You two are just friends, right?"

"I don't know what we are," Shelly said. "At the moment, he's certainly not my favorite person."

"Meerreew," Smokey said. She'd walked over to Shelly while Shelly had been talking. Now she jumped into Shelly's lap and snuggled up against her.

"Yes, my dear, you are my favorite person," Shelly murmured as Smokey began to purr loudly.

"I hate to say it, but Smokey isn't a person," Fenella pointed out.

Shelly laughed. "I'm so upset, I don't even know what I'm saying," she said after a moment. "Which is crazy. Even if I was falling for Gordon, and I'm not even sure I was, it isn't like we had a decades-long romance or anything. We'd never even kissed and I'm carrying on like my husband died again or something. Just ignore me. I intend to."

Fenella laughed. "You and Gordon were spending a lot of time together. Maybe you just miss having someone to do things with."

"There is that," Shelly agreed. "When you've been half of a couple for nearly all of your adult life, it's horrible suddenly being on your own all the time. Gordon was nice to have around."

"He seems like a nice person."

"He is a nice person. I just wish I knew what he was thinking."

"If he's like most men, he probably isn't thinking anything," Fenella said. "Except maybe about the football scores."

Shelly laughed. "You could be right. Maybe I'm reading too much into all of this. Maybe he is just busy with work and I'm worrying unnecessarily."

"Maybe she needs to find another man," Mona suggested.

"I'm meant to be having dinner with Donald tonight, but I can cancel if you need me," Fenella offered.

"Oh, goodness, no," Shelly said quickly. "Gordon is going to ring later and we might get dinner together if he finishes work in time, but even if he doesn't, I don't want to interfere with your social life. Smokey and I will be fine on our own if we have to be."

Smokey sat up on Shelly's lap and nodded at her before jumping down and pouncing on Katie. The pair rolled around on the floor for a minute before Katie raced away again. Smokey followed for a few paces and then gave up and curled up near the windows for a nap. A moment later Katie came back and joined her.

"Where are you and Donald going?" Shelly asked.

"He said something about trying a new restaurant in Peel," Fenella replied.

"I heard some top chef from London has opened a tiny little restaurant in Peel," Shelly said. "Apparently there are only a handful of tables and he's only open one or two nights a week, but the food is said to be fabulous."

"It sounds very fancy," Fenella said worriedly.

"It's Donald," Mona said. "Of course it will be fancy."

"You'll have to borrow something from Mona's wardrobe again," Shelly said.

The pair spent a happy afternoon trying on various dresses from Mona's wardrobe. Shelly found two dresses that fit her perfectly and that weren't at all to Fenella's taste.

"Take them," Fenella insisted. "I won't wear them and they're perfect for you. Let's look to see if there are matching shoes."

"Of course there are matching shoes," Mona said from where she'd been sitting and watching the fun. "And matching handbags."

"I can't take the shoes and the handbags, too," Shelly protested.

"What am I going to do with shoes and handbags in those colors?" Fenella asked. "They go with the dresses and would be useless to me."

"Are you absolutely sure?" Shelly asked.

"I'm positive, and I know Mona would be, too," Fenella replied. She looked over at Mona, who winked at her.

By the time Donald arrived to pick her up for their dinner date, Fenella was wearing her favorite dress out of the five or six she'd tried on that afternoon. It seemed as if there were dozens more in the wardrobe, but she'd stopped looking when she'd found this one. The matching shoes were comfortable and pretty and the matching handbag was just the right size for what she needed to carry.

"Stunning as ever," Donald said when she opened the door to him. "Shall we?"

13

The restaurant in Peel was everything that Fenella was coming to expect from an evening out with Donald. The food was perfectly prepared and beautifully presented, if a little fussy for Fenella's taste. Left to her own devices, she was quite happy with simple foods, although she would never think of complaining about even the fanciest of desserts.

"Work has been taking up far too much of my time lately," Donald said over drinks, after they'd ordered. "I'm hoping to start delegating more to my assistant so that I have more free time. And I'm hoping to spend some of that extra time with you."

"I am supposed to be writing a book," Fenella replied. "But I don't seem to be doing very well with that."

"Maybe you need to get away. I understand some writers find it useful to go on a retreat where they don't have television or Internet access, or some such thing. I'm sure there must be cottages in the wilds of Scotland that would take you away from the real world and let you focus on your work."

"I'm not ready to lock myself away yet," Fenella laughed. "I couldn't justify the expense, anyway. I very much doubt that I'll ever find a publisher for my masterpiece, even if I ever do get it written."

"I have friends in the business. Once you have a solid draft, let me know."

Fenella thought about the offer for a moment. While she really wanted to find a publisher based on the merit of her book, she also knew that getting published was an enormous challenge. If Donald could help her rise to the top of the slush pile and actually get someone to read her book, she might actually have a chance.

"Your starters," the waiter intoned, placing plates in front of each of them.

Fenella's mouth watered as she picked up her fork. Her salad, with spicy grilled chicken and warm walnut dressing, was every bit as good as it had sounded on the menu.

"Would you like to try the caviar?" Donald asked after a few bites.

"Not even a little bit," Fenella replied. "But you're welcome to try my salad, if you'd like."

Donald shook his head. "I'd really like to hear how you've been and what you've been doing lately," he told her. "I feel as if I haven't seen you in weeks."

"You saw me on Tuesday," Fenella reminded him. "And I haven't been doing all that much, really. If you take away all my conversations with the police, I haven't been doing anything at all."

"The police? Do you mean Daniel, or is there something going on that I don't know about?"

"I have spoken to Daniel a couple of times, but mostly I've been talking to Inspector Mark Hammersmith. He's investigating the three accidents that have recently taken the lives of three women that I'd only just met. He seems to think the deaths might not have been accidents."

"I'm not sure how you fit in?" Donald made the statement a question.

"Anne Marie Smathers told someone that she was coming to see me the day that she died," Fenella explained. "And I had plans with Margaret Dolek the day she died. Hannah Jones passed away the day after we'd had lunch together."

Donald took her hand. "I'm so sorry," he said staring into her eyes. "I had no idea. Are you okay?"

"I'm fine, just frustrated. All three deaths look like accidents, but now that there have been three of them, that seems like too convenient of an explanation. I know Inspector Hammersmith is taking a good look at all three cases."

"He can't possibly think you're involved in any way."

"I don't know what he thinks. I barely knew the women, of course, so that has to be a point in my favor."

"If they weren't accidents, I assume the police are thinking murder. Who could possibly want to murder three harmless older women?"

"I don't know. You're part of their social circle. Can you think of anything that might link them together and motivate a killer?"

Donald shook his head. "Off the top of my head, no, but I'll think about it."

Fenella finished her salad while Donald nibbled on his food, staring into space. After a while, the waiter cleared their dishes.

"I'll have your main course for you in just a few minutes," he promised.

When he'd gone, Donald shook his head. "My father knew all three women well. I'm a generation younger, but I remember many years of social occasions with them present. I can't think of any reason why someone would want them dead after all these years."

"Phillipa Clucas was pretty upset at the party. According to Paulette, her mother found her father's memoirs on his computer and it was full of stories about his infidelity."

"And you think Phillipa is killing all of her husband's former lovers?" Donald asked incredulously.

"It was just one possibility," Fenella said quickly. "Apparently, when Paul checked the computer, he couldn't find any trace of the memoirs. Paulette is sure that her mother dreamed the entire thing. Apparently Phillipa is taking very strong sleeping pills that cause vivid dreams, I've been told."

"Even if the memoirs were there and she'd found them, Phillipa wouldn't hurt a fly," Donald said. "I've known her my entire life. I'm sure she was devastated when she thought that Paul had cheated on her, but there's no way she'd try to get revenge in that sort of manner."

"What about Paulette or Paul?"

Donald blew out a long breath. "I've known both of them forever. I just can't see it. Paul, Junior, knew his father well, and Paulette? It just isn't in her nature."

"Was Paul unfaithful to Phillipa?"

"I don't know anything for sure," Donald said. "Certainly, once Anne Marie Smathers was widowed, she seemed determined to have affairs with every man she met. I doubt Paul would have resisted. I can't see either Hannah or Margaret actually sleeping with him, though."

"Here we are," the waiter said brightly, delivering plates. Fenella's chicken with rice and steamed vegetables looked wonderful, even if she couldn't remember the names of all of the fancy sauces that decorated the plate. Donald's steak looked good as well, smothered in peppercorn sauce, with vegetables and baby new potatoes.

"Anne Marie told me as much the night we met," Fenella picked the conversation back up when the waiter had gone. "But I don't know about Margaret or Hannah."

"You're asking me to remember things that happened a long time ago, when I was pretty young," Donald protested. "As I said, even I knew about Anne Marie. She was not interested in discretion. But the other two women were married. I would assume, if they did have affairs with Paul, that they did so very discreetly."

"What did you mean when you said that Paul, Junior, knew his father well?"

"Just that Junior must have known about his father's other women. Phillipa never came to the parties or charity events, so Paul wasn't always as discreet as he probably should have been, especially once his son started coming along."

"But you don't remember him with Margaret or Hannah?"

"I knew about him and Anne Marie because that was Anne Marie. The only other woman that I'm certain he had an affair with is Patricia Anderson, and I'd rather you didn't repeat that to anyone."

Fenella nodded. "Do you think Paul, Junior, knew about his father and Patricia?"

“Probably. He would have been at all of the parties by the time it happened.”

Fenella sighed. “The food is delicious,” she said. She was working hard to try to remember to taste everything, as her mind was elsewhere.

“I’m glad you’re enjoying it,” Donald said. He topped up her wine glass and then patted her hand. “Maybe all three women did have accidents,” he said.

“If they didn’t, can you think of any other motive? Someone suggested that it might all be tied to Herbert Smathers’s death.”

“Ah, poor Herbert. My father used to talk about him. He loved Herbert’s car and very nearly bought himself the same model. When Herbert crashed, he was awfully glad he hadn’t.”

“I understand Anne Marie drove the same type of car.”

“Anne Marie had her own unique approach to life,” Donald said with a laugh. “I’m sure she’s in the afterlife now, laughing at the fact that she ended up dying in the same way Herbert did.”

“Did your father ever suggest that Herbert’s death was anything other than an accident?”

“Oh, yes. He used to say that Anne Marie had finally had enough of the man and eliminated him. It was something of a joke within the group.”

“Hardly funny.”

“I think it was all just teasing. I was never sure, but Anne Marie never struck me as the type to know enough about cars to deliberately cause a crash.”

“Were there any other mysterious deaths or scandals or anything that you can remember? Maybe some money or jewelry disappeared or charity funds were misappropriated?”

“Nothing is leaping to mind immediately, but I will give the matter some thought. I have a few friends across that might be able to help as well. Men who were friends with my father back in the day who have retired to the UK. I visit them once in a while when I’m across. I’ll ring them both up and see if they have any ideas.”

“I’d appreciate that,” Fenella told him. “It’s worrying to think that the deaths might not have been accidents and I hate that the police think I'm the thing that links them together."

Donald gave her hand a squeeze. "I'm sure Daniel will step in to defend you if Inspector Hammersmith has any concerns. And if he doesn't, I can ring the chief constable and have a word. You really mustn't worry."

As the waiter cleared their now empty plates, Fenella took a drink of wine. "Let's talk about something more pleasant over dessert," she said. "Something inconsequential so I can focus on my cookie cake with its molten chocolate center."

Donald told her stories about some of his travels as they ate. His jam roly-poly didn't tempt her in the slightest as she broke open her chocolate chip cookie cake and a river of hot chocolate sauce poured out. She was slightly annoyed when Donald asked for a bite, but she tried hard not to show it. He was buying dinner, after all.

He held her hand all the way out of the restaurant and back into his car. The small sports car felt uncomfortably intimate as they drove back across the island.

"I'm not going to try to persuade you to let me stay tonight," he said as they went. "I'm still letting you set the pace, so I shall wait to be invited. Having said that, if you were harboring any doubts about my feelings for you, if you did ask me to stay the night, you might find it difficult to get rid of me in the morning."

Fenella turned his words over in her mind. She wasn't ready to sleep with him, but it was flattering to know that he wanted her. Jack hadn't made her feel at all desirable, at least not for a great many years. That was part of her reluctance, of course. It had been a long time since she'd been intimate with a man and the thought of taking things to that level with worldly and sophisticated Donald Donaldson terrified her. The thought of taking things to that level with anyone at all terrified her, she realized. Maybe she was too old to be contemplating such a thing.

Donald walked her to her door and then pulled her close. "Something for you to think about when you're snuggled up in bed tonight," he whispered in her ear. The kiss reminded her that she was not too old at all, and that she and Donald had incredible chemistry between them. For a scary moment, she thought about inviting him in, but then her heart rate began to return to normal and she simply thanked him for dinner and let herself into her apartment.

"He isn't going to wait around forever," Mona told her. "You should really tell him you aren't interested."

"Maybe I am interested," Fenella countered.

"If you were interested, you'd have invited him in," Mona said.

"I'm not ready to take things there."

"Tell me about the evening," Mona changed the subject. "Did you talk to him about the murders?"

"I mentioned the accidents to him," Fenella replied, emphasizing the word accidents. "He's going to think about possible motives, just in case they weren't accidents, though. He said he'd ring a few of his father's old friends who are across as well. They might have some ideas."

"I wonder whom he's going to ring," Mona said. "I never understood people moving across to retire, but some people did. Most often because their wives were from across, or their children moved there. Never mind, it will be interesting to see if he comes up with anything."

Fenella got ready for bed and then curled up with Katie. She was trying hard not to think about her plans for the next day. Tea with Patricia and Melanie didn't appeal in the slightest, although she would rather do that than find out that Patricia was dead. She sighed and flipped over, annoying Katie, who jumped down and wandered away. Of course, Katie could sleep whenever she wanted the following day. Fenella didn't have that luxury.

After tossing and turning for what felt like the entire night, Fenella was finally fast asleep when Katie jumped on her chest. "No, go away," she muttered.

"Meerreew," Katie replied.

Fenella opened one eye and frowned at the clock. "Is it really eight?" she asked the kitten. "You've actually let me sleep in for a bit. Thank you."

"Meeoowweerroww."

Fenella slid out of bed and headed for the kitchen. She filled

Katie's bowls and then poured herself some cereal and switched on the coffee maker. Once she'd eaten and had her first cup of coffee, she felt pretty good. A shower and a second cup helped even more.

"Okay, today I'm going to try writing a little bit," she announced. "I'm going to start with an early diary entry and just write something about Anne's childhood."

Katie watched as Fenella set up her laptop and sat down to work. Fenella selected a date at random and began to write. It wasn't long before she found herself sighing deeply and regretting that she'd ever started.

"I can't get inside the girl's head," she complained to Katie. "Her life was too different from mine. I can't even begin to imagine what she was thinking or feeling."

Fenella forced herself to type a complete diary entry, as she felt she needed to make some effort. It was only just over a hundred words, but at least she'd done something. "I think that's quite enough for today," she told Katie as she shut the laptop down. "And now I shall read a good book and relax."

Katie was happy to snuggle up next to her on the couch while Fenella read one of the Rex Stout books she'd brought from Buffalo with her. It was only when her stomach started rumbling that she noticed the time.

"It's one o'clock," she exclaimed. "I haven't had any lunch. I'm not dressed for afternoon tea, and I still have to get to Ramsey."

After changing quickly while munching on a slice of bread, Fenella rushed outside and was thrilled to find a taxi waiting in the rank nearby. The drive to Ramsey seemed to take forever, but it was still a few minutes shy of two o'clock when she paid off the driver and headed into the Seaview.

"There you are," Patricia said, getting to her feet as Fenella approached. "Traffic was horrible, wasn't it? I hope you aren't having too much trouble getting around our little island?"

"No, not really, but I've not taken my driving test yet, so I'm relying on taxis."

"I wish I'd known. I would have been happy to collect you. You must let me drive you home. I've always wanted to see Mona's flat. Have you made many changes since you moved in?"

"I haven't changed anything," Fenella replied. "Everything Mona had is wonderful."

"She acquired a great many valuable antiques over the years. She seemed to have unlimited funds at the auctions. I always wondered where all of her money came from."

Fenella ignored the unspoken question. "I'm quite happy to take a taxi home, but if you'd like to give me a ride, I'd be more than happy to show you Mona's apartment."

"Of course, it's yours now," Patricia said. "Do you plan to keep it or are you thinking of selling it and finding something else?"

"I can't imagine finding anything else that I would like better than where I am. The building is centrally located, the apartment is beautiful, and the furnishings are splendid. I can't see any reason to move."

"I thought maybe you'd prefer something larger. I'm sure there's plenty of money if you did."

"I live alone. I don't even need two bedrooms, so I definitely don't need anything larger."

"Perhaps, if you and Donald get more serious, you'll change your mind," Patricia suggested.

Fenella opened her mouth to protest and then bit her tongue. Patricia was the last person she wanted to discuss Donald with, really.

"I feel as if I need to apologize," Patricia said after a moment. "Melanie is always late for everything. I don't know where she gets it from. I've never been late for anything in my life and my husband was much the same."

"Perhaps she's tied up with the police," Fenella replied.

"The police?" Patricia said in a shocked tone. "Why on earth would she be tied up with the police?"

"When I talked to Inspector Hammersmith last, he mentioned talking to you and to Melanie," Fenella said. "He's looking for things that might tie the three recent accidents together."

"I don't know what you're talking about," Patricia said coolly.

"You haven't spoken to the man yet?" Fenella asked, surprised. "He was concerned that Anne Marie, Margaret, and Hannah might have been murdered."

"Murdered?" The color drained from Patricia's face. "Anne Marie crashed her car and Margaret fell down her stairs. They were both accidents. As I understand it, Hannah slipped in her bath. That was an accident as well."

"The inspector was concerned that the three deaths, all of women of a certain age from the same social circle, might be connected. He felt they were too close together to be coincidental."

"Nonsense," Patricia said briskly. "Accidents happen every day. I'm sure those three aren't the only people who've died on the island in the past week. If he works hard enough, maybe the inspector can find some way to link every single accident to one common cause. Perhaps it's all a conspiracy to get rid of elderly women who take up more than their fair share of the health service's resources. He should look into that."

"I didn't mean to upset you," Fenella said. "I thought you'd already spoken to him."

"He's been leaving messages on my phone since yesterday morning," Patricia admitted. "Now that I know what he wants, I'm even less likely to ring him back. Don't get me wrong, I'm terribly sad about all three deaths. They were my friends, after a fashion, and they were also reliable supporters for the Manx Fund for Children. Maybe that's the common link. Maybe someone is trying to destroy all of my years of hard work by eliminating my supporters, one at a time."

Fenella flushed. "But what did you want to talk to me about?" she asked, wanting to change the subject.

"We have a huge event coming up at Castle Rushen, but I really don't want to get into too many details until Melanie arrives. She's the driving force behind the event and she's in charge of organizing all of the volunteers."

"Did you want to order or are you waiting for one more?" the waitress asked.

"We're waiting for my daughter," Patricia said. "When she arrives, we'll all be having afternoon tea, but don't bring anything until she gets here."

"Of course, madam," the waitress said. She nodded at Fenella and then walked away.

"I can't imagine what's keeping Melanie," Patricia said, glancing at her watch again. "She's always late, but she knew today was important."

Fenella checked the clock on the wall. It was only ten past two, which didn't seem all that late to her. "So tell me more about the Manx Fund for Children," she said, wishing she didn't have to be polite. "I understand you founded it."

"Yes, many years ago, after a personal tragedy," the woman replied.

"I'm sorry."

"I had a son," Patricia told her, staring at something in the distance. "And I lost him. I felt I had to do something to honor his memory."

"I can't imagine your pain," Fenella said.

"You never wanted children?"

"I can't have them," Fenella told her. While she was touched by Patricia's story, she didn't feel like sharing her own.

"I wanted to name the charity after my son, but my husband didn't think that was wise. Sometimes I'm sorry that he got his way, but he was probably correct." Patricia sighed.

"The Manx Fund for Children is a good name," Fenella said.

"Yes, I know. It tells people what we are trying to raise money for, which is a good thing. I just wish, that is, it would have been nice to feel that my son's legacy was in the name, that's all."

"I've heard you do very good work."

"When we started out, I was hoping to raise a thousand pounds. It seemed a lot of money to me. I'd married very young and had never held down a paying job. I thought that it would be difficult to get people to give away their hard-earned money."

"I'm sure it is."

Patricia shrugged. "Perhaps I simply move in the right social circles for this sort of thing. People have been incredibly generous and terribly kind over the years. I raised that first thousand in less than a week, and by the end of the first month I was able to give ten thousand pounds to Noble's for the children's ward."

"My goodness, how wonderful."

"Things grew from there. I'd only planned on helping Noble's, but over time we've added more and more organizations to the list of those that we help. I still remember taking that first check to Noble's, though. All of the doctors and nurses knew me from my son's many stays. It was almost like a family and it was wonderful to be able to support them."

"What did they do with the money?" Fenella asked, wondering if it was a rude question.

"They made over the children's play area. They had a nice big space for the children to use, but the carpet was torn and the walls were marked and stained. They put in fresh carpet, painted, and replaced nearly all of the toys. It became a much brighter and happier place for the children to play."

"That must have brought you a lot of satisfaction."

Patricia nodded. "But all of that was a long time ago. I must tell you about all of the good that we do."

She'd only just started telling Fenella about some of their recent projects when they were interrupted.

"Mrs. Anderson? I'm Inspector Hammersmith of the Douglas CID. I'm sorry to interrupt, but it's rather important."

Patricia looked up at the man and frowned. "I don't have anything to say about the sudden and unfortunate deaths of my friends," she said. "I'm quite certain they were all tragic accidents."

The inspector nodded. "Thank you, but that isn't why I'm here. Could I have a minute of your time in private?"

"Perhaps, after we've finished," Patricia said. "I won't be interrupted, though."

Inspector Hammersmith took a step closer and leaned down toward Patricia. He spoke quietly, but Fenella was able to overhear every word. "I'm terribly sorry, but there's been an accident. If you'd like to come with me, I can get you to Noble's quickly. Your daughter is probably already on her way into surgery."

"Melanie? An accident? What happened?"

"We're still investigating. I've left the experts going over the car and came to find you. She told us you would be here," the man explained.

"So she's okay?" Patricia demanded.

"She was conscious when she was pulled from the car. I don't know the extent of her injuries."

"I'm terribly sorry," Patricia said to Fenella, getting to her feet. "We'll have to reschedule."

"Yes, of course," Fenella agreed. "I hope Melanie recovers quickly."

"Thank you," Patricia said. She picked up her handbag and began to walk away.

Inspector Hammersmith frowned at Fenella. "You were meeting Melanie for tea?" he asked.

"Yes."

"And now she's had an accident."

"I barely knew the woman."

"Yes, that's what you keep telling me about everyone," the man replied. "I have a number of questions for you, but they'll have to wait for later." He turned on his heel and walked quickly out of the room, catching up to Patricia near the door.

Fenella sat back in her seat and took a shaky breath. Melanie certainly hadn't had an affair with Paul Clucas. Where was the connection? What was she missing? And how could she persuade Inspector Hammersmith that she wasn't involved?

"Is everything okay?" the waitress asked, looking confused.

"I'm afraid Patricia had an emergency and had to leave," Fenella explained.

"Do you still want tea?"

"I'm awfully sorry, but I don't think I'll bother. I think I'd rather just go home. But I've been taking up a table for half an hour. You must let me give you something for the trouble." Fenella opened her handbag, but the other woman held up a hand.

"Don't be silly. I haven't done anything for you at all and half the place is empty today. If you weren't here, the table would have been sitting empty. I hope we'll see you again another day, though."

"I hope so, too. I had tea here last Sunday and it was delicious." Fenella got to her feet and headed for the door. While she was disappointed that she wasn't going to get to enjoy another sumptuous tea, she was happy that she didn't have to try to find excuses for why she couldn't help with Patricia's fundraiser. With Melanie very much on her mind, she pushed open the restaurant's door, nearly hitting a woman who was approaching it.

"Oh, I am sorry," she exclaimed.

"It's quite all right," the woman said. Fenella was surprised to recognize Phillipa Clucas.

"Fenella?" Paul said. He was only a step behind his mother. "But what are you doing here?"

"I was meant to be meeting Patricia Anderson for tea, but she had a family emergency and had to go," Fenella explained.

"I do hope everything is okay," Paul replied, looking concerned.

Fenella wasn't sure how to respond to that. No one had told her not to mention Melanie's accident, but Inspector Hammersmith had done his best to keep his voice down when he'd told Patricia. Feeling as if she ought to keep quiet, Fenella shrugged. "I hope so as well."

"But does that mean you didn't get any tea?" Paulette asked. She had been a few steps behind Paul, but she'd caught up in time to hear the conversation between Fenella and her brother.

"I didn't."

"You must join us," Paulette said. "I'm sure my mother would love a chance to get to know Mona's niece."

"I don't want to crash your family party," Fenella protested.

"It isn't anything like that," Paulette assured her. "Mother and I try to have tea here every Sunday when she's well enough, and today we've invited Paul to join us for a change, but it isn't anything special."

"Except I'm just out of hospital," Phillipa said. "It feels special to me after nothing but dry toast and broth for a week."

"You were only in overnight," Paulette said.

"Well, it felt like a week," Phillipa replied.

Paul chuckled. "I promise there won't be any broth or dry toast at tea," he said. "Please join us," he added, giving Fenella a smile.

"If you're sure," she replied, still hesitant.

"Of course we're sure," Paulette said. "Do come along." She hooked her arm around Fenella's and led her back into the restaurant. Only moments later they were shown to the same table that Fenella had just left.

When the waitress came over, she grinned. "I know you said you'd be back, but I wasn't expecting you quite this soon."

"I ran into some friends at the door," Fenella explained, feeling slightly foolish.

"Sometimes it seems as if this is a terribly small island," the woman said. "Is it afternoon tea for everyone?" she asked.

The waitress walked away, making a note on her pad, after a chorus of "yeses."

14

"My daughter is right," Phillipa said as soon as the waitress was out of earshot. "I am happy to meet you, although I feel as if we've met before."

Fenella glanced at Paulette, trying to remember what Paulette had said about telling her mother that she'd dreamed the encounter at the charity auction.

"Mother, you did meet Fenella at Tynwald Day," Paulette said. "I hope your memory will return to normal now that you're off all of those tablets."

"Tynwald Day?" Phillipa echoed. "I don't really remember," she said to Fenella apologetically.

"There was a lot going on that day," Fenella said, waving a hand.

"I've been having such odd dreams, you see," the woman added. "I actually dreamed that I found evidence that my husband cheated on me. It was horrible."

"I'm so glad it all turned out to be just a bad dream," Fenella said. She looked over at Paul, trying to signal that he needed to join in the conversation.

"Anne Marie Smathers and I used to have coffee together every Thursday," Phillipa said. "I felt so sorry for her when she lost her husband that I insisted that we start meeting regularly. She was all alone, you know."

Fenella nodded and glanced over at Paulette, who shrugged.

"Mother, maybe we should talk about something else," Paul said. "Oh, look, here's our tea."

The waitress passed out the teapots. "I'll be back in a minute with everything else," she said.

"I had the children, you understand," Phillipa said. "But poor Anne Marie hadn't been blessed with children during her marriage. They were only married for a year or so, I believe, before Herbert's tragic accident. I fell pregnant with Paulette within a few months of my wedding, but poor Anne Marie was left alone and childless."

"She didn't mind," Paul interjected.

"Of course she minded," Phillipa corrected him. "She should have remarried, of course, but there were so few men available. Everyone married much younger in those days. The men who chose to remain single weren't very nice men."

"It was good of you to spend time with her," Fenella said.

"Yes, it was the least I could do. The poor woman was left with a great deal of money. She didn't need to work, but she had nothing else to do with her days."

"I met her at the charity auction," Fenella said. "I was very sad to hear about her death so soon after we'd met."

"I always warned her about that car of hers," Phillipa replied. "She was obsessed with it. It was the one place she could feel close to Herbert, she told me. I warned her that she drove it too fast, especially now that it was getting older. So many things can go wrong with cars. I did warn her."

"Mother, what's been happening on that program you watch on the telly?" Paul asked.

"Nothing," she replied with a wave of her hand. "Margaret and I were friends, too, although we never grew as close as Anne Marie and I were. Margaret was as busy with her children as I was with mine, of course, although she did still manage to attend a lot of the charity functions and other social occasions that my husband simply had to be a part of."

"Social connections are important for small business owners," Paul said in a patient tone. "In those days more deals were made over drinks at some pub than in any meeting room."

"Yes, and most of the wives went along for those drinks," Phillipa told Fenella. "I always felt that my place was at home with my children, though. It was unseemly for married mothers to be out drinking and dancing in the evenings."

"I only met Margaret briefly, but she seemed very nice, too," Fenella told her.

"She was nice. Both of her children moved across, which was difficult for her. I'm so fortunate that my children have chosen to stay here, well, aside from Paula, of course."

Fenella didn't know how to reply to that, so she was grateful to see the waitress heading their way. "Look how lovely," she exclaimed as the waitress placed tiered trays on their table.

"I do love an afternoon tea," Phillipa said happily.

For several minutes everyone filled plates and then began to eat. Fenella was just starting to relax when Phillipa began again.

"Margaret should have sold her house and moved into a retirement community," she said. "I warned her about all of those stairs. She had problems with her knees and she shouldn't have been going up and down the stairs all day. She didn't listen, of course. She loved that little house."

"Mother, you won't listen, either," Paul said. "You know I think you should move, but you won't listen to me."

"I'm taking care of Mum," Paulette said sharply. "She's happy at home, aren't you?" she appealed to Phillipa.

"Of course I am," Phillipa replied. "Paulette takes good care of me."

"But if you moved into a retirement community, Paulette would be free to do other things," Paul suggested.

"I don't have other things I want to do," Paulette snapped. "I've been looking after Mum since I was old enough to do so. I can't imagine doing anything else."

Paul looked as if he wanted to argue more, but instead he grabbed a finger sandwich and took a large bite.

"Of course, dear, sweet Hannah shouldn't have been on her own, either," Phillipa said after a moment. "She could barely walk. It's no wonder she slipped in the bath. Two of her children moved across, too. I can't imagine how difficult that must have been for her."

"Well, I'm not going anywhere," Paulette said, patting her mother's arm.

"No, dear, you aren't, are you?" the other woman said, looking at her daughter as if she were seeing her for the first time. "Why didn't you ever find a husband?"

Paulette blushed. "Like you said, there aren't very many men out there," she muttered.

"I always wanted grandchildren," Phillipa told Fenella. "I always thought that I would have some one day, but now it doesn't seem very likely. I suppose Paul could still find someone and settle down, but it would be a huge surprise if it happened. Still, perhaps it's for the best, under the circumstances."

"What does that mean?" Paul asked.

"Because of Paula," Phillipa replied.

Paul and Fenella exchanged glances. Fenella had no idea what the woman was talking about, but there was no way she was going to ask.

After an awkward pause, Phillipa sighed. "But you don't know about my Paula, do you? She was my baby. I was so happy when I fell pregnant again after I'd had Paul. My husband didn't really want any more children, so I felt incredibly blessed when I found out."

"Mother, let's not talk about this," Paul said.

"Oh, hush," Phillipa told him. "I'll talk about whatever I want to talk about. Fenella deserves to know the whole story."

"Yes, Mother," Paul replied. He began refilling his plate with more sandwiches and cakes while Phillipa took a sip of tea.

"I was delighted to have another girl," she continued. "Paulette didn't really like frilly pretty things, so I was looking forward to having a daughter who I could dress in pink and ruffles. Unfortunately, it quickly became apparent that there was something terribly wrong with Paula."

"I'm sorry," Fenella said.

Phillipa nodded. "Thank you. I suppose, if all of this had happened today, that I would have had all manner of tests during my pregnancy. Perhaps I would have been able to prepare for the shock. As it was, though, I had no reason to suppose that my baby was going to be anything other than completely healthy."

"I think Fenella's heard quite enough," Paulette interrupted.

"And if it happened today," Phillipa continued, ignoring her daughter, "they probably would run all manner of tests to try to work out what was wrong. Maybe they could even treat whatever was wrong with Paula, but I doubt it. I think she had some sort of genetic abnormality. Whatever was wrong, though, once I recovered from my shock, I fell madly in love with her. She was a beautiful baby. She rarely cried and she had a way of staring at you, watching everything that you did, all the time."

"I remember that," Paul said. "Even when she was very little, she used to lie on the floor and watch every move I made."

"She never learned to walk or crawl," Phillipa said. "She couldn't even sit up by herself, although she loved to sit on my lap and watch the world go by. She couldn't talk, but she used to communicate with noises. I could understand her, even if no one else could."

"She was very sweet, in her own way," Paulette said. "But she was also a lot of work. As soon as I was able, I tried to help as much as I could."

Phillipa nodded. "Paulette was a great help. She used to take Paula for long walks along the promenade. We had a special pushchair made for her that could accommodate her as she grew. She never gained weight the way she should have, but she still got too large for me to carry around easily. The pushchair made everything a little bit easier."

"I was too young to be much help," Paul said. "I was probably more of a nuisance than anything else," he added ruefully.

"You were fine," Phillipa told him, patting his hand. "You were just a typical boy. You were full of energy and needed to be entertained. It was hard for me to keep you happy and look after Paula as well. You started spending more time with your father as soon as you were able to do so."

"Yeah, I remember going to his office after school and just running up and down the corridors. He never complained that I was too loud or in the way," Paul said.

"And I did," Phillipa said sadly. "You couldn't run and make noise at home because Paula needed her naps. She was still a baby in many ways, even when she was older. She took naps twice a day and if she didn't get her sleep, she would be nearly impossible to deal with."

"It was fun, spending time with my father," Paul said. "I never minded."

"I minded," Phillipa told him. "But I couldn't seem to work out a better solution. Paulette was happy to help out, but you just wanted to play."

"Paulette was the perfect child, even then," Paul said.

Fenella thought she could detect a hint of mockery in his tone.

"I was never perfect," Paulette argued. "All I wanted was for Mum to be happy. I've been working on that for the last forty-odd years."

"When Paula was ten, she started to lose weight," Phillipa said sadly. "The doctors couldn't work out why, but her health began to fail. She'd go into hospital and rally and then come home and get worse again. That went on for about six months. One morning, when I got up to get her breakfast, she wouldn't wake up."

The woman stopped talking and opened her handbag. While she was wiping away tears, the waitress exchanged empty trays for full ones, carefully averting her eyes from Phillipa's distress. "Do you need anything else?" she asked in a soft voice.

"We're fine," Paul said.

The waitress nodded and walked away while Phillipa was taking a few deep breaths. Finally she looked up at Fenella. "It shouldn't have been a shock. She'd been so poorly for so many months and the doctors had always told me she could go anytime, but it was still a shock. I, well, I lost my mind for a while. My husband sent me away to hospital until I was able to function again."

"I'm so very sorry," Fenella said.

"It was so long ago, but I can still feel the pain," the woman told her. "It was that pain that brought me and Patricia Anderson together. She'd lost her son, you see. We understood one another."

"Yes, she told me that she'd lost her son," Fenella said.

"I was fortunate that I still had Paulette and Paul. They were the only things that pulled me out of my misery. Patricia didn't have any other children, not yet. I was quite jealous, actually, when she fell pregnant with Melanie. My husband refused to even consider having any more children, and she always told me that her husband felt the same way. I wish I knew how she'd changed his mind."

"Mum, have another sandwich. You've barely eaten anything," Paulette urged.

"Almost as soon as she fell pregnant, she stopped coming to visit me," Phillipa said, sounding hurt. "I never knew why, but it made me sad."

"I didn't know that," Paulette said.

"I tried to hide so much from you both," Phillipa replied. "I did my best to pretend to be happy as much as I could."

"I should have tried harder to understand how you really felt," Paulette sighed.

"You were a child," Phillipa said. "You couldn't possibly understand how I felt, losing your sister."

"Does anyone need more tea?" the waitress interrupted. She refilled everyone's drinks, chatting about the food and the weather as she did so. Fenella was pleased that something had broken the tension at the table, but as soon as the waitress walked away, it came back.

"Our father should have been there for you more," Paulette said. "He was always working, even right after Paula's death."

"Your father worked hard to give us a comfortable life," Phillipa told her. "I never had to worry about money, and neither do you, even though you've never held down a paying job."

"I did try," Paulette said tightly.

"I know you did, dear," Phillipa replied, patting the woman's hand. "But you mustn't resent the long hours that your father's job required. He did it for us, you know."

"He went to a lot of parties and social occasions after hours," Paulette replied, pulling her hand away.

"That sort of thing goes hand in hand with having a small business on a small island," Paul said. "I go to one event or another at least three nights a week."

"But you don't have a wife and children at home," Paulette pointed out. "Our father should have been home more."

"Where is all of this coming from?" Phillipa asked. "You always loved your father so much."

"I'm sorry," Paulette waved a hand. "Thinking that he was unfaithful was upsetting. It made me think a lot about my childhood and how few of my memories actually include my father. He wasn't home very often. He could have been unfaithful and we would have never known."

"Let's not start talking about that again," Phillipa pleaded. "I was so angry at him and my friends, and then so relieved to find out that it was just a bad dream. I really don't want to even think about it anymore."

"Tell us about your childhood," Paul said to Fenella.

"Oh, goodness, my childhood was very different, of course," she replied. "I grew up in America. We moved there when I was two. I have four older brothers who never seemed quite sure what to do with their unexpected little sister. Sometimes they could be quite wonderful to me, and other times they were horrible, but that was a long time ago. We all get along now." More or less, she added silently to herself.

"I'd just assumed you were an only child, since you're the only one who has moved into Mona's flat. Did she leave her estate to all five of you, then?" Paul asked.

"No, she left everything to me," Fenella replied. "And I've no idea why, really, unless it was because I was the only girl."

"I could see Mona thinking that," Phillipa said. "Men were playthings to her. I was always just a little bit jealous of her life. She seemed incredibly happy all the time."

"She did," Paul agreed. " She lived on her own terms and she was unapologetic about it. Some people didn't like it, but she simply didn't care."

"I didn't approve of her morals," Paulette said. "I understand she had affairs with married men."

"I don't know about that," Paul countered. "She flirted with every man she met, but I think she was truly devoted to Max."

"But she never even married him," Paulette replied. "If she was truly devoted, she should have married him."

"They were engaged once," Phillipa recalled. "I remember your father telling me that Max had bought her an engagement ring worth thirty thousand pounds. I couldn't imagine it."

"And then she threw it into the sea," Paul laughed. "I remember that evening. It was a spectacular fight."

"What were they fighting about?" Paulette asked.

"I've no idea," Paul replied. "They were always fighting about something. They were madly in love, but they didn't much like each other."

Paulette shook her head. "That just seems all wrong to me."

Fenella was relieved when the conversation moved on to other subjects, like a new bookstore that was opening in Ramsey and the uncertain future of a once popular but now disappointing restaurant in Foxdale. As the waitress cleared the table, Phillipa sat back with a sigh.

"I feel as if I must be extra careful now," she said. "All of my friends keep having accidents, and I'm afraid something might happen to me, too."

"Mum, you mustn't think that," Paulette said sharply. "Nothing bad is going to happen to you."

"I'm getting old," Phillipa replied. "I am going to die eventually."

"Not for a very long time," Paulette said, taking her mother's hand. "I plan on looking after you for many more years."

While Phillipa and Paulette went to the restroom, Paul insisted on paying for tea. "It's the least I can do after the rather miserable conversation," he told Fenella when she objected. "I'm just grateful you were here. I can't imagine how much worse it would have been without you."

"Are you sure your mother is okay?" Fenella asked.

"No, not at all," he replied. "Her doctor switched her medications again, but I'm not convinced he's worked out the right combination yet. Paulette doesn't seem to mind, but I don't like seeing her on too many drugs at any one time."

"Paulette still seems angry with your father, even though the memoirs don't exist," Fenella said.

"As I said, when she first told me what our mother had told her, I may not have sounded surprised enough. Now she's realized that our father was never around and that he had more than adequate opportunities to cheat. It's difficult for her, as she always thought the world of him."

"I'm surprised she hasn't asked you outright about it."

"She'll probably get around to it at some point," Paul said. "I think she'd rather not do it in front of Mother, for which I'm grateful."

"But your mother has her suspicions."

"She must know. That has to be why she had the dream in the first place. But I suspect she'd rather not know for certain. Otherwise, she'd be asking everyone about it, I suspect."

"I'm surprised she didn't say anything to Anne Marie at the charity auction."

"I believe my sister dragged her out before she could talk to anyone else after her confrontation with you. Paulette said she was trying to keep Mother away from anyone who had been friends with our father. Obviously, she didn't know who you were."

Fenella nodded. "Perhaps she shouldn't have taken her to the party in the first place," she said, feeling as if that party had been the catalyst behind a great many unhappy events.

"Mother wouldn't have missed it. She insists on supporting Patricia. I'm sure it dates back to the time when they were very close, after they'd both lost their children."

"She's still very sad about losing Paula."

"Yes, and so is Paulette. I don't remember all that much about her, except that she was always on the floor in our sitting room, taking up a lot of space and making a lot of noise. That sounds terrible, but I was twelve when she died, and I'm afraid I wasn't nearly as sorry as I should have been."

"I'm sure having your mother disappear after her death was harder to deal with," Fenella said.

"It was, definitely," he replied curtly.

"I think we're all ready to go," Paulette said. "I've left Mum in the lobby. She was too tired to walk all the way back here."

Paul nodded and stood up. Fenella was quick to follow. She waved to their waitress as the trio made their way to the door. In the lobby, Fenella stopped at the couch where Phillipa was sitting.

"It was nice to see you again," she said.

"I'm not sure that's true," Phillipa replied. "I don't think I was very good company today."

"I had a lovely time," Fenella insisted.

"I get too lost in the past," Phillipa told her. "There are so many things I would do differently if I could. Sometimes I wish I could go and talk to my eighteen-year-old self. I'd tell her so many things."

"It's probably best that we can't do that. I suspect we'd all make significant changes in our lives if we could," Fenella replied.

"I just hope all of the deaths stop now," Phillipa said solemnly. "No matter what happened in the past, no one deserves to die." She turned her gaze from Fenella to Paulette, staring at her daughter for a moment before sighing. "And now I must struggle to my feet, mustn't I?"

Paul held out a hand and helped her up. Paulette quickly took her arm and began to lead her away.

"Are you free for dinner one night this week?" Paul asked as he and Fenella followed the pair toward the door.

"I'll have to check my calendar," Fenella replied. "Call me sometime."

"I'll do that," he said.

Fenella watched as the trio crossed the parking lot and got into a large car. When the car was out of sight, she climbed into a convenient taxi. She was eager to get home, but her mind was racing. Something that Phillipa had said was bothering her, but she wasn't sure what it was.

"How was tea with Patricia?" Mona asked when Fenella walked back into her apartment.

"Cancelled," Fenella replied. "Melanie had an accident."

"Melanie? What happened?"

"Apparently she was in a car accident."

"Is she okay?"

"I'm not sure. Inspector Hammersmith took Patricia to Noble's. I'd call to ask, but I'm sure they wouldn't tell me anything."

"But that doesn't make any sense," Mona complained. "Why would the killer target Melanie?"

"Maybe she just had an accident," Fenella snapped. "People have accidents every day. Maybe everyone is just having sad and unfortunate and oddly timed accidents."

"Are you okay?" Mona asked, clearly concerned.

"No, I'm not okay," Fenella admitted. "I ended up having tea with Phillipa, Paul, and Paulette, and it was disturbing; that's probably the best word for it."

"Tell me everything."

Fenella took some pills for her pounding head and then obliged her aunt. When she was done, Mona shook her head.

"They're a strange family," she said. "I think Paulette is behind the killings and Phillipa knows it."

"Based on what?"

"I don't know, instinct, maybe."

"Well, I'm thinking something even worse," Fenella told her. "I think Paulette killed her little sister."

Mona gasped. "She was only a child herself when Paula died."

"She was fifteen."

"Still, her own sister?"

"Is that much worse than killing several elderly women because you think they might have slept with your father?"

"Yes, it's much worse," Mona said. "She was meant to be looking after Paula. I can't believe she'd hurt her."

"I still don't see where Melanie fits into it all, though."

"Maybe Paulette wanted to inflict maximum pain on Patricia, so instead of killing her, she decided to kill Melanie," Mona suggested.

"What a horrible thought."

"What are you going to do now?" Mona asked. "You need to ring Daniel."

"I can't ring Daniel. He's working, and anyway, what would I say?"

"Tell him about your tea with the Clucas family. Tell him what you're thinking about Paulette. Find out how Melanie is doing."

"He's working," Fenella repeated herself.

She was still trying to work out exactly what she wanted to do when Inspector Hammersmith knocked on her door.

"I was going to ring before I came, but I was in the neighborhood," he explained. "I hope you have time to answer a few questions?"

"Of course," Fenella said with a sigh. "Come in."

It was nearly time for dinner, but Fenella wasn't hungry after eating so much at tea, so she set a pot of coffee brewing and put out a plate of cookies for the man.

"Thank you," he said, helping himself. "I don't remember when I ate last."

Fenella thought about offering to cook something for her guest, but she didn't really want to make him feel too welcome. When the coffee was ready, she poured them each a cup and then sat down across from him at the kitchen table.

"Can you tell me how Melanie is doing?" she asked.

"They think she's going to be fine," he replied. "She's badly bruised and banged up, but nothing is broken. She was lucky that her car had several airbags, all of which deployed."

"That's good news, anyway," Fenella said.

"And you were meeting her for tea today," the man said.

"Okay, you know what? I'm tired and I'm sad and I'm a little angry," Fenella said. "So I'm going to just tell you exactly what I think is going on, even though you'll probably think I'm insane."

"That sounds promising," the man said.

"He's going to think you're crazy, but I think you're doing the right thing," Mona said encouragingly.

"I think Paulette and her mother did find something on that computer. I don't think it was actually any memoirs, I think it was more a fantasy piece, but I think Paulette believed it was all true and I think it sent her over the edge. I think she's been trying to kill everyone on her father's list of conquests and as far as I can tell, she's been pretty successful."

"Why tell you about the memoirs if she was planning on killing everyone? Surely she had to realize that would make her a suspect?" he asked.

"I don't know, maybe she didn't think it through before she talked to me. She certainly backtracked quite quickly after that, though."

"Yes, she did," he agreed. He made a few notes in his phone and then looked up. "Why target Melanie?"

"Maybe Melanie's accident really was an accident," Fenella suggested.

"Actually, we're pretty sure it wasn't," the man told her. "There was fairly clear evidence that the car's brakes were tampered with. So clear that the reporter from the local paper who arrived not long after I did noticed it."

"So maybe Paulette got Melanie's car mixed up with Patricia's, or maybe she wanted to hurt Patricia by killing her daughter, or maybe the cases aren't even connected," Fenella said, feeling frustrated.

The inspector nodded. "I appreciate your sharing your thoughts with me," he said. "I was planning on speaking with Paulette Clucas again. I'll keep what you've told me in mind when I do so."

"Tell him about Paula," Mona suggested. "He should have all of the facts."

Feeling as if this was really going to make the man think she'd lost her mind, Fenella cleared her throat. "Paulette had a little sister called Paula," she said. "Paula had lots of health issues and died when Paulette was around fifteen."

"Does that help explain Paulette's motive in some way?" the inspector asked.

"Phillipa said something about Paula getting sick at home and then getting better when she went to the hospital," Fenella explained.

"That is generally how we expect hospitals to work," the man replied.

Fenella flushed. "She said something about how it kept happening over and over again until Paula died. There was just something about the way that she said it that made me wonder, that's all."

"Made you wonder what?"

"Made me wonder whether Paulette, under the guise of being a helpful big sister, wasn't doing something that hastened her sister's death," Fenella said in a rush.

The inspector was silent for several minutes, typing on his phone without looking up. Eventually he took a sip of coffee and then spoke.

"I know you've been through a lot since you've been on the island," he began. "We see it a lot in the police, actually. Once you've been through a few murder investigations, you start seeing every death as suspicious. I don't blame you for starting to question every story that you're told."

Fenella nibbled her way through a cookie, trying to work out what she wanted to say. "Just ask her about Paula," she suggested after a swallow of coffee.

He nodded. "I may do that," he said. "After I've read through any information we have in the files about the case. Thank you for your time and for sharing your thoughts. Daniel said I should listen and take seriously anything you said. He said you have good instincts."

"I hope he's wrong this time," Fenella said. "I'd really like all of the deaths to have been accidents."

"Because we know that Melanie's crash wasn't an accident, we have a police guard at her door. Her mother is planning on staying with her for the time being, so we're hopeful that she'll be protected as well. I'm going to have Paulette brought in for a little chat tomorrow morning. If I were you, I'd try to avoid the entire Clucas family for the next twenty-four hours or so."

"Can you let me know what happens?" Fenella asked as she walked the man to the door.

"Probably not," he said. "But maybe Daniel will be able to answer some of your questions, seeing as you two are close friends. If you're right about any of this, it should all be in the papers and the courts eventually, as well."

Fenella shut the door behind him and leaned against it. She felt like screaming or crying or something, but she wasn't sure exactly what.

"You need a glass of wine and a man to rub your back and tell you that you're wonderful," Mona said. "Ring Donald. I'm sure he'd be happy to indulge you."

"I'm not calling anyone, but I will have a glass of wine," Fenella said.

In the kitchen, Katie demanded her dinner. Fenella made herself a sandwich, since she was standing in front of the refrigerator, and then sat down in front of the television. "I wonder what Shelly's doing," she mused as she flipped through the channels.

"She's out with Gordon," Mona told her.

"Oh, good," Fenella replied, not questioning how Mona knew.

The pair watched television together for several hours before Mona got up and stretched. "This has been fun, but I have to go and talk to my guardian angel. He seems to think I should move on now and I'm going to have to persuade him to let me stay a while longer."

"You have a guardian angel?"

"He's more like my immediate supervisor or something," Mona shrugged. "He's supposed to make sure that I behave, but I dare say he's rather fond of me. He never complains when I do things I'm not meant to do."

"So you aren't leaving?"

"Not yet, anyway. Not while you still need me." She faded away before Fenella could reply.

15

Patricia rang a few days later. Fenella had been scouring the local paper every day for news about Paulette, but hadn't found anything. She hadn't heard any gossip either and was starting to think that she had been wrong about everything.

"I just wanted to let you know that I haven't forgotten your willingness to help with our upcoming event," Patricia said. "But we're putting everything on hold for a short while."

"I hope Melanie is okay," Fenella replied.

"Physically, she's recovering well. Knowing that someone wanted to kill her has taken an emotional toll, though. We're going to be taking an extended holiday in the south of France. I'll ring you when we return."

Fenella put the phone down and looked at Mona. "Patricia and Melanie are having an extended holiday in the south of France," she repeated.

"The police must have the case solved, if they're letting them go away," Mona speculated.

"Patricia seems like the type who would threaten to bring in her lawyers if the police tried to tell her they couldn't go away."

"Advocates, dear," Mona corrected her. "But you're right. Patricia may have made a fuss. You should ring Daniel."

"You've been saying that several times a day since Sunday," Fenella replied. "And I'm still not doing it. He'll call me when he can, or else he won't, and we'll read all about it in the local paper. I'm not comfortable calling him to ask for information."

"So just ring him to see how he's doing," Mona suggested.

Fenella ignored her and got back to work on her book. Both she and Mona were delighted when Daniel called that evening. Fenella thought she was being very kind when she put the call on speaker for Mona's benefit.

"How are you?" Daniel asked.

"I'm well. How are you?"

"Tired. I'm one of the older students on this course. No one else seems to mind the late nights, even with our early starts, but it's taking a toll on me."

"And you're there through August. You'll be too tired to come back to work."

"I may be," he chuckled. "I wish I had time for a good long chat, but I've a lecture in half an hour. I just wanted to bring you up to date on Paulette."

"Is there news? I keep checking the local paper, but there hasn't been anything there and I haven't seen anyone to ask."

"There is news, but you can't repeat any of what I'm going to tell you, not even to Shelly," he said.

"I won't," she agreed quickly.

Daniel sighed. "I shouldn't be telling you any of this, but I feel that your help was instrumental in working out what was going on. I think you have a right to know the whole story."

"If you're really uncomfortable with telling me, then don't," Fenella said quickly, earning herself a furious look from Mona.

"As long as you promise not to repeat it, I'd like to tell you the story," he countered. "Especially since you worked out most of it yourself."

"Paulette killed all those poor women?"

"Not exactly. She's been talking to Mark and he's passed along what she's told him. I don't know that we'll be able to find any evidence of any of this, but for what it's worth, I think she's telling the truth, at least as she sees it."

"So what happened?"

"She and her mother did find her father's memoirs, or something like that, on his computer. She stopped her mother from reading more than a little bit, but she read everything. Mark has a copy, and from what he's said, if it were all true, the man wouldn't have had time to hold down a job. He claims to have slept with just about every woman he ever met."

"Most of us were not at all interested," Mona said.

"Paulette claims she was upset with what she read and worried about her mother's reaction. That's why she started playing around with her mother's medications. She wanted to help her mother forget about what she'd seen."

"Poor Phillipa," Fenella exclaimed.

"Yes, she's at Noble's being monitored for a few days after the cocktail of drugs that her daughter had been giving her. But I'll get back to her at the end. According to Paulette, when she met you for tea and told you all about the memoirs, hurting anyone was the furthest thing from her mind. It wasn't until after she'd heard about Anne Marie Smathers's accident that she did anything."

"So Anne Marie's death really was an accident?" Fenella asked.

"As far as we can tell, yes. Paulette said that when she heard about Anne Marie's death, it made her happy because she knew that Anne Marie had slept with her father. Once she realized how happy she was with what fate had done, she decided to give fate a helping hand."

"So she started killing the other women in her father's notes," Fenella sighed.

"She claims she didn't kill anyone," Daniel told her. "She says she just did little things that might cause little accidents. She seems to think that she shouldn't be in any trouble for anything she did."

"So what did she do?" Fenella asked, feeing confused.

"She admits that when she visited Margaret she tripped on the carpet at the top of the stairs and may have torn it a little bit. She meant to warn Margaret, but she concedes that she might have forgotten to do so."

"Of course she's lying," Mona snapped.

"She also admits that when she went to visit Hannah she dropped a bottle of bath oil in the tub and that it spilled everywhere, which may have made the tub slippery. Apparently she suggested to Hannah that she might want to have a bath because she thought the bathwater would wash away the oil."

Fenella sighed. "Those poor women. What about Melanie?"

"Ah, that's where things fall apart a little bit for Paulette. Melanie's brake lines were clearly cut."

"What does she say?"

"That she was walking down the road and saw a huge tree branch under Melanie's car. She reckons that a sharp bit on the branch must have sliced the brake line as she was trying to be helpful by removing it."

"That would be funny if it wasn't so awful," Fenella said.

"Yes, I know," Daniel replied.

"What happens next?"

"Mark is working with the doctors at Noble's. Paulette is going to get locked away for treatment for a very long time. She's clearly mentally unstable."

"What will Phillipa do without her?"

"Thrive," Mona said firmly.

"I get the feeling from what Mark has said that Phillipa is somewhat relieved. I think she always had some idea that Paulette was unbalanced, dating back to Paula's death."

"Did Paulette say anything about Paula?" Fenella asked.

"Again, Paulette insists that what happened to her sister was just an accident. Apparently she'd been looking after her and she accidently left a plastic bag near her sister's head when she tucked her into bed for the night."

Fenella and Mona both gasped.

"When she went to check on her the next morning, she found the bag on Paula's face and took it away because she knew she'd be in trouble if her mother found it. She knew she was meant to keep plastic bags away from Paula. Allegedly, she was so worried about the bag that she forgot to check on Paula while she was removing and getting rid of the bag. An hour later, her mother found Paula dead."

"Poor Phillipa," Fenella said sadly.

"Mark thinks that Phillipa suspected what had happened, which was why she encouraged Paul to spend so much time with his father and why she did everything she could to keep Paulette at home with her. He also reckons that she had some suspicions about all of the accidents that were suddenly happening, but all of the drugs she was being given made it impossible for her to think clearly."

"You said she's in Noble's?"

"Yes, for another week at least. Then she's going to go and stay with Paul for a while, I understand."

"It's all so awful and sad," Fenella sighed.

"But at least Paulette has been caught and stopped," Daniel pointed out. "Mark is pretty sure that Patricia would have been next on the list."

"But why did she try to kill Melanie?" Fenella asked.

"According to the notes on Paul Clucas's computer, Melanie was his daughter," Daniel said.

"I didn't see that coming," Mona said. "She certainly doesn't look anything like him. She's the spitting image of her mother."

"Does Phillipa know?" was Fenella's question.

"I don't know. Mark talked to Patricia and she's denied it. I don't think she'll tell Melanie, and it's critical that you never repeat it."

"I won't," Fenella assured him.

"It could be true," Mona said thoughtfully. "The timing would have been about right."

"I need to get to my class," Daniel said with a sigh. "I'm going to try to ring you a bit more often over the next month. I miss talking to you."

"I miss you, too," Fenella admitted.

"I really hope you'll be able to avoid getting mixed up in any more murder investigations, at least until I get back," he added.

Fenella bit her tongue. She would happily go for the rest of her life without getting mixed up in any more murder investigations. Somehow, though, based on recent experience, she didn't think that was likely.

ACKNOWLEDGMENTS

Thanks to my wonderful editor, Denise.

Thanks to Linda at Tell-Tale Book Covers, who does the amazing covers for this series.

Thanks to my beta readers who help fine-tune my stories.

And thanks to my readers who keep me writing!

FRIENDS AND FRAUDS

RELEASE DATE: FEBRUARY 16, 2018

Since she's been on the Isle of Man, Fenella Woods has had the chance to make many new friends. Her closest island friend is her next-door neighbor, Shelly. When a man appears on Shelly's doorstep claiming to have been a childhood friend of Shelly's recently deceased husband, Fenella is quick to try to help Shelly deal with the surprise.

As Shelly tries to work out whether she wants to talk to the man or not, Fenella meets, and dislikes, several of the man's friends who are visiting the island. But when Shelly finally agrees to have meet the man, they find out that he had at least one enemy as well.

Police Inspector Mark Hammersmith isn't happy when Fenella finds yet another dead body, even though she barely knew the dead man. Inspector Daniel Robinson, Fenella's friend, is still off the island, though. Fenella has to deal with Mark, whether she likes it or not.

As they learn more about the man and his friends, Shelly and Fenella find themselves caught up in yet another murder investigation. Can they help Mark find the killer before he or she strikes again?

ALSO BY DIANA XARISSA

Aunt Bessie Assumes

Aunt Bessie Believes

Aunt Bessie Considers

Aunt Bessie Decides

Aunt Bessie Enjoys

Aunt Bessie Finds

Aunt Bessie Goes

Aunt Bessie's Holiday

Aunt Bessie Invites

Aunt Bessie Joins

Aunt Bessie Knows

Aunt Bessie Likes

Aunt Bessie Meets

Aunt Bessie Needs

Aunt Bessie Observes

Aunt Bessie Provides

Aunt Bessie Questions

Aunt Bessie Remembers

Aunt Bessie Solves

Aunt Bessie Tries

Aunt Bessie Understands

Aunt Bessie Volunteers

Aunt Bessie Wonders

The Isle of Man Ghostly Cozy Mysteries

Arrivals and Arrests

Boats and Bad Guys

Cars and Cold Cases

Dogs and Danger

Encounters and Enemies

Friends and Frauds

Guests and Guilt

Hop-tu-Naa and Homicide

Invitations and Investigations

Joy and Jealousy

Kittens and Killers

Letters and Lawsuits

The Markham Sisters Cozy Mystery Novellas

The Appleton Case

The Bennett Case

The Chalmers Case

The Donaldson Case

The Ellsworth Case

The Fenton Case

The Green Case

The Hampton Case

The Irwin Case

The Jackson Case

The Kingston Case

The Lawley Case

The Moody Case

The Norman Case

The Osborne Case

The Patrone Case

The Quinton Case

The Rhodes Case

The Isle of Man Romance Series

Island Escape

Island Inheritance

Island Heritage

Island Christmas

ABOUT THE AUTHOR

Diana Xarissa grew up in Erie, Pennsylvania, earned a BA in history from Allegheny College and eventually ended up in Silver Spring, Maryland. There she met her husband, who swept her off her feet and moved her to Derbyshire for a short while. Eventually, the couple relocated to the Isle of Man.

The Isle of Man was home for Diana and her family for over ten years. During their time there, Diana completed an MA in Manx Studies through the University of Liverpool. The family is now living near Buffalo, New York, where Diana enjoys writing about the island that she loves.

Diana also writes mystery/thrillers set in the not-too-distant future under the pen name "Diana X. Dunn" and fantasy/adventure books for middle grade readers under the pen name "D.X. Dunn."

She would be delighted to know what you think of her work and can be contacted through snail mail at:

Diana Xarissa Dunn
PO Box 72
Clarence, NY 14031.

Or find Diana at:
www.dianaxarissa.com
diana@dianaxarissa.com